Love Finds You™

in the City at Christmas

Love Finds You™

in the City at Christmas

RUTH LOGAN HERNE
ANNA SCHMIDT

summerside
PRESS™
New York

Love Finds You in the City at Christmas

ISBN-10: 0-8249-3436-9
ISBN-13: 978-0-8249-3436-1

Published by Summerside Press, an imprint of Guideposts
16 East 34th Street
New York, New York 10016
SummersidePress.com
Guideposts.org

*Summerside Press™ is an inspirational publisher offering fresh, irresistible books
to uplift the heart and engage the mind.*

Distributed by Ideals Publications, a Guideposts company
2630 Elm Hill Pike, Suite 100
Nashville, TN 37214

Guideposts, Ideals, and *Summerside Press* are registered trademarks of Guideposts.

The town depicted in this book is a real place. References to actual people or
events are either coincidental or are used with permission.

All Scripture quotations are taken from The Holy Bible, King James Version.

Cover and interior design by Müllerhaus Publishing Group, Mullerhaus.net.

Printed and bound in the United States of America
10 9 8 7 6 5 4 3 2 1

Red Kettle Christmas

RUTH LOGAN HERNE

Dedication

. . . .

To Zach, for always believing, laughing, and caring . . .
and the coffee gift cards were a total bonus! Love you!

Acknowledgments

....

Huge thanks to the Salvation Army Greater New York Division for their help on this very special project! The ongoing work of this ecumenical organization finds its way to hard-pressed people in times of crisis, past and present-day.

To Major William Groff, retired, a special round of thanks for filling in some very important blanks and chatting with me. Bill, your information was huge, and now we can work on your book!

To Reverend Edward Jay Sinclair, for his advice and help in steering me to Bill.

And to Zachary Blodgett, Esq., Associate Contract Attorney for the Greater New York Salvation Army. Your willingness to ask questions and help your mother are wonderful traits!

And to my agent Natasha Kern who called and said, "Would you like to write a Christmas story set in Manhattan?" The answer was a resounding "Yes!" I live in the rolling hills of upstate, but I love New York City!

And they, continuing daily with one accord in the temple, and breaking bread from house to house, did eat their meat with gladness and singleness of heart, praising God, and having favour with all the people. And the Lord added to the church daily such as should be saved.

ACTS 2:46–47

Chapter One

....

*New York City, Midtown, Thanksgiving morning
1947*

The bell's clear trill beckoned NYPD Patrolman Mike Wolzak. The welcoming chime brought warmth to the chill of gray November.

Mike aimed for the sound and the corner that would lead him to his assignment, keeping watch over the Macy's Thanksgiving Day Parade.

Memories surged. Childhood images recalled the wonders of Christmas in the city, his little sister held tight in his father's arms, his mother's hand grasping his as the parade went by, both parents straight and tall, proud of their part in the American dream.

So much gone.

So much different.

So much sorrow.

But he had a job to do, a task he did well. He rounded the corner, intent, then stopped.

A lone woman stood between him and the parade route. A cloak covered her beneath an old-style bonnet. Damp tendrils of hair clung to her cheeks. Rain misted her face.

Gloves too thin for the cold, wet conditions shielded her hands. Her right hand rocked a bell, the small sound sweet in the dank, dark day. A heavy red kettle stood off to the side, suspended from a tripod base.

She glanced his way and smiled, and that smile . . .

A look that touched her face, her eyes, her mouth . . .

Drew him closer.

"Good morning, Officer. Happy Thanksgiving."

His day promised to be anything but happy, but she knew nothing of that. Nothing of him. Seeing her there, tucked beneath an overhang that offered scant help from the wind-driven mist, an urge to help swept over him. But how?

"Mommy, may I move closer to the parade for just a little bit? Please?"

Mike's attention veered down. A child stood tucked in the lee side of the doorway, a little girl, a miniature of the woman before him. The inset doorframe protected the child from the elements, while her mother dealt with less hospitable conditions. He moved forward, drawn to serve, and put out a hand. "Mike Wolzak, NYPD."

The woman raised her gaze and accepted his gesture, placing her wet, gloved hand in his. "Karen O'Leary."

Her voice warmed him. Soft, full of welcome, as if she weren't cold and wet, soliciting financial help from people too caught up in the crowd's noise to hear the bell's plea.

"And this is?" He turned his gaze down. The child returned the look with an expression so honest and sweet he couldn't help but smile, and smiles had been a rare commodity of late.

"I'm Laurie." She tipped her head back and chin up, clearly proud of what she was about to say as she held up one small hand, fingers splayed. "I'm five."

"And clearly smart for your age," Mike told her.

The girl beamed.

Her mother's gentle smile said she appreciated his overture. "It seems we're both working this day." She indicated the growing crowd of people lining Broadway with a tilt of her head. "How blessed we are to have the freedom to work as we should."

Her words struck a sour chord within him.

He hadn't felt blessed a few moments ago, and he was pretty sure sorrow would drag him as the day wore on, but right now the hope and promise in her gaze made him feel more optimistic than he had in a long time.

The rousing rhythms of Glenn Miller's "St. Louis Blues" heralded the coming parade. Bright music to warm the day, celebrating the end of war, the joy of returning soldiers, a new tomorrow. Movie house newsreels lauded the excitement of the troops' return, but not all came back. Some had made the ultimate sacrifice. And Mike knew others whose tomorrows would ever be affected by the remnants of war, mentally and physically.

"It's coming, Mommy!"

The child's voice called him away from dark remembrances. Innocent joy uplifted her eyes and her tone.

The young mother aimed her gaze down. "I must stay here. This is my assignment for today. You know that, Laurie, but if you let me tie your hat nice and snug, you can come out here and watch."

Mike measured the child's vantage point with a quick glance. She'd see very little, if anything, a full block up from the parade's path, with people four-deep lining the road.

Should he offer?

No. Not when he was on duty. What if something happened? What if . . . ?

"May I take her closer?" He uttered the words before common sense could stop them. "We'll go right down to the end of the road.

You'll be able to see us from here. And there aren't too many safer places to be on parade day than with one of New York's finest."

Indecision shadowed Karen's face, but her eyes said she couldn't disagree.

"Oh, Mommy, please?" Laurie gripped her mother's hand, her voice imploring.

"We do not beg." Karen's voice stayed calm but stern.

The child quieted, but while her mouth went silent, her eyes pleaded.

Mike turned away to hide a smile. He would have caved at the kid's initial entreaty. Clearly parenting wasn't as easy as he might have thought.

"You will be good?"

More hopeful now of a positive answer, Laurie nodded earnestly. "*So* good."

"And you will not ask for things?" Karen posed the question with one brow thrust up, a no-nonsense expression.

"I promise, Mommy."

"And you're sure this is all right?" Karen turned her gaze up to his, and a tiny breath of hope eased the tightness in Mike's chest, a clench that began mid-war and hadn't let go yet.

"It's fine."

"Well then." Karen handed him the bell for a moment. She leaned down and secured the girl's hat with a tighter bow beneath her chin. Soft brown ringlets tumbled from beneath the hat's edge. Tenderly, she pulled the child's collar up and tucked the hair beneath. "I know you don't like your hair tucked in, but"—Karen kept her voice firm but gentle—"we need to ring the bell until one o'clock. You'll get very cold if your hair gets soaked in the rain, so you must keep it inside your coat. Okay?"

"I will. I promise."

"All right."

She stood, reached out a hand for the bell in Mike's hand, and met his gaze. "Thank you."

Two simple words. No embellishment. But in those two words, he read the gratitude of a woman who cared for her child despite the odds. A woman like his mother had been.

"No problem." He flashed her a smile, lifted the child, and hiked down the street, not wanting the girl to miss a minute of the day's festivities. Yes, they'd get wet. And they'd probably get cold. But she'd have a memory to hold forever, much like the ones he held close. And no one could take those good memories away.

* * * * *

Only a foolish woman allows her child to be carried into the sprawling crowds of New York City on parade day.

Karen knew this and made the decision anyway. Foolish? Well. She'd been called worse in the past. She'd gazed into the man's eyes, read the shadows of life and loss, and seen his pain. But alongside the pain she discerned honor and protection, and on that note, she let her precious daughter go.

And then watched from her post a block away, the bell chiming tiny reminders of want and need.

"Some coffee, miss?"

Karen turned toward the thick accent, half Yiddish, part Brooklyn. A man not much taller than her waved to the one lit store behind them, a bagel shop, bright and fragrant. From it, the scent of warm bread kneaded the morning mist. "We're only open until noon this day, the holiday, you understand . . . "

She nodded, knowing not everyone got holidays off.

"But the coffee is fresh, hot, and good. And if you don't mind doing an old man a favor, my nephew and I will pack up the extras at the end of the day and send them home with you and the little girl."

Warm bagels, fresh from the oven, boiled just so before being baked. Rarely did she indulge in such a treat, but wouldn't the girls at the Booth Memorial Home be delighted by this man's generosity?

She nodded, elated. "I have people who will be truly gratified by your generosity."

"And the coffee, miss? What do you like in it?"

Temptation mounted. What she liked was cream and sugar, but why tease her senses with what couldn't be on a regular basis?

It's a holiday. Treat yourself. Why do you insist on going without? Doing without? The war is over. Stop punishing yourself.

While the war had ended, her life continued, and that meant providing for herself and her daughter. Eking out a living. Providing a home. Spoiling herself with nonessentials could make it more difficult to sacrifice when needed. With no further hesitation, she smiled at the bagel maker. "Black is fine."

"All right." He hurried back to the shop. Bright light shone a triangle onto the wet, gray pavement when he opened the door. Exhaust fans in the upper side wall pumped the scent of baking dough into the street. The fragrance warmed her, the thought of taking extra food to the expectant mothers at the home adding solace from within.

The parade's joyous noise pulled her attention back down the road. Laurie was now perched on the officer's shoulders, an enviable vantage point for any child. This would be a day to remember, an event to jot into the girl's memory book. At five years old and precociously bright, Laurie wouldn't care about a big meal or a family tradition she'd never known. But she'd remember this parade, viewed from high atop a policeman's shoulders.

The bagel scent made Karen's stomach gurgle.

She pushed the longing aside.

There would be little turkey at the home today. She'd seen the cook's face last evening. Donations were down as men and women scrambled to regain footholds lost while fighting a war on multiple fronts. But Major Dennison had a knack for turning out delicious meals from scant supplies, while volunteers and paid nursing staff looked after the young mothers. And they'd been given two fifty-pound sacks of surplus potatoes from the farmers' market. Potatoes could go a long way toward stretching meager turkey and gravy.

Karen smiled as she thought of Major Dennison, the Salvation Army officer in charge of the Booth Home kitchen who possessed a drill-sergeant persona. No one called Major Dennison by her first name. But the major's strict tactics covered a heart of service and sacrifice, two marvelous traits, well hidden.

"Here you go, miss."

Karen turned back. The bagel maker's earnest smile of understanding made her glance down.

"I thought a little cream and sugar might warm you better," he said, almost apologetic, as if striving not to hurt her pride.

Her eyes smarted. His gesture, kindly and good, sweetened the coffee more. "It's perfect. Thank you, Mister—?"

"Arnie." He pointed to the sign above the small shop. "Arnold Mencher." He shrugged and pointed east toward the cop and the little girl. "Mike's family has done business with us a long time, since the first war. Once neighbors. Now friends."

World War I. Karen nodded, following the path from his arm to the pair watching the drawn-out festivities. "You've made a lot of bagels, sir."

Her appreciation for sticking with a job deepened his smile. "First my father, then me. My father, he came over before the troubles grew worse. With Mike's grandfather."

Karen pondered his given name. "You are Polish."

"And Jewish." The man squared his shoulders, proud of his heritage. "Not all came over when there was a chance. And now . . . "

Karen read his shrug and understood the "now." Concentration camps had taken a huge toll on Eastern European Jews. "You have family, Arnie?"

He nodded and stepped aside as some passersby paused to drop coins into Karen's kettle. The sharp noise of the coins said few had stopped on their way to the parade. She hoped more would part with loose change at the parade's end, but something was always better than nothing.

"Two boys. One girl. In Brooklyn."

"Do they help?" she asked.

He shook his head. "I am typical American father now. I want much more for them. They have American schools, American citizenship, American dreams. They will have college. Many choices. It is a parent's wish to watch his child's success surpass his own. But my sister's boy, Stanley, he is my apprentice now. And he does well."

His words rang true in some ways. Didn't Karen want more for Laurie than she'd had herself? But also, in a time of increasing success, she worried that her child might one day have too much and not appreciate simple things. Like a mug of sweet coffee on a cold, rainy Thanksgiving. Leftover bagels formed by a hardworking immigrant's hands.

"The staff of life." She smiled at his shop as a few local customers went in, older folks more drawn to the warmth and smell of hot dough than to the parade a block away. "I think you've done fine for yourself, Arnie."

His frank expression thanked her. He hurried away as the strains of the last marching band faded to her right.

Short minutes later, crowds streamed by her, aiming for a subway station, happy folks heading home. Some dropped coins into her bucket. Most did not, but a few tipped their caps in her direction as she wished them a happy Thanksgiving.

Mike's expression said he noted the lack of participation, but Laurie's face . . .

Bright and animated, bursting with stories . . .

Pink cheeks and shining eyes meant a great deal. A day begun in the shadows of a doorway, brought into the light of joy with no change in the weather. Such is the power of a good remembrance, Karen knew.

"Your kettle isn't filling all that quickly." Mike took a few coins from his pocket and dropped them into the metal bucket.

"I think it's normal for Thanksgiving Day," Karen replied. "People have spent their money on food for a feast. And for some, shopping tomorrow is a big occasion."

"And you?" he wondered as he tugged his glove back on. "Will you be shopping tomorrow?"

"No. Working." She paused ringing for a moment to change hands. She wondered how much she should say as she stuffed her empty hand back inside the cloak to warm her chilled skin.

"Me too." He hesitated, then asked, "Do you work nearby?"

Karen wasn't a foolish woman. She'd seen a light of interest in the policeman's eyes, a sheen of appreciation. But she'd vowed never to be fooled by a man again, and now she had so much more at stake than a tarnished reputation.

Now she had Laurie.

So she shook her head and answered offhand, "Near Union Square. And you? Do you take the train into Manhattan?"

"From Brooklyn, yes. So . . . " He hemmed, then put out his hand again, much like he did first thing that morning. "Thank you for letting me walk Laurie down to the parade. We kept the peace together." He winked at the little girl, and her returned smile made Karen feel good about her decision.

"It was a great pleasure to her." She leaned down and covered Laurie's cheeks with butterfly kisses. "And a wonderful service to me, so we're both grateful."

The streets had pretty much cleared. The *clink* of a key in the lock said Arnie's Bagels was closing for the holiday.

The older man hurried their way, a large box in one hand and a small sack in the other. "Bagels." He set the box in the doorway alongside Laurie. "And cream cheese, of course."

"Of course." Mike exchanged grins with the older man as if cream cheese was a given. Karen had lived on nickels and dimes long enough to understand the true luxury of both treats.

"I had onion, sesame, and some plain leftover, and I made a batch of pumpernickel late in the day." Arnie clapped his hand to his head as though chastising himself. "What was I thinking?"

As Karen leaned down to set the bag of cream cheese next to the box of bagels, the tender, warm smell of the fresh breads assailed her.

Her stomach churned in wishful anticipation.

Her mouth watered.

But she didn't dive into the box the way she longed to. Instead she slipped off her damp glove, turned, and gave Arnie a hearty smile and her hand. "You will have made many people happy this day. Your generosity will not go unrewarded."

Arnie dismissed her thanks with a wave. "It is, of course, nothing. Happy Thanksgiving, miss."

"Karen," she told him. She waved a hand toward the usually busy intersection below them. "And I'll be ringing the bell each morning outside Macy's until Christmas Eve, so we'll see each other again."

"Each day?"

Too late, she realized that Mike might take her revelation the wrong way, as if she were flirting with him. Or hinting to Arnie for more food.

She was doing neither, but a part of her would like to see Mike again. So had she blurted out the information on purpose?

Kind of. And that was most likely foolishness on her part.

Arnie's smile said it was all right with him. "I will make sure you have coffee," he promised. "Ringing the bell for so many days is a big sacrifice. Maybe too big?" he wondered out loud, one gray brow cast up in question.

Major Flora had made the same argument a few weeks ago, but Karen remained adamant despite the hospital director's concerns.

The Salvation Army had fed her body and nourished her soul when she'd been homeless. Major Flora Parker had given her so much from an organization that catered to the least among mankind.

Karen had been among those "least." With the army's help, she was now a registered nurse, a professional woman. So getting by on a little less sleep for four short weeks was nothing in the grand scheme of things.

Karen raised her chin and shook her head. She knew what her past had wrought. She understood what the Salvation Army had done for her in her hour of need.

Now she was the one helping. Reaching out. Caring for those less fortunate. She'd been on both sides of the financial divide, and she understood that sometimes things happened. Sometimes, circumstances and emotions made for bad choices.

But from that choice came a precious blessing.

She palmed Laurie's head. "Most days Laurie will be in school. And my replacement will come at noon—"

"It's almost one," Mike interjected, but then he stopped when an old-style car rumbled up to the curb.

"Except for today," Karen finished. She indicated the old car and offered a quick greeting. "Major Flora. This is Officer Mike Wolzak and bagel maker Arnie Mencher."

The older woman climbed out, dressed in formal Salvation Army attire. She nodded to the men, but her smile went deep and wide as she faced Karen and Laurie. "I expect you two are ready for warmth. And food."

"I am quite starving," Laurie announced.

Mike grinned. Arnie's face softened, as if the child's words both amused and berated him. "I should have brought you a bagel earlier," he scolded himself. "I will be more aware next time."

"You have done many a great service." Karen reached out and enveloped one of his hands between both of hers. "We thank you, Arnie."

"And I thank you, Officer Mike!" Laurie barreled into Mike, hugging the big guy's legs. "You made me so happy!"

"Major Flora, look." Karen bent to retrieve the box of bagels. "Arnie has sent us a treat."

Major Flora's face went quiet. She turned to the Jewish baker. "When I was hungry, you fed me. Naked, you clothed me."

"In my books it is written that we please God by doing good for others. Happy Thanksgiving to you both."

"And you."

Mike helped load the bagels into the back of the car. Carefully, he stowed the mostly empty cast-iron kettle alongside the bagel box. Karen folded the tripod into a thin bundle of three legs and then laid it on the floor of the back seat.

"Karen, hop in," Major Flora said as she rounded the front of the car. "I'll take you and Laurie with me. Save you the subway fare."

"That would be a help." A part of her didn't want Mike or Arnie too privy to her tight financial status. But another part understood that humility was of God.

It was a lesson she'd struggled with since childhood, and didn't have much of an easier time today. "Gentlemen." She faced them both from her side of the car. "Thank you so much for your kindnesses."

"I will look forward to seeing you back here." Arnie's expression seemed to say that she'd just become his do-good project for the holiday season.

"And I'm working this section for the holidays, so it appears we'll meet again, ladies."

"Oh, I would like that a lot!" Laurie proclaimed her attraction to the big, robust policeman with a wide grin.

Karen chose a more refined reply. "As God wills."

His gaze followed her when she climbed into the car. As Major Flora pulled away from the curb to head to Lower Manhattan, Arnie hurried toward the subway station and a home filled with the scents of the day. Roast turkey. Mashed potatoes. Stuffing and pie.

But Mike stood strong and singular, legs braced, arms by his side, alone in the street now that the crowds had dispersed. The image he presented, a lone avenger, guarding the day, filled Karen with mixed emotions.

His honest and gentle strength drew her.

Her promise to herself said there was no room for more mistakes in her life, and unless life came with guarantees . . .

Which it did not . . .

She'd make it as she had, one day at a time, just her and Laurie, making do. They'd done all right so far.

And they'd continue to do just fine.

Chapter Two

. . . .

"Mike, we're short today. I know it's the holiday, but I figured you, bein' single . . . "

Temptation pulled Mike to say yes. He'd much rather catch a second shift and welcome the quiet anonymity of the empty streets than go to his aunt's house in Brooklyn and pretend it was a wonderful feast day while his mother's family recounted their happy memories of Irina Wolzak. They'd fuss over him and his sister like a clutch of old hens, sweet, sympathetic, and more than a little bossy.

Filial duty forced him to refuse the overtime. His parents would have expected him to take care of his sister, regardless of the circumstances. He owed them that and so much more. "I can't, Jack. Sorry."

"Ach, it's a formality anyway." Jack hooked a thumb, indicating the quiet city beyond street-dusted windows. "You go home. Maybe catch the game on the radio."

A radio at Aunt Frannie's? On Thanksgiving? That would never happen. The only reason she'd approved the purchase a few years ago was to stay updated on war news while the family served. "My aunt considers technology an intrusion and an unnecessary evil. We're eating there because—"

Jack waved a hand, sparing him from voicing the words. "I know. The first one's the toughest, Mike. It will get better."

Jack had lost a couple of family members early in the war, so he understood loss firsthand. A few days ago, Mike might have believed him that things would get better, but then Mary Lynn dropped her bombshell on him. He hadn't been able to eat or sleep for three days. A recent glimpse in the mirror said the stress was catching up with him. How could he face the family today if the aunts figured out Mary Lynn's delicate and disappointing condition? He accepted Jack's advice with a slow nod, then turned to go. "I'll catch the news in the paper, like always."

"See ya, Mike."

"Yeah."

Mike pulled his jacket collar higher. Teeming rain began as he trudged, head down, to the subway stop. The downpour made the walk to and from the subway thoroughly inhospitable, which suited his mood just fine.

"Mike, you're here! Ach, you're soaked, come in, come on, let me help you!" Uncle Joe reached to help peel off Mike's thick jacket, then he took the coat and hung it on Aunt Frannie's prize possession, a thick oak hall tree he'd pulled close to the fire.

"That's a hazard, you know," Mike warned, ever the cop. Then he smiled. "But it sure will feel nice to put on something warm and dry in a few hours."

Uncle Joe grabbed his arm and kept his voice low. "We've got the early game on upstairs, Irv and me. Detroit's getting pounded." He thumped Mike on the back, driving home the point with physical force.

"Remember how Dad loved baseball?"

Uncle Joe paused. Nodded. "Loved it like butter."

Mike laughed. The old family joke equated anything really good with butter. During the Depression, his father's family went without butter for years. When things eased up and wages rose, his father and his family tied all good things to God . . .

And butter.

"Mother got the best brand for today." Uncle Joe announced the butter procurement like he was describing the latest radio system in a car, as if nothing could be grander. "And Idaho potatoes."

"Wonderful."

Uncle Joe started to lead him to the stairs, but Mike waved him off. "I need to say hello to the ladies first. And I hear a pesky kid running around."

"Cousin Mike!" Little Joe burst out of a back room and slammed into his legs, much like Laurie had done earlier. Mike snatched the kid up and swung him around. Little Joe's shriek brought his mother running.

"You're on clean-up duty if you make him sick," Maggie warned, but she laughed as she said it, right up until she scanned the first-floor playroom with a mother's eye. "Joey, did you get out every toy Grandma has in there?"

Guilt stamped the kid's face. "Mostly."

"Well, put half of them back," Maggie scolded. "We have to catch the seven o'clock train back to the island, and if we miss it, Dad and I will not be happy."

"All right." The boy shuffled his feet and scowled. "I wish there were other kids around here. This house is boring."

Maggie's face went sad.

Mike stood, tongue-tied, longing to ease the moment. His cousin had lost two babies after giving birth to Joey. Her expression said she accepted the blame for her kid's loneliness. It was crazy to think like that. Mike might not know a lot about pregnancy, but he understood guilt real well. He hooked an arm around Maggie and gave her a half hug. "We keep praying, right? That one of these times, everything will be perfect for you guys."

She made a face that said enough was enough. "I'm just stinkin' tired of being sad, Mike. You know?"

Oh, he knew all right. But God hadn't installed an on/off switch for human emotion, and that meant they'd have to plod through the ups and the downs, same as always. Lately, though, there'd been too many downs.

For no reason he could fathom, the image of Karen's face came back to him. How she met his gaze and smiled, so sweet. The way she secured the child's hair beneath the coat's collar, thinking ahead. And how many folks sacrificed hours each day to ring the bell for a local charity?

Very few.

So that made Karen O'Leary special beyond words, but Mike had sensed her reticence when he inquired about her job. She wore no one's ring; he'd noticed that when she slipped off her gloves. But she'd clearly put him off, and that meant she had a reason to put him off. Was she a war widow, raising a child alone? Maybe.

"Mike! You're here, you have made it!" Aunt Frannie burst through the swinging door, interrupting his thoughts. She stopped short of hitting him with it, then grabbed his face in her two hands. "Every day I pray to God to bring you and Mary Lynn peace. Joy. Warmth. Too much, too much, I say to Him." She waved a fisted hand in the air as if hailing God's attention, then brought the hand back to his cheek. "And He listens to me, Mikey."

His look of doubt must have shown because Aunt Frannie rolled her eyes and firmed her look, an expression his mother had used. "He listens to all. Our trials, our sorrows. You believe *that*, the rest will come."

Mike bit back a sigh.

Aunt Frannie meant well, and she loved and missed her sister, but she still had her husband and kids, her family unscathed by the war.

Mike's father had perished in France, and Mike hadn't gotten word of his death for nearly a month. By that time it just made sense to stay put and continue the fight.

And then he'd come home, ready to help his mother and sister, only to have his mother's cancer diagnosis revealed. In less than three years' time they'd lost both parents.

He went back to police work and caring for his younger sister, insisting he could do the job on his own, despite his aunts' and uncles' offers of help.

And now Mary Lynn was pregnant. Unwed. Unpromised. And no way on earth would he let that scumbag kid near his sister with a ring, even if the kid offered.

Which he hadn't.

He accepted Aunt Frannie's words with a halfhearted shrug. "I don't find much time to pray these days, Aunt Frannie."

"Time is nothing," she scoffed, then drew closer, her soft blue eyes boring into his. "For you, me, for us." She waved the left hand around again. "We do best when we live our lives as a prayer."

"That's hard for a cop."

"Bah." Aunt Frannie's expression deepened. "A cop is like a good dog, protecting the sheep, the lambs. The dog means no harm but protects as needed. And that is what a good policeman does. You. Your father. Your uncle, your grandpa."

A whole line of Wolzaks and Carmichaels had manned the force for three generations, a history that held the family in good stead. Law and order was bred into their blood, their bones, bolstered by righteousness. But Mike hadn't felt very righteous of late.

"Uncle Mike, did you get to see the parade?" Joey came back into the room, his face wistful.

Mike nodded. "I did."

"Did you love it so much?"

Mike couldn't pretend otherwise. "Yes."

"Can I maybe go next year? Please?"

"Joey, don't pester your uncle." Maggie started bringing things to the table, pretty china plates and old-style silverware, just polished. "He's been working all day."

Mike knew that wasn't exactly true. He'd kept an eye on his parade grounds while holding a small child, a beautiful girl, giving her a joyous morning. He'd delighted the child and therefore the mother, and he wasn't about to pretend he wasn't pleased by both outcomes. "Yes, I'll take you next year. I promise. That way Mom can help Grandma, okay?"

"Okay!" Joe ran back off to the playroom.

Mike moved to go into the kitchen.

Maggie stopped him. Gave him a hug. "Thank you."

"For?" He kept his voice gruff to stave off any more rising emotions. He'd had enough of those already and he'd barely gotten in the door.

"You bring hope, Mike." She backed off and smiled at him. "It's your gift."

Hope, huh?

His hope hadn't helped his little sister all that much, and he had no idea how to handle the situation. He could barely talk about her condition without wanting to wring the boy's neck.

And maybe hers.

He'd been young once, but it seemed so long ago now. He understood temptation. And truth to tell, he was no saint, but society allowed different standards for men.

God doesn't.

The truth of that made Mike sigh.

Eventually he'd matured. Being a soldier had a way of doing that to a man, and serving on multiple fronts deepened the process. But he'd never been a young girl, bereft of parents, longing for love while her big brother worked away his grief protecting the streets of New York. Which meant he'd failed to serve and protect the most important person assigned to him, his little sister.

The swinging door opened once more. This time Mary Lynn came through, carrying a pile of freshly ironed linen napkins. She didn't look up, didn't meet his eye, and the pain of that pierced deep.

Did she hate him?

Fear him?

Was she scared to death of what was to come? Because frankly, he was.

She set the napkins around the table, then the silverware, chin down, her blonde hair a curtain drawn over half her face.

He'd stopped at a church early that morning, grateful for the open door. The softly lit sanctuary called him forward. He sank to his knees on a leather-wrapped kneeler and folded his hands, but when he looked up at the cross, anger skewed his emotions. He saw no sacrifice in the burnished oak. All he saw were two planks of wood, crossed in geometric simplicity. And that made him feel even more alone.

"Mare? You need help?" He offered the words as a gesture, because they both knew she needed more help than he could give, but today, for the holiday, they'd pretend everything was all right. Even though it wasn't.

* * * * *

"You be good for Jane, okay?" Karen gave Laurie one last kiss and then turned her attention to the morning volunteer who had offered to watch her. "And you're sure you don't mind having Laurie here? The weather—"

"She's fine. Go. Ring that bell. No reason for Laurie to be out in the cold today."

Karen gathered her cloak close as she walked to the Lexington Avenue station. Wind whipped beneath her layered bonnet, and she wished she'd had time to knit a warm hat and scarf for herself, but work and Laurie took the bulk of her time. She was blessed to have a room at the hospital, though, a cozy corner where she and Laurie could be safe and unencumbered with extra bills. Living practically rent free meant a slightly lower salary, but in Manhattan, low rent was nothing to shrug off. And the hospital provided a safe and secure environment for her daughter, and that was nothing Karen took lightly.

She exited the subway in Midtown and hurried to her kettle station, east of where she'd stood yesterday.

Throngs of shoppers made walking slow, and her nursing watch told her she was already five minutes late. She passed Arnie's Bagels on her right. The warm dough scent was just as good, maybe better, than yesterday because now she understood the delicious chewiness of his hand-turned, fresh-baked bagels.

The girls would eat the second half of the bagels tonight with their dinners, and that was a thought to savor.

She spotted the kettle on the edge of Broadway and paused to collect her bearings. The drop-off person had set it too close to the road, but foot traffic and the cumbersome tripod made it almost impossible to shift the heavy kettle easily. The lock on the kettle made stealing more difficult, but it also meant the whole assembly had to be moved as one.

She drew a breath and started to encircle the unwieldy setup with her arms.

"Let me help."

She knew that voice. That tone, deep and steady. Firm but kind. "Mike."

He smiled down at her and lifted two legs of the tripod while she grasped the third. "Where would you like this?" he asked.

"Closer to the buildings," she told him. "I won't be collecting anything that close to the road. Unless the taxi drivers decide to throw me their fares."

His laugh said he didn't expect that to happen.

Neither did Karen. But then, she hadn't expected Mike to be on hand to help her get settled with the kettle, and he'd appeared out of nowhere, a knight in shining armor.

Or a man on a mission, with one thought in mind.

"Where's Laurie today?" His face, gently humored, made her think of long walks and chess games, peaceful afternoons. But his eyes still showed the depth of old aches.

"With a friend." She wouldn't say anything more than that, no identifiers. "It's kind of nasty to have her out here."

"It's nasty for you, too." His voice scolded just a little, as if he cared about her comfort and warmth. "How long are you here today?"

"Two hours." She made sure the kettle and tripod were secure before withdrawing the bell from her cloak pocket. She started tolling the bell, its cheerful noise drawing smiles from happy shoppers.

"Let me start you off." Mike reached into his uniform pocket and withdrew a folded bill. As he pushed the folded bill into the money slot, a few folks noticed what he was doing.

Another person filed up to the kettle, slid some quiet money into the slot, and hurried away. He was followed by a mother and two teenage daughters. They fussed as they dug into purses and pockets for every bit of spare change they could find, and when they started inserting the pile of coins, the steady *Clink! Clink! Clink!* turned heads her way.

"Merry Christmas!" Karen sang the words out, cheerful and sweet, just the way she'd heard others do in the past, remembering a night when a bell ringer's voice hailed her to warmth and safety. She'd been saved that night, in more ways than one.

Now it was her turn.

More folks stopped by, dropping loose change and the occasional folded bill into the shiny red kettle.

"And you're on your way." Mike's look congratulated her on a good start.

"Thank you for seeding the pot," she whispered, and when he drew close . . .

So close she could count specks of pale green in sky-blue eyes . . .

He reached out and grasped her hand. "You're welcome. I'll see you later."

His words spiked her heart rhythm, but wasn't that exactly how she'd felt six years ago? As if Gilbert's promises meant something?

They didn't and she'd been foolish, but now she considered herself wiser. Especially where romance was concerned.

For nearly an hour she rang the bell, nonstop. The steady stream of well-wishers and contributors made her feel as if she was accomplishing something today. Making a difference. And wasn't that another part of why she opted to take the less lucrative job with the Salvation Army hospital? Because these kind, good people made a difference in down-and-out lives, every single day. And she wanted to be part of that.

"Karen? Try this."

Karen turned with just over an hour to go. Hands numb, she'd been alternating them beneath her cape to maintain some warmth, but it was a feeble gesture in the face of the low temperatures and cold, wet wind. She pulled up a smile from somewhere down deep. "You're back."

"Mm-hmm." Firm hands looped an extra-long, bright red knitted scarf around her neck. Then Mike handed her a matching hat, thick-knit and lined with red cotton. He smiled approval as she pulled the hat down over her head, then drew the bonnet back up to provide another layer of protection.

"Better?"

It was embarrassing to admit, but . . . "Much," she told him. "I can feel my ears again. Almost."

He smiled, then held out a pair of costly black gloves. Karen recognized the quality right off and took a full step back, concerned. "I can't accept those, Mike."

"You can't wear warm gloves?" His eyebrows spiked sky-high. "That's the silliest thing I ever heard."

She frowned, exasperated, unsure what to say. "I can't because that's an expensive gift." Her gaze swept the lined leather gloves. "I don't accept gifts from strangers. As a police officer, I'm sure you understand the logic in that."

"Well." He stood firm at her side, allowing plenty of room for people to feed the kettle in front of her. The duller sound of the coins meant today's kettle would help feed many. "These aren't gifts. They were my mother's, and she'd be insulted if they sat in our house, unused, while someone stood out in the cold. She'd be affronted by the very idea."

"She's gone?"

He drew a breath and nodded, but the ache in his eyes said more than his next words. "Four months ago. Cancer. And if you were to have met her, you'd realize that nothing in her house went to waste or sat unused. The very thought would be a travesty of her faith. So, please." He held out the gloves again. "On behalf of Irina Rose Wolzak, accept these gloves to keep your hands warm. It is the least she would do if she were here. I brought them to the station this morning, in case I saw you."

His words opened her heart and touched her soul. She reached out and Mike peeled her thin gloves from her hands. Then he held out the leather ones, one hand at a time, allowing her to slip her fingers into the fur-lined hand protectors.

Her smile inspired his, and it broadened as she wiggled her fingers. He grasped her hands in his for just a second, but what a sweet second it was. "Better?"

"So much."

He dipped his chin with a victor's grace, as if he'd just won an important battle. "Good. Stay safe." He tipped his policeman's cap and moved on, walking the beat with an easy air. But then, he was carrying a night stick and a gun, so he could walk most anywhere un-accosted.

The thick scarf warmed her neck and chest. The hat was snugged tight against her head, and while her hair would look dreadful once she arrived back at the Booth Memorial Home, no one there would care. And she felt so much more comfortable bundled up this way.

But the gloves were the best. Warm fur blanketed both of her hands, from palm to the tip of each finger. Slowly the iced feeling left her, and warmth replaced it.

How did he know to bring her things?

As she watched his broad shoulders move south on Broadway, she realized that his days were exposed to the elements as well. So of course he'd know what she needed to stand out here hour after hour.

But why does he care? What's in it for him?

A tiny corner of her heart longed to wish for the sincere interest of a good man, a gentle soul, but her track record didn't bode well in that department.

Maybe Mike was as nice and sincere as he seemed.

Maybe he wasn't.

But in any case, she was blessed by what he shared, his mother's accessories, to keep her warm.

The soft scent of sweet vanilla perfumed her face, her chin. Irina had chosen a welcoming aroma, a smell that reminded Karen of vintage kitchens and fresh-baked cookies.

She might do just that tonight, she decided. Once she had a nap, that is. Tonight's overnight shift would end just in time for Laurie to visit a friend tomorrow. Karen would catch a few hours of sleep first thing in the morning, ring the bell, and then catch another nap before doing the weekend overnight shift.

And then have a quiet Sunday with her daughter. Those hours together made everything else totally worth it.

Chapter Three

He'd pleased Karen.

A silly grin leaked up from nowhere Mike recognized, a smile in response to a young woman's look of pleasure and comfort.

He felt good, but when a young thug made off with an elderly woman's purse two storefronts ahead of him, Mike took off in hot pursuit.

The kid was quick.

Mike was quicker. Of course it didn't hurt that the clutch of shoppers held the kid up, thwarting his idea of a swift escape. And by the time Mike had the cuffs on him, backup had arrived. The new cop on-scene put in a call for a pickup, but the harried note in the dispatcher's voice said it wouldn't be arriving any too soon.

"Great." The second cop glared at the miscreant, then his watch. "My wife has company coming over tonight, kid. The first time she's had guts enough to plan anything since we got married, and I'll be late getting there because you had to knock off an old woman for six dollars and forty-two cents."

The kid stared down, silent and still.

"Call his mother," Mike advised. That got the kid's attention. His chin jerked up and his eyes raked the street, searching for a means of escape.

There was none.

"I bet his mother doesn't know sonny-boy is out here ripping off old ladies. Does she, son?" Mike laid the question out as if the kid was a long-lost best friend. He leaned in as the kid showed signs of remorse. "She'll be disappointed, I expect."

"Mike, we've got another situation." Reggie Smith jerked his head north. "Two kids just ripped off a Salvation Army bell ringer up Broadway. They knocked her down and ran off with the kettle. Some people tried to stop them, but they hopped into a car waiting a block up and sped off."

Mike heard one thing only. *"Salvation Army bell ringer."*

He tossed Reggie the keys to the cuffs and set off at a run. "I'm covering the bell ringer. Call Bucci to help you here."

"Will do."

Three blocks separated him from Karen. He'd felt pretty light on his feet when he walked away from her a half hour before. Her accepting attitude made him appreciate things, and he hadn't had a lot to feel good about lately. Karen's smile changed that.

Now his feet felt leaden, even though they ate the ground with a speed he didn't know he possessed.

What if the kids hurt her? Visions of her lying there, injured, took over his senses.

Anger rose inside him, raw fury, a thrusting surge he hadn't felt since returning home from the front. He cut through lights, bounded the curb, and nearly plowed two older women over in his hurry.

The women scolded something in Italian but went silent when he paused before Karen. Then the two old ladies adopted a more interested posture, along with the small crowd gathered at the cor-ner's edge.

"Are you all right?" He said it too gruffly, too overwrought, making it sound like the mugging was her fault.

She swung his way and looked happy to see him. "Mike, I'm so glad you came."

He stared, confused, because the woman before him didn't look roughed up, or even all that riled. Maybe Reggie was wrong. Or maybe . . . and he hated that he welcomed this idea with more joy than he should have . . . it was a different bell ringer needing his help.

But no. One glance around showed her kettle was gone, tripod and all. "Of course I came." His inner fury lessened a little because she looked no worse for the wear except for a long streak of muddy water staining the back of her cloak. "Are you okay?"

"I'm fine, a little wet. Mussed up, for sure. But, Mike"—she leaned closer, her face pinched in worry—"the money is gone. The kettle is gone. And we were doing so well today."

"The important thing is you," he insisted. He spun her around, making sure there was no hidden damage, but stopped when she squared her shoulders and faced him down.

"I am fine." She stretched the words out, enunciating each one, convincing him. "But that money is meant for people down on their luck. The poor. The impoverished. How on earth am I going to replace it?"

"Replace it?" Did he sound as dumb as he felt? He hoped not, because they had quite a crowd gathered around them now, a crescent-shaped group, murmuring. Whispering. Wondering. "Karen, don't worry about that. It's just money."

"Just money?"

Her mouth dropped open. Her eyes went wide. Clearly the concept of "just money" didn't ring her bell. She looked so put out that Mike almost took a step back, but that would be silly. Right?

"That money feeds babies." She poked a finger at him, narrowly missing his chest, but only because he retreated slightly. "It provides food and shelter for the poor. And Mike, it wasn't *my* money. It was the army's, and I was the guardian of it. I failed, and I need to replace it. How can I do that? Do you think you'll find the kids that took the kettle? Get the money back?"

They'd try, but most likely the kettle would be found in less than pristine condition, sawed open and the money extracted. "We might."

"But you might not." Worry creased her brow, and he found himself in the awkward spot of wanting to soothe the furrow away. Hug her close to make her feel safe. Only she didn't seem the least bit frightened.

Mad? Yes.

Concerned? Assuredly.

Frightened? Not a bit, and he wondered why that was. She'd just been mugged, for heaven's sake. Shouldn't she be?

"And how do we figure out what might have been in there?" She puzzled the question, pacing in front of the shop, seemingly oblivious to the crowd. "It's not like I keep track of what folks contribute or anything like that."

"Allow me to help." A well-dressed man stepped forward and handed Mike a twenty-dollar bill. "Add this to her kettle funds whether or not you find it, okay?"

What choice did Mike have? "Um, sure. Of course. I—"

The Italian women walked up and gave him five dollars. "For the young lady's kettle."

A louder murmur swept a wave across the gathered crowd. As more and more people pressed forward to hand Mike money to keep for Karen's kettle, other passersby paused, wondering what was going on. As the story passed on, how the bell ringer with the merry red scarf and hat was attacked and her kettle stolen, good-hearted people from every direction pushed in, wanting to add to the funds.

Before too long, Mike's hands couldn't hold the wad of bills and coin. Ignoring the cold, he took off his patrolman's hat and put the money in there.

The crowd cheered.

Karen smiled, a look of gratitude and wonder so dear that a tiny latch on his somewhat rusty heart opened, seeing it. For that moment, with people gathering around them, replenishing the stolen funds, he *felt* like a hero.

"Here you go."

"Take this!"

"Here's a fiver. Merry Christmas."

Dialects from every borough resounded, and Mike got a solid glimpse of something understated and wonderful: When New Yorkers rose to an occasion, lines of division didn't stand in their way. Except for the possibility of Major League Baseball, in which case he was Brooklyn born and raised in the shadow of Ebbets Field, a Dodger fan from birth, even though the Yankees had just taken another World Series title.

The bums.

"Nice assignment, Mike."

Al Bucci approached from the right-hand side. He nodded to Karen and bent lower, solicitous. "Are you all right, miss?"

"She's fine." Mike could have snapped the words with more professionalism, but while Al was a great cop, he was a guy who played the field romantically, and Mike wasn't about to stand by and watch Al sweep the bell ringer off her feet with his usual charm.

"Ah." Al lifted his eyes to Mike's, and Mike was pretty sure the other guy was laughing at him quietly. "We had the kid picked up."

"Good."

"And I think he was part of the group that caused this ruckus here." Al indicated Karen with a thrust of his chin. "He created a diversion a block away, we chase him down, these kids take out the bell ringer and get the money pot. Notice they waited until she'd been here a while."

"They planned it?"

Al hiked a shoulder. "It appears so. The kid ratted his buddies out because his mother's threatening to let him stay in lockup indefinitely. Says he's incorrigible and needs to have new friends."

"I can't argue with that." Karen scowled but then faced the crowd, brighter. "I hope you all know just how thankful I am. How grateful the army will be." She moved into the crowd, shaking hands, giving thanks to all she could. "This money, your donations, they will bring a better tomorrow to the least of us."

"Glad to help, ma'am."

"Merry Christmas, miss."

"Nice copper you've got there, young lady!"

The last comment brought a blush to her cheeks. She glanced around, her face wondering if Mike heard.

Oh, he'd heard all right. He smiled. Winked.

Her color pitched higher, and Mike was pretty sure the chill temperatures had little to do with it.

Gradually the crowd dispersed, but not before a shopper combined her purchases into a large corded-handle bag and gave them a smaller variety to hold the cash.

"There's nearly two hundred dollars here," Mike estimated as he put the bills in the bottom and topped them with coin. "Karen, that's amazing."

"That's the Holy Spirit, touching hearts. Saving lives. It *is* amazing, isn't it?"

"It is, but we've got a problem." He faced Al and frowned. "We can't leave her alone with this money. And we're not off duty for nearly four hours."

"I can have dispatch call the army. They can send someone to collect this," Al proposed.

"Can they tell them we need a new kettle, too?"

Mike aimed what he hoped was a stern gaze down. "You are not staying another hour to finish your shift. You've had enough trauma for one day. Can the army give you a ride home again, or will you use the subway?"

* * * * *

Karen squared her shoulders and drew herself up to her full height, because no matter how handsome and strong the policeman was, no one charted her destiny but her. And the Good Lord. "I will stay. And you want to talk about trauma?" She raised a hand and ticked off her fingers. "Soldiers with limbs amputated from fighting a war. Widows, scraping a living, barely getting by, trying to make ends meet. Children with no food, no warm shoes or socks with winter coming. Old folks unable to get out and get food, no one to care for them. Young women with child, on their own, fearing to give birth much like Mary in Bethlehem. When I was hungry . . . " She let the quote trail off as she sent a smile over his shoulder. "Arnie!"

"I brought a treat for you to eat as you work, miss." He held out a waxed-paper-wrapped bagel, fresh and good. Heat from the bagel steamed the inside of the paper, the curved bread was that fresh. In his other hand he toted a mug of coffee, a replica of the day before. "I did put a little of my favorite cream cheese on the bagel," he added, almost apologetic again, as if he didn't want her to feel guilty over his gesture. He spoke in run-on sentences, his quick, patchwork speech underscoring his immigrant status. "This cheese, they make it in a little town up north, now it's here"—he waved his hand, showing he meant in New York City—"so delicious, I think. I hope"—he put his hands out in an inviting gesture of kindness—"you like."

"Of course I will." She beamed at him, but then Arnie turned his attention to the two policemen.

"There is much to watch on this corner, gentlemen?"

Mike read the older man's meaning and laughed, then shrugged, admitting, "You're a quick study, Arnie. Unfortunately today there is a reason for us to be here *besides* the pretty girl."

His look made heat rise to her cheeks a few minutes ago. His words, now? They warmed her from within, but she did her best to ignore them, even if there was no way she could ignore the speaker. Not with his broad shoulders, square chin, and big blue eyes.

Mike angled his gaze her way. "Karen got mugged a little while ago."

Arnie said something in another language, something short and curt and probably not meant for a lady's ears, but Karen was deeply touched by his quick, protective emotion.

"And then all these people started pushing money on us," Karen added.

"Money?" Arnie raised a brow in disbelief.

Mike held the bag open. Arnie whistled. Al nodded.

"But I don't know when the army officer will get here with another kettle," Karen fussed, "or to pick up this money. It isn't safe out here on the street. Arnie?" She waited until the older man turned her way. "Could we keep the money at your shop? Just until the officers come by to do a pickup?"

Arnie clapped a hand to his heart. "It is my pleasure to help."

"That's a great idea." Mike's look of approval made her feel good, and if she wasn't careful, she'd be seeking his approval in other things. Would that be bad? Wrong? One look at the kind but firm set of his chin said it was neither.

Mike clapped the older man on the shoulder. "Thank you, Arnie."

"I'll walk back to the shop with him," Al decided. "Just in case these little thugs have friends hanging around, waiting for the uniforms to take a hike."

"Thanks, Al."

"Yes." Karen reached out and touched Al's sleeve. When he turned, she shook his hand. "Thank you for coming over here. For helping to keep us safe."

"You're welcome, miss . . . ?"

"Karen." She stuck out her hand. "Karen O'Leary. I'm—"

"And that's all he needs to know right now, isn't it, Al?" Mike sent a pointed look toward the baker as he edged closer to Karen's side. "Because Arnie needs to get back to his shop. I'll watch out for Karen."

Al's grin said he understood the unspoken message while Arnie moved toward the road's edge, waiting for the light to turn green. "You are right, Michael. This is a busy day."

"Let's go." Al fell into step next to Arnie, the bag tucked beneath Arnie's arm.

"Well then." Mike moved a step closer to Karen, not touching her but not all that far from touching her, either. And it felt nice to have him there, to stand in the shadow of his warmth and strength. As long as she realized that was all she could do.

He switched his attention to her as the men crossed the busy street. Careful, he laid his hands on her shoulders. "Are you sure you're all right? Really?"

All right? With his blue eyes boring into hers? With the pressure of his big, rugged hands on her shoulders making her feel like the safest woman in the world? The scents surrounding them, fresh bread, car exhaust, roasted nuts, and him.

A scent that was uniquely Mike, clean, fresh, but manly.

"I'm fine." She shrugged away from his grip, refusing to let herself go there. She'd learned a tough lesson as a teenage girl. But faith, hard work, and determination had moved her to a more stable point in life, at long last. She would do nothing to risk that, now or ever.

Chapter Four

....

Would Mary Lynn be home? Or would she be out someplace, leaving him no word? And had he given his mother this much trouble as a teen?

He knew he hadn't. But then he'd had a solid, stable family life from day one. For over five years, all Mary Lynn had known was war and want, a time of sacrifice, then loss. He couldn't equate his behavior with hers. And while she wasn't a young seventeen by any means, she was a gentle-hearted girl, seeking love.

Intellectually, he understood her actions. Emotionally, he felt like the biggest loser in the world. One job, one not-so-big job, to look out for his almost grown sister, and he'd blown it.

The brownstone's stairs gave a familiar squeak. His mother said she could always tell when Dad was coming home by the way the staircase creaked, just so. The melancholy memory pinched. Only two sets of footsteps would echo on these stairs now. That seemed plain wrong.

The scent of warm turkey greeted him as he opened the door. He breathed deep and bypassed the living room to step up, into the kitchen. "You cooked?"

Mary Lynn made a wry face. "Aunt Frannie dropped it off. Said all I had to do was heat it up, and I figured that couldn't be too hard." Her expression didn't seem to agree with Aunt Frannie's assessment, though. Tear streaks ran down her face, and she stared at the stove as if traumatized.

"Did you burn yourself?"

She shook her head, then drew a breath.

The breath did her in. Her face paled to some shade of gray green Mike had no name for, and she raced for the bathroom.

Mike stood frozen in place, wondering what to do. He wanted to call Maggie, ask her how he could help, but Mary Lynn begged him to keep things quiet, at least for now. But how could he when she was so clearly sick and he had no means of help available?

"Mare? Can I help?"

"No." She sounded tired. Maybe disgusted. With herself? With him? With her condition? He didn't know.

"Why don't you rest? Take a nap? Are naps good for you?"

A half laugh, half cry came from beyond the golden oak door. "I don't know. I have no idea. But if I sleep now, I'll never sleep tonight. And tomorrow I'm supposed to go to a baby shower for Cousin Tess."

A baby shower? Sympathy welled within Mike. "Can you handle that okay? Emotionally? Physically? Won't the smells bother you?" A Polish party was a celebration of foods, including cooked cabbage rolls. Spiced sausage. Chewy bread. And amazing pastries to round out the day, but the combination of odors couldn't be easy for Mary Lynn if the simple, single aroma of heated turkey and gravy sent her scrambling to the bathroom.

She opened the door and faced him, looking pinched and miserable. Without a word he extended his arms. She fell into them, crying like she had years ago, when someone broke her favorite toy. Or when their little dog went missing, never to be seen again.

Mom had fixed her toy almost good as new.

Dad had gone to the country and found a likely batch of pups and let her pick one out. Bogey had been their dog for nine years now, a sweet, shaggy thing with not a bit of guile. Just a good old dog.

But Mom and Dad were gone, and Mike had no clue how to fix the current predicament, so he just held her close, letting her cry, offering the only thing he had: love.

"I don't know what to do, Mike, what to say. I know that pretty soon people will realize I'm pregnant and they'll be staring at me, shocked. Surprised. Disgusted. And I don't know how to handle any of it. And then today, Danny called."

"I don't want him anywhere near you." Mike didn't release her, but he loosened his hold enough to look down, into her eyes. "He's no good, Mare. No matter how cool he seems or seemed, he's the kind of guy who puts himself first, always. You don't believe he was thinking of your welfare when he—" Mike arched an eyebrow.

Mary Lynn huffed a breath, understanding him without words. "No. He wasn't. Not then and not now. He thinks I should get rid of the baby, Mike."

"You mean have someone adopt it? When it's born?"

The answering look on her face said that wasn't the kid's intent, which meant . . .

"An abortion?" That the kid had the audacity to suggest an illegal and immoral act heightened Mike's anger.

"He said there was a doctor he heard about in Queens, but . . . I can't do that, Mike." She teared up again and Mike pulled her close, hugging her. "It's not the baby's fault that I'm stupid."

"You're not stupid." He toughened his voice, ready to do battle. It was all right if he thought her actions were dumb. It wasn't all right for her to think so. "We all make mistakes, Mare. We're all young at one time or another."

"Not you, Mike." She pulled back, grabbed a hanky, and blew her nose. "You're always doing the right thing. Working. Protecting. Fighting wars. I'm the one who messes up. I couldn't even fold the stupid bandages right when Mom took me to Ladies' Day to help get things done."

"You were twelve."

"Old enough to help." Mary Lynn heaved a sigh, then worried the cotton hanky in her hand. "I'm not smart enough to be a mom. Not yet. But I would never do what Danny said."

"What'd you tell him?"

"I told him to never call me again. And to stay away from me and my kid."

Mike liked that scenario. And because he did approve it, he figured it might not be the best one, but for now he'd let it ride. Because keeping Mary Lynn healthy and calm was taking top priority on his list.

He nodded toward the kitchen. "You hungry or no?"

Her skin washed out again. She shook her head.

"Then why don't you go rest. If you don't feel like going with Aunt Fran tomorrow, stay home. I'm working tomorrow, but I'm off on Monday."

"I have school Monday."

He nodded. "But we need to find you a doctor, a woman's doctor. We need to make sure you're okay, Mare." He turned to go back to the kitchen.

Mary Lynn's voice stopped him. "Do you hate me, Mike?"

He shook his head. Turned. "Never."

"But you're disappointed in me."

Mike eyed the wall, the ceiling, the floor. He sighed, then brought his gaze back to hers, reached out an arm, and tugged her down to sit beside him on the step. "I'm ten years older than you are."

She nodded.

"Until that war came along, I had everything going for me. Family. Home. School. Baseball."

She smiled at that, because they'd been brought up to love baseball. The ball park was their home-away-from-home. The game was second nature. They'd played ball in the park from the time they were small children. Neighbors joined in, parents. Friends. Playing ball was woven into the fabric of their lives.

"I went to war knowing who I was, what I was doing, what I was fighting for. And being a soldier grows you up, hard and fast." He reached his arm around her and gave her a gentle squeeze. "But being home alone is hard on women. The extra work, the worry, the waiting so long between letters. When you're in the trenches, time just passes. You lose track, you just go from one battle to the next, praying.

"Back here?" He raised his right shoulder and sighed. "I guess I didn't know how hard it was to be left behind, waiting for that telegram. I can't even think of how difficult that was for you and Mom, with Dad and me gone. Mom going out to work. You coming home to an empty house, day after day. And then Dad died, and you guys bore that alone too. You handled Mom's illness on your own until I got back. Mare, it's not that you're a mess-up. It's that you had too much on your plate, and I didn't realize that until you told me about the baby."

"Too late," she whispered.

The drama in her voice challenged him.

It *wasn't* too late. He'd tackled his share of hard work in the army. And it wasn't going to be easy to deal with this new circumstance. Was she going to be sick every day? Emotional? On the verge of tears constantly? Was this normal?

He hoped not, but he had no idea, which meant they needed to seek professional help. That meant owning up to a doctor—a stranger—about his sister's condition. He wasn't about to consult his two buddies who'd recently become new fathers. Keeping Mary Lynn's condition quiet for the time being was important.

To whom? You or her?

Both, Mike decided. His parents hadn't aired dirty linen in public. Neither would he. And if he needed a little time to figure out the best course of action, he'd take it.

"I'm going to lie down for a little bit." She raised her gaze to his, and he knew what she longed for. He read the petition in her tear-filled eyes. She wanted forgiveness and absolution, but Mike had been a black-and-white, right-and-wrong kind of guy for as long as he could remember. Those qualities made him a good soldier and a great cop. Right now, Mary was looking for a shade of gray he couldn't offer her, and frankly? He wasn't sure he ever could.

* * * * *

Quieter streets greeted Mike on Sunday morning. He strode up one side of Macy's, then down another, reality sinking in.

No Karen.

He moved across the street, walking the beat he'd been assigned, watching for a glimpse of her shiny, red kettle.

Nothing.

Perturbed, he walked into Arnie's shop midday and ordered a bagel loaded with cream cheese, olives, and pastrami. And while Stan put his sandwich together, Mike nonchalantly approached

Arnie. "Have you seen our Salvation Army ringer this morning, Arnie?"

Arnie turned from the boiling pot, surprised. "It's Sunday, Mike."

It was. Mike nodded.

Arnie's expression said Mike was a little slow on the uptake. "Salvationists don't work on Sunday. Unless it's a necessary job like yours."

She wasn't there.

Queer how his heart tightened in disappointment, knowing he wouldn't see her today. *Or tomorrow.* He was off tomorrow, and he'd be spending his morning checking out how to take care of Mary Lynn's situation. Finding a doctor.

"Here you go, Mike." Stan handed over the bagel sandwich. Mike handed him a five, accepted his change, and started to walk out the door.

"Mike?" Arnie's voice made him pause.

"Yeah?"

"Our bell ringer." He pointed toward the shopping district corner Karen had been assigned. "You think she is all right after yesterday's scuffle?"

Mike didn't want to admit he'd been wondering the same thing. Mental trauma sometimes reared its head well after the fact. "I don't know. But she's feisty, so I'd say yes."

Arnie shrugged agreement, but his face still showed concern. "Feisty, yes. And beautiful. With a story, I think, which is why she rings the bell."

Mike moved closer. He had no idea why people rang the bell, just that they did. Christmas bell ringers had been around as long as he could remember shopping Midtown at Christmas.

Just another holiday tradition, right? "You need a story to ring the bell? Is that like a prerequisite?"

"It is a payoff," said Arnie.

"Payback," Stan corrected him.

"Ach, yes, payback." The older Mencher made a face. "If the army helps you, you help them."

Karen had needed help? For what? Mike wondered. He knew the army had actively helped troops in Europe and Asia. Did they do the same here, for those left behind? He filed the information and held his sandwich aloft. "Gotta go, guys. See ya."

"Thanks, Mike." Stan's voice followed him out into the cool day, but it was Arnie's words he focused on. If Karen was paying back for kindnesses rendered, what had the army done for her? He didn't have the least idea, and there was no one to ask but Karen herself, and she wasn't there.

* * * * *

"Mommy, may I ring with you tomorrow?" Laurie hopped onto the bed they shared in their army-provided studio apartment on Sunday morning.

"And miss school? I think not." She grinned at the little girl, shooed her off the bed, straightened the covers with a few quick flicks, then extended a hand. "Grandma has invited us to go to their church today. Would you like that?"

Laurie eyed her, suspicious. "My real grandma?"

Laurie's tone said she hadn't forgotten the last time they'd visited her grandparents. The only time, actually. Karen nodded. "Yes. The grandmas around here just like to remember their grandchildren, so they like it when you call them grandma." A few of the local volunteers at the Booth Memorial Home had semi-adopted Laurie.

"Like a game."

"Yes."

"But my real grandma will be there." Laurie hemmed and hawed, indecisive. Her hesitation meant she'd held that wretched day in her mind all this time. Karen hated that. She'd been so careful to keep Laurie's life free from grown-up drama, but that day Karen's father had greeted them in rare form, spewing four years of pent-up anger.

She'd vowed to stay away forever, but her mother's call sounded sincere, as if willing to fix broken fences. Make amends. Karen's spiritual heart welcomed the overture. Forgiveness was of God. She understood the command of "seventy times seven," but understanding and acting were sometimes at odds.

Her mother heart said nothing was more important than protecting Laurie from the bitterness Karen knew as a child. But if God was truly a God of second chances, shouldn't she follow along?

Yes. As long as her parents were nice in front of Laurie. And Karen wasn't sure that would be the case.

"Do you think we should go?" Laurie asked. "I'd rather go see our new friend Mike."

Mike's image came to mind. More than his image, his kindliness tempted her. And it shouldn't. Couldn't.

Why? Her conscience scolded. *A nice man, sweet and caring. Upright and honest. A policeman, a protector. Why is that bad?*

Not bad, Karen decided. Risky. Mike's goodness might disappear in a puff of disappointed smoke once he realized she was an unwed mother. She'd seen him study her hands, looking for a trace of a ring. Here at the home, the girls believed she was a war widow and she let the assumption slide. Laurie didn't need the details of her birth discussed around impressionable ears.

But she wouldn't lie to Mike when he asked, and she had a solid feeling he'd be asking. Probably soon. And she wasn't sure she could bear the expected look of disenchantment she'd see in his eyes.

"I love you, Mommy." Laurie reached up and grabbed Karen, and that childish embrace bolstered Karen's strength and her faith. "But I don't want to go to Grandma's church."

"Then we won't." Karen hugged her, then waved toward the closet. "Find your navy blue dress, your white tights, and your white shirt to go underneath, please. I'll call Grandma and tell her."

She went downstairs to use the communal hall phone. When her mother's voice came through the line, she sounded surprised that someone was calling her. "Hello?"

"Mom, it's Karen."

"Oh!" A momentary pause stretched, then her mother's voice came back, sharper. "You're not coming."

"Not this time. But I'd like to come another time if I may."

"Without Laurie."

Karen hadn't said that, but it's what she meant. She nodded, unseen, and added, "She's a little nervous, still."

"Because your father yelled at you."

Screamed, berated, raged. Karen had left all that behind when they kicked her out of the house as a pregnant teen. "Laurie's life has a gentler focus. She's not used to people yelling. And she's smart as can be, so she remembers for a long time."

"Your father had his say. You had yours. I say that's the end of it."

How Karen wished that were true, but she knew her father's temper. A dogged Christian and long-time alcoholic, he'd quoted chapter and verse about her loose morals. At the top of his voice. Meeting her mother at church was a better choice than their walk-up in the Meatpacking District, but still . . . not today. She refused to force Laurie into an uncomfortable situation. "Maybe you and Laurie and I could have lunch together sometime? My treat," she added, because she understood her mother's tight financial circumstances.

"I'll have to think on that. Good-bye." Trudy O'Leary hung up without waiting for Karen to reply.

"Bye, Mom."

Karen re-cradled the phone. A noise behind her made her turn, surprised. "Major Flora."

Major Flora eyed the phone, then her. "I heard. A difficult circumstance."

It was, but . . . "Made more so by a lack of tolerance and love for the bottle."

Major Flora accepted the words with her typical grace. "Then we shall cover them with prayers and give God gratitude that He brought you to our door all those years ago."

"Amen."

Major Flora stepped to the phone, then waved Karen away. "If you're staying here for service, that's lovely, but if you'd like to take a few girls to the Catholic church down the road, I'd be grateful."

"Glad to. I'll just finish getting Laurie ready and round up the girls."

"Perfect."

It wasn't perfect for the girls, Karen recognized that. Going out in public pregnant and unwed gave some folks reason to stare. But the beautiful church dedicated to Francis Xavier had a lovely staff of good people, staunch believers with kind hearts. And that made taking the girls to church there so much easier.

Chapter Five

....

"You have returned."

A strong Yiddish voice drew Karen's attention Monday morning. She turned and shared a smile with Arnie. "I have. Did you miss me?"

"I did." He handed her a wrapped bagel and the customary mug of fresh-brewed coffee.

"You spoil me." She laughed but couldn't hide her enjoyment. "You know you don't need to do this every day, Arnie. You have been too kind already."

"Bah." He made a face, and a wealth of wrinkles creased his cheeks, his forehead. "One thing I know. There is no such thing as too much kindness, and we are instructed to help others, be kind." He pointed upward, giving God credit for the rule. "Who am I, a simple man, to argue?"

His words made her smile, and when he saw that, his face went a shade more serious. Almost fatherly. "And while today is nicer, you will be here in many days of cold and maybe even snow." He met her gaze and creased his brow again. "You feel the need to do service. So do I. We both do good, right?"

"Yes. And thank you."

"You are welcome." He started to move toward his narrow

store, tucked amid a collection of big, sprawling establishments, then turned back. "Mike came looking for you yesterday."

Karen's heartbeat spiked. She missed Mike this morning, and while she hated to admit it, she'd been ringing the bell with one hand while trying to spot the patrolman with her eyes. "We don't ring on Sundays."

"And that is what I explained," Arnie said. "I don't think he knows a lot about your army, but he served ours in the war."

"A soldier." That knowledge stirred memories she'd pushed aside on purpose. A young woman, seventeen, thinking she fell in love with a soldier, a full-grown man. She'd been so foolish. Young. Naïve.

But from bad came wondrous good in the form of her daughter, and she'd helped serve the war effort in her own way by being accepted into the Cadet Nurse Corps. The war had ended by the time she graduated, but the government-funded training set her on a path to independence. A career, not just a job. A way to care for her child without relying on anyone else.

"I think he is off today." Arnie called the information over his shoulder as he crossed the busy road, eyes darting right, then left. "I will see you when you drop the mug off."

"Gladly," Karen replied. She sipped the coffee and swallowed the sweet, hot brew with appreciation as she shoved disappointment aside. She hadn't seen Mike yesterday. She wouldn't see him today.

But she longed to see him, and that was ridiculous. Wasn't it? Weariness assailed her by noon. She'd be able to get back to the home, catch a quick nap, and have dinner with Laurie, then sleep for three hours before her night shift began. She sipped the last of the now-cool coffee, gathered her wrap closer, and smiled as her replacement ringer approached. "Helen. Good to see you. Merry Christmas!"

"And you." The older woman moved somewhat slowly, but she reached out and gave Karen a hug as she took her place opposite Macy's department store. "This is your assignment each day?"

"Yes." Karen swept the bright, busy streets a quick look. "Isn't it marvelous? I am surrounded by so much beauty. And with so many people passing, our kettle fills quickly."

"While you have so little." Helen's expression disparaged their surroundings, the wide store-front windows filled with tempting treasures. "I hate being in the middle of things I can't have. It's annoying."

Helen was wrong. The sights and sounds surrounding Midtown at Christmas made Karen sigh with delight, not envy. Ornaments strung overhead. Christmas lights festooning windows along the shop-filled streets. Decorated trees, bright and winsome, marking each empty nook. Window displays artfully designed with lovely settings and moving figures. One clever group of windows was set up *as* windows of a traditional New England home. Shoppers walking by peeked through lace-curtained, colonial-style panes at children trimming a tree. A family seated at dinner. Tiny tots tucked into a sweet, comfy bed, sound asleep. Reindeer, heads bowed, seemed to munch sweet hay in another window frame. The next held a toy factory manned by hardworking elves, tiny wooden people swinging mallets and plying paint. She loved the whimsy, the sweet promise of childhood dreams fulfilled. No matter what Helen said.

"Karen?"

Mike's voice called to her. She turned, surprised, and nearly dropped Arnie's mug to the concrete. Mike wasn't in uniform today, but he held himself square, tall and mighty, a man who carried his strength with ease.

He grabbed the mug, held it close, and gave her a smile that made her think of long walks. Holding hands. Exchanging looks. All things she'd sworn off.

But here and now, with this man?

It all seemed so possible.

"You're done?"

She nodded, then remembered her manners. "Mike Wolzak, this is Helen Gearing. She's my replacement so, yes. I'm free to go."

Mike reached out a hand to Helen. "Nice to meet you."

Helen ignored the gesture and aimed a sharp gaze at Karen. "You got a boyfriend?"

Karen started to shake her head, embarrassed, but Mike put a single hand on her shoulder and looked down at Helen. "Maybe."

His single word, quirked smile, and hiked brow eased Helen's chronic frown. She half nodded, smiled slightly, and took the bell from Karen's outstretched hand. "Well, good."

Good? It wasn't good, nor was it something Karen bantered about. Romance, love, life . . . Those were serious issues. She moved to cross the street, ready to return Arnie's mug, but then stopped. Mike had the mug and when she turned, the smile he sent her was about the nicest thing she'd ever seen. "Forget something?"

"It seems I did."

"I'll walk you up to Arnie's. And then the subway," he decided as he fell into step beside her. "That is unless you have time to grab a cup of coffee with me? I could wrap my hands around a hot mug of coffee about now."

She shouldn't. She was short on sleep already, and she recognized the sparks of attraction she felt for this man. Two good reasons to offer a polite smile and decline.

One glance at his face negated her decision.

Sadness deepened the gaze behind the smile. Loss furrowed his brow. He'd been at war and recently lost his mother. His need called to the caretaker in her, and his ruggedly handsome face wasn't anything to dismiss casually.

Yes, she should go back to the home and catch a nap before Laurie got home from school, but the idea of sharing coffee and a conversation with Mike rejuvenated her. "I'd like that."

"The tea room in Macy's?"

She loved Macy's. Who didn't? Laurie had begged to see the summertime movie about a little girl who didn't believe in Santa Claus, but somehow the real Santa had ended up working at Macy's and helped the child and her mother know the true meaning of Christmas: faith.

But money had been tight, and Karen couldn't justify the cost of admission. Not when her nursing uniforms set her back a pretty penny and Laurie's school clothes put a similar bite on her finances. "That would be lovely, Mike."

The store was quieter today than it had appeared the two days following Thanksgiving. They picked a table, and when Mike held out her seat, a sigh of pleasure rose within her.

"Two coffees," Mike told the waitress when she stopped by. He switched his attention to Karen, one brow thrust up. "Are you hungry? They make great sandwiches here."

"I'm not, but thank you. Arnie sent me a bagel."

"Of course he did. He's a good man."

"He is." Karen accepted her coffee from the waitress and stirred milk and cream into the tall stoneware mug. "He told me he's known your family for a long time."

"Yes." Mike grimaced, then smiled. "He's known us through good times and bad times. He had a shop in Brooklyn, not far from our place in Flatbush. Stan and I played street ball together as kids, but then things changed."

Karen arched a brow, inviting him to continue.

"Not everyone in the neighborhood made the Menchers feel welcome."

"Because they're Jewish."

Mike frowned, eyes down. "You'd think that wouldn't matter, wouldn't you? In America, where there are so many people, so many choices. And we just fought a war because one group hated and distrusted another group." His face said he hated the war but believed in the cause, and Karen recognized the true man's struggle within. "Arnie and his family moved to the Brighton Beach area. He ran the Flatbush shop with his cousin until the one over there"—Mike hooked a thumb toward Broadway—"got established. Then he had a cousin take over Flatbush. It's okay if they work in the old neighborhood because everyone loves their bagels. It just wasn't okay that they lived there."

Karen touched her hand to his. "People get foolish and protective with little cause. But I believe things will get better." She shrugged. "They must, because we're all more connected now. Automobiles. Phones. Radio. And now television. Just look at baseball."

Mike sat straighter and squared his shoulders. "You know baseball?"

She sent him a sharp look as she sipped her coffee. The creamy deliciousness kick-started her sleep-deprived brain. Although with Mike, she didn't feel tired. She felt warm. Happy. Energized. "I don't just know baseball. I love it. My aunt and uncle were huge Yankees fans. When I was little, they took me to games. It was crazy, so many people. Such a big stadium. I was scared they'd lose me and kind of excited to think what adventures I'd have if they did," she confessed, laughing. "The major had seats for one of the World Series games this past October, donated by a businessman in Lower Manhattan. She invited me to go because she knows I love the game, but I sent one of our girls instead." She leaned forward. "Although I longed to see Jackie Robinson play. Having him on the Dodgers, giving him a chance to shine in the major leagues?" She pressed her hand to Mike's and gave him a warm smile. "If you want proof things are changing, it's in your own back yard. Ebbet's Field."

Sensible and beautiful, Mike decided. And a baseball fan, although for the wrong team since the Yankees beat his Dodgers in the World Series less than two months ago. "Do your aunt and uncle still take you to games?"

Her smile dimmed. Her eyes calmed. "I haven't seen them in over a dozen years. My father had words with them when I was twelve and told them to never come back."

"Karen. I'm sorry." This time he took her hand in empathy. "Are they still at odds?"

"They are at peace, Mike."

He frowned because the way she said it didn't sound quite right.

"Aunt Lonnie and Uncle Bill were killed in the Great Hurricane. They lived on Long Island and they'd gone to the movies for the evening."

Mike knew the rest. The eastern side of Long Island had taken a direct hit from the storm. The entire movie theater had been washed out to sea with the combination of wind and storm surge. "Karen, I'm so sorry." He squeezed her hand gently, wishing pain and death away, but no such wishes were granted to mere mortals.

"Thank you." She met his look of concern with a smile. "But while I miss them, I'll see them again. We'll rejoice in heaven, at the King's throne, and Uncle Bill's arthritis will be healed and Aunt Lonnie will have a host of children surrounding her. What cannot be in this life is always possible in heaven."

"She couldn't have children." Maggie's struggles with pregnancies had given Mike a deeper understanding than most single guys could embrace. "But they had you."

"For those first twelve years, yes." She smiled approval at his understanding.

"Did they keep in touch with you after your father fought with them?"

He'd said the wrong thing. He knew it right off because pain laced her gaze. She faltered, then made a face of quiet acceptance. "It would not have been good for them to contact me. My father doesn't possess a forgiving nature."

Mike read between the lines.

Her father had been mean to her. Abusive, maybe. It was there in the downcast look, the slight tremble of her jaw, the flash of angst he'd witnessed. Time for a change of subject. "Have you taken Laurie to see Santa Claus yet? And did she see *Miracle on Thirty-Fourth Street*? when it came out last summer? It was set right here, at Macy's."

She made a face of regret. "I didn't."

"Because it was a Christmas movie in summer," he agreed. "I took my younger sister, Mary Lynn. She loved it, regardless of the season. Now she's got posters of it decorating her room. Does Laurie like movies?" He leaned closer, holding her attention. "And would you allow me the honor of taking you both to the movies, Karen?"

She backed away physically and emotionally, as far as the

chair and the busy restaurant allowed. "Mike, how nice of you, but I must refuse. I'm—"

"Is there someone else, Karen?" Her quick reaction made him cut to the chase, because if there was no one else in her life, no man, he'd like to get to know her better. Much better. Her innate warmth and sensibility calmed his inner turmoil. The fact that she was downright beautiful?

Didn't hurt matters at all.

He reached for her hand and raised one brow, waiting for an answer.

She stood. "I must go."

He stood as well. "You didn't answer my question, which means you don't want to answer."

She didn't hesitate to meet his gaze. "I suspect you do quite well when interviewing suspects. You have good timing, but it isn't fair to use those skills on me."

"A simple question isn't an interrogation." He halved the short distance between them and smiled gently as he reached out to help her adjust the folded collar of the long cloak. "It's merely a question. And I'd like an answer. Please."

The "please" did it. She sighed, glanced down, and acknowledged his question with a slight frown. "There is no one."

Her expression said she wasn't comfortable with the topic. Having lost family recently, Mike understood that quite well. "Then—"

"And there can be no one," she added. She took a firm step back, rounded the table, and moved to the door.

She had the advantage because Mike had to stand in line to pay for their coffees. He watched her leave, head high, the movement of the cloak offering silent testimony to her speed, but he wouldn't chase her down to demand more answers. He didn't need to, because he knew where she'd be tomorrow. And the next day. And the one after that.

She'd be ringing the bell in front of Macy's Department Store, and with over twenty days left until Christmas Eve, he'd have plenty of time to stop by and talk on his daily assignments.

He might not be all that old, but he was experienced enough to recognize the gleam in her eye. A flash of interest she dimmed purposely.

He'd made it through a daunting Police Academy class filled with out-of-work professors and engineers, victims of the Great Depression, and he'd excelled. He'd survived nearly four years of a war that cost him his father and a good share of his faith and innocence.

But he felt more faithful around Karen, as if her gentle beliefs called to him. Her soft gaze, earnest looks, quick smile, thoughtful silences.

If there was no man in her life, there was a reason why, because Karen O'Leary was more than special. She was exceptional, and he'd be honored to keep her company. The trick was convincing her of that, but Mike remembered how shy Bogey had been when he came to live with them in Brooklyn.

The pup had come around. Mike hoped the woman would do the same.

Chapter Six

Helen Gearing was right.

Surrounding yourself with things you could not have was cruel punishment. Karen hadn't thought so about the pretty windows, bright lights, or evocative displays of home and family. This year's windows weren't the utilitarian wartime versions of a few years back. These windows screamed love, life, and the pursuit of happiness in full color.

But Mike Wolzak was off-limits for more reasons than she could list, so why had she gone for coffee with him? Why did she let those big blue eyes entice her?

Head down, she walked to the subway stop, determined to disavow the spectacle of Christmas present. She'd place her mind in a stable, a manger, a tiny babe, born to the poor.

Swaddling clothes. Hay. Maybe a big, brown cow, chewing her cud. Sheep, grazing in fields.

Yes, that is where she'd find her Christmas joy. In a far-off land of want and need, a people oppressed.

* * * * *

"Mommy, are you awake?" Laurie bounded into the two-room apartment at full tilt three short hours later.

"I am now." Karen stretched, yawned, and smiled into her daughter's delighted eyes. "What has you so excited?"

"Santa!"

"You have seen him?"

"No, of course not!" Laurie laughed and draped herself over her mother. "But I want to so badly! Katie Thompson and Jimmy Mancuso went to see him on Saturday, and they said he's going to bring them presents. Will he do that here, Mommy? *Can* he?" Her voice implored Karen to reaffirm a myth, a story untrue. Should she cast aside the girl's optimism for a cold dash of reality? Was there harm in a child's imagination?

"Oh, I think St. Nicholas will stop by as he comes through town," Major Flora said from the half-open door. Her brown-eyed gaze warmed as she regarded the child. "He has a heart for children, for sure."

"Major, I—"

"Of course, we must never ask for too much." Major Flora ignored Karen's interruption and stooped to Laurie's level. "We must always remember that the best gift of Christmas is a child."

"Baby Jesus." Laurie breathed the words and sighed. "My mommy puts yarn on him."

Major Flora turned a puzzled look toward Karen.

"The crèche." Karen pointed out the small, inexpensive manger scene on the dresser. The tiny, wooden feed box was lined with bits of rainbow-toned yarn. "For every time Laurie is good and kind, she gets to put a piece of yarn in the feedbox."

"And my good deeds will help keep the baby warm on Christmas," Laurie continued. She grabbed the major's hand and tugged her forward. "You can see I've been very good already, Major Flora."

"Indeed you have." Major Flora hugged the girl's shoulders and exchanged a smile with her. "But that is no surprise around here. You are known by many to be a delightful child."

Laurie's eyes went wide. "For real?"

"Oh, yes." Major Flora's musical voice pitched up. Optimism brightened her aging face as she turned back toward Karen. "And did you know that the word *crèche* also refers to a place for small children? A safe haven?"

"I didn't." Karen stood and stretched. She'd enjoyed having coffee with Mike, but right now her body was missing that extra two hours of sleep. "Fitting, though. As are many things in life."

"Yes." Major Flora nodded. "And what better time than the season of miracles to begin anew?" Hope and joy blossomed in Major Flora's tone, despite the cold, drab gray December afternoon, and that meant one thing and one thing only:

Helen must have told Major Flora about Mike.

Karen choked back a sigh, sent Major Flora a look of frustration, and moved toward the aluminum coffeepot on the two-burner unit at the kitchen end of the room. "Or stay the chosen course."

Major Flora laughed out loud, and the determined little major didn't give herself to laughter often. "As God wills, child."

Karen sent her a mock scowl, but Major Flora's words opened a new door of thought. Was this meeting with Mike part of God's plan? Did the handsome cop happen upon her accidentally as he walked his beat, or was this man part of her destiny?

"When God closes a door, somewhere He opens a window," Major Flora reminded Karen of the comforting phrase as she moved to the door. Before stepping through, she turned. "But it takes courage to brave the windows of life, Karen. To trust. To love."

Her words impaled Karen's heart.

She'd trusted her parents.

They'd failed her miserably.

She'd trusted her aunt and uncle. Their good hearts and shining souls had lit a path of joy for a struggling adolescent, but they'd been snatched away from her in her father's fit of rage.

She'd trusted Gilbert. Loved him. He'd been her knight in shining armor, so handsome in his uniform. Strong. Courageous. Full of promises. And oh, how she longed to be a person of promise!

He'd kept none of them, so she'd embraced a more "Thomas-like" mindset as she struggled through pregnancy, nursing school, and work. She'd found a community of caring at Booth Memorial. That was enough.

A quiet nursing shift that night would have offered more time for introspection. Three babies in five hours barely allowed time to breathe.

"You're needed in room four," Dana Roberts told her as dawn approached. "Susan's going into labor."

"She can't." Susan was a seventeen-year-old girl who was just entering her eighth month. "It's too early."

Dana's face said more. Much more.

Karen hurried down the hall and around the corner. She'd developed a rapport with Susan. Like Karen, she'd been thrown out of her home because of her pregnancy. Major Flora had stumbled upon the girl in a cold, shadowed corner of Chelsea, alone and despondent. She'd brought the girl home, to Booth Memorial. She'd been here for six weeks, but her baby wasn't due until February. Seven-month babies . . .

They'd lost one last year, a beautiful, tiny baby boy born to a girl named Genevieve. They'd sat and cried together, Karen and

Gen, knowing little Samuel's soul was safe with God, but the girl's empty arms ached to hold her newborn son.

Karen knew the odds went against survival, so therefore she'd pray they could stop Susan's labor. Or save the child.

"Hey." She slipped into the room. Susan's tear-stained face told the story. "How are we doing, sweet girl?"

"Scared."

"Because of the pain? Or the timing?"

"Both," the girl whispered. She buried her face in the pillow. Karen reached out and massaged the girl's shoulders. Slowly, Susan's muscles relaxed. She uncurled some. But her face wore the stamp of grief and fear, two emotions Karen remembered well.

"Have you decided on a name yet? Just in case this baby decides to come early?"

"I think Christina if it's a girl." Susan blew her nose, swabbed her cheeks, and sat up slightly.

"Don't sit up," Karen cautioned. "Lying down might put off the labor. It might not. But it can't hurt, right?"

"Okay."

"And for a boy?" Karen wondered as Susan slid back down. "It was Michael, right?" It made her smile to say the name out loud. Images of Mike Wolzak sprang to mind, the square-jawed look of warmth and quiet determination. The smile that lit those blue eyes from within. She could see a tiny Michael, a rugged baby boy with sturdy arms and legs, impatient to tackle the world.

The thought of Mike's child brought heat to her cheeks and a longing to her heart. Was Major Flora right? Should she examine God's will more closely, or was that simply a convenient excuse to let herself go off course? Her current plan was safe: just her and Laurie, one day at a time.

But sitting with Mike today, seeing the frank interest in his gaze, hearing his words of question made her rethink her choices. Mike's simple presence enticed her.

Karen had promised herself to never allow temptation to rule her life again. But was that the promise of a frightened girl, or a mature woman? The former, most likely, and that meant she should reexamine her choices and her chances, as God allowed.

"Christopher Michael, I think." Susan sighed. Her eyes looked heavy as stress waned. "If I decide to give him or her up for adoption, at least I'll know my little Chris is out there someplace. Happy. Safe. Secure."

"And that's a blessing to any child, Susan. I'll pray for your decision. And whichever way you choose, I'll pray that God guides you every step of the way."

"Thank you, Karen."

She sat quietly, praying, as the girl fell asleep, then eased away and tiptoed out the door on silent feet. Major Flora met her just beyond. "How's she doing?"

"Sleeping now and no signs of labor."

"Praise God."

"I must go." Karen waved a hand toward the back of the small hospital. "I'm going to get Laurie ready for school and then take the train to Macy's."

"We'll watch over Susan."

"I know." Karen turned slightly. Susan's door was shut tight against sound, but still she whispered. "After losing Gen's little boy last spring, my heart aches every time a young mother goes into early labor. There is so much we don't know. So much we can't do. Perhaps if we had Isolettes . . . "

"Too expensive for our budget, I'm afraid," the major replied. "But I pray each day that we might be able to provide better care to the tiniest of God's children."

"I hate that lack of money makes life-and-death decisions," Karen admitted.

"I do as well," Major Flora replied, "but we must trust God's will to guide us. The Lord giveth and the Lord taketh away. Blessed be the name of the Lord."

Karen made a face of sorrowful understanding. "But empty arms and idle hands are never a good combination." She'd witnessed the heartbreaking sorrow of lost pregnancies. Surely there must be a way, a means of making things better? "I'm going to pray that God guides the hands of the researchers who want success as much as we do. That science can help the tiniest souls of all."

Major Flora smiled and kissed her cheek. "I'll join mine with yours. Together we'll make a formidable noise unto the Lord."

Although the major was small and quiet, Karen had no doubt that she could be considered formidable as needed. The knowledge made her smile. "Amen."

* * * * *

"Did you find a doctor today, Mike?"

Mike turned, wishing he had better news, wishing he was smarter. "No, but I'm still looking. Give me another day, okay?"

Mary Lynn looked embarrassed to have asked, as if helping her was a bother. Mike put the last dish in the cupboard, crossed the room, and hugged her. "I'll find one. I promise."

She nodded against his chest, but he sensed the fear within.

She'd been keeping her silence, carrying her secret, offering up her burden of sickness as a punishment for sin.

Was it?

His mind muddled. Didn't the Old Testament speak of women travailing in childbirth as a reckoning for eating the forbidden fruit? Was God like that?

"Blessed are the meek. . . . "

Jesus had preached faith, hope, and love. He'd reached out to the sick, the lame, the woman about to be stoned for her sin of adultery. . . .

Christ had intervened and evened her path to righteousness. Surely God didn't inflict pain on all women for one person's actions, but the little he knew about pregnancy left him aggravated.

He'd hated fighting in the war but believed in a just cause and did his duty as he was trained.

He disliked crime and danger but knew his skills kept people safe, the faithful sheepdog guarding the flock.

But a pregnant teenage girl in his care?

That left him stymied.

Tell someone. Talk to someone, a woman, someone who has gone through the experience. Someone who might know what doctors are good. In combat, you sought advice. This is no different.

But it was, and that knowledge cut Mike to the core because discussing Mary Lynn's pregnancy brought it into the open. He'd been hiding her condition for weeks, and he knew why. Illegitimate children brought shame to a family, and this was his shame to bear because he hadn't looked out for her properly.

They ate a quiet supper. Outside, the neighbors had strung lights to celebrate the Christmas season. Multicolored clotheslines stretched between buildings, the gay colors brightening the darkness. The Szepanskis had put their tree in their front window as always, a postcard-perfect display of Christmas cheer, a childhood memory his mother had copied in their front window.

He hadn't brought up the topic of a tree, and Mary Lynn hadn't asked. Their front window stood unadorned, framed by the green embossed drapes his mother loved, but those drapes provided a border for the pretty display across the street, and that made their place even more austere.

"Do you have homework?"

Mary Lynn nodded. "A ton. We've got our senior paper due in mid-January, and I've got a stack of research books from the library. Plus the regular stuff. And I'm glad I had all my Regents work done by last year so I could take some business classes this year. If I decide to keep the baby, I'm going to need a job. The business courses will help me with that."

"A job?" Mike carried his plate to the sink and rinsed it. "Instead of college?" He shook his head, grim, and retook his seat. "Mom was excited about the thought of you being the first girl in our family to get a college degree. You've done so well in school."

"Until now."

She meant that she'd messed up totally by getting pregnant and Mike couldn't disagree, but giving up her dream of a college education?

No. He'd promised to look after her. He'd made a pledge, a solemn oath. Yes, they'd messed up, but that just meant they needed to try harder. "There will be a way. I'm not sure how, but I know that your dream was to go to college. And that was Mom's dream, too. So we're not going to worry about a job. I have a job and I'm doing all right with money, and there's the insurance money, too. You're going to school, Mary Lynn. End of discussion."

She gripped his hand. "I can't use the insurance money to cover up what I've done."

Mike leaned over and planted a kiss on her forehead. "Sure you can. That's what money's for. And Mom and Dad would be the first to make sure you and the baby are taken care of. One thing I learned in that war, sis: take each day and rejoice in it. We've lost a lot these past three years."

Sorrow shadowed her face. "Yes."

"Now we need to regroup. And we'll do it, Mare. I promise." He wasn't sure how, and no answers fell at his feet that day, but he'd pledged his help, and Mike never went back on his word.

His words calmed her gaze. "I'll do dishes."

"Nope. You study. I'll clean up the kitchen and then do a little research of my own."

The doorbell rang as he put away the last dish. He tossed the towel onto the table and crossed the living room to open the door. "Mrs. Szepanski."

Their across-the-street neighbor smiled as she handed him a foil-wrapped loaf. "I made bread today. I thought you and Mary Lynn might enjoy a bite. I noticed she was looking peaked these last few weeks, and there's nothing like homemade bread to stick to the ribs."

A part of him longed to confide in his mother's friend. Maybe she could offer advice on a discreet doctor, an office that wouldn't make Mary Lynn more guilt-ridden than she already was.

But would the neighbor keep their predicament quiet?

Mike sighed inside.

Jana Szepanski was a talker and she might pretend to mean well, but she'd have Mary Lynn's plight all over the old neighborhood in record time. Mike smiled, kept his counsel, and held the loaf of bread aloft. "Thank you for this. We'll enjoy it."

"Good!" She smiled up at him, then noted the sparse look of the home behind him with a glance. "It's hard to gussy things up for Christmas when you're grieving, isn't it?"

Hard?

Impossible, Mike thought. He shrugged, silent.

"If you decide to decorate, call me. Packy and I will come help. But Michael, if you leave it for this year, that's okay too. Although I'd get your mother's *szopka* out of storage. That nativity scene made by her mother was your mama's pride and joy. Other than you two kids, of course."

The crèche, handmade in turn-of-the-century Poland, was carefully stored each year. It had caused a family rift over a decade ago, when his grandmother passed the jewel-toned scene to his mother. Aunt Frannie thought it should come to her, but she'd gotten Grandmother's wedding ring instead. She'd even offered a trade to Irina, but Mike's mother had clung to the ornate, handmade Christmas scene. She'd even fashioned extra figures of her own over the last years, a way to fill the time while he and his father fought overseas.

The handmade foil, paper, and bejeweled Krakow nativity might make them miss their mother less. They certainly couldn't miss her more than they did right now. "That's a great idea. We'll see to it, Mrs. Szepanski. And thank you for the bread."

She peeked around him as if looking for something. Mary Lynn, perhaps?

But then she smiled and waved before she walked back across the street to her decorated home.

Mary Lynn appeared at his side once Mrs. Szepanski had gone. She indicated the festive neighborhood with a dip of her chin. "During the war, no one used decorations. Or lights. And the storefronts were filled with books and things about how to be a better war wife. How to make do. There was no tin foil or metal, so everything seemed darker, even at holiday time."

"Longest nights of the year," Mike remarked as he shut the door. He held out the loaf of bread. "Mrs. Szepanski was kind enough to bring this by. She said you looked peaked when she saw you."

"She came over because she suspects," Mary Lynn corrected him. "I got sick coming up the street from school a few days ago. She saw me. I said it was the stomach bug going around, but I could tell from her eyes that she knew, Mike. Or at least suspected."

"Oh, Mare." He pulled her into his arms, knowing he could only protect her from so much. Loose talk, neighborhood snipes, cruel looks . . . he had no way to control those. If he could, he would tuck her away someplace safe, away from the questioning glances and the backyard gossip. Maybe he should look into that, to find her a place where her secret and shame could be hidden away for six months, more or less.

Would that be better for her? Worse?

Reason said he should do anything he could to allay her fears and discomfort. The question was, what should he do?

He wasn't sure, and since he and God had fallen out awhile back, he wasn't about to bring his concerns to the altar. His father had raised him to be decisive once he'd chosen a course of action. Right now he didn't know which path to take, but he'd examine the options and figure it out. He always did.

Chapter Seven

....

"I brought your coffee today. But Arnie said the bagel is his gift to you."

The husky warmth of Mike's voice negated every mental barrier Karen had erected since the previous afternoon. She turned, trying to hide her pleasure, but the moment their eyes met, she recognized the impossibility.

He saw it too. And he smiled, his gaze drawing hers, his steadiness grounding her. "I shouldn't eat so much, and not while I'm working," she said. Talking about food shouldn't get her into too much trouble, and the streets weren't too busy with shoppers yet. The work rush had abated nearly an hour before and stores were just opening, so this was the perfect time for Mike to stop by. She suspected he knew that.

"From the size of you, I don't think eating too much is ever a problem." Mike's tone said he didn't find her size unappealing, and that made her smile grow wider.

"Thank you. I think. And while normally I wouldn't agree with you, we were swamped at work last night, and I'd delivered three babies by five o'clock this morning. That meant I ran from room to room, helping."

"You're a nurse."

She saw his expression and tilted her head. "You thought I only rang the bell?"

He frowned and scrubbed a hand to his jaw. "No, well . . ." He hemmed and hawed and shrugged. "I had no idea. I didn't know they even had women bell ringers until I came across you on Thanksgiving. They had guys dressed up as Santa when I was little."

She nodded. "Those were often clients who had been helped by the services the army provides. But I would look ridiculous in a Santa suit."

"I'm not so sure that's true." Flirtation layered Mike's comment. Not flirting back was getting more difficult by the day. "I can't believe what a coincidence this is, though. I've been trying to help a friend find an obstetrician."

"Your friend is expecting?"

"Yes."

Karen heard the single word of affirmation, but what she saw was anxiety in his eyes. "And she hasn't seen a doctor as of yet. How far along is she?"

"Nearly three months. Is that bad?"

Karen sent him a look of reassurance. "Women have had babies from the beginning of time. Yes, it's good to have medical care, but pregnancy isn't an illness. It's a natural part of our lives."

"I don't know how something so natural can make someone so sick," he protested, and his expression told Karen he was closer to this woman than he'd let on.

Well then. What she didn't need was to become involved in some kind of silly love triangle. Mike's unveiled concern for this woman's plight meant he was invested in her. Then why was he here, caring for Karen? Flirting with her?

Another girl-in-every-port kind of guy? Like Gilbert?

She pushed that idea aside. Mike wasn't like that. He couldn't be.

But a much younger Karen had thought that about Gilbert too. Her naïveté around men appalled her. She took a firm step back, mentally and physically. "The body changes during pregnancy. Those changes can cause nausea. But when you consider the miracle of life, the blessing of a child, a few months of morning sickness isn't a big trade-off."

For one brief moment he looked helpless, but then her words registered. "That's a sensible way of looking at it. I'd never thought of it like that."

Karen slid the leather gloves over her fingers now that the kettle was properly positioned. She waggled her fingers at him. "My hands are grateful to you daily. What a difference these make."

"I'm glad, Karen." He stepped closer, maybe pretending he didn't notice she'd stepped back deliberately? "Do you know any good baby doctors? Here or in Brooklyn?"

"They're everywhere, Mike." She tipped her gaze up, trying to read between the lines and failing, but determined to avoid the drama of messy human relationships. She'd been surrounded by that as a child, and caused her own in youthful indiscretion. Never again. "But I do know that Doctors Fillmore, Fillmore, and Bartlett are in Brooklyn. They're with Kings County Hospital. Is that close to you?"

"Practically in my back yard. And they're good?"

She nodded firmly. "Yes, they're good. I've been studying about nurse-midwives, though. If I ever get the chance to go back to school, that's what I want to do."

"Be a midwife? Isn't that kind of an old-fashioned way of doing things now that we've got doctors and big, modern hospitals?" he wondered.

"Delivering babies is a specialty, but I sometimes wonder if making birth too antiseptic takes the joy out of it. But for the moment, I'm happy where I am. And because the opportunity for further schooling may never open up, I'll honor God by doing what I do, the best I'm able." She turned her gaze outward as she talked, the clear song of the bell tolling rhythmically. "I love working with new mothers. Holding those newborns." The smile that brightened her gaze came straight from a sincere heart. "Each one a miracle, Mike, no matter how they are delivered into this world. Or by whom."

Her words made him think hard. Each child a miracle, even when conceived out of wedlock? Was she kind or naïve to see things that way? No matter. She'd given him the best piece of information he could have asked for: the name of a practice to care for Mary Lynn. He'd stop by there on the way home and set up an appointment.

"Thank you for being frank with me. I know things have changed since the war. I forget that sometimes."

Consternation darkened her profile, an expression that said she understood. She drew in a deep breath, smiled at someone walking by, wished them a merry Christmas, then turned toward him. "There *has* been a lot of change in little time, all around the world. And you were gone, fighting a war, so it's hard to come back and find everything different. Some in good ways. Some not. And for you"—she faltered, and the look of concern changed to sympathy as her voice went soft—"things changed more than most. I shouldn't take offense in any case."

"The war changed a lot, that's true." He raised her hand lightly and gave it gentle pressure from his hand, a silent message of comfort. "But I didn't mean to offend you, Karen. I would never do that intentionally."

Her eyes said she longed to believe him.

Her bearing said something else. "Thank you for the coffee."

He'd been politely dismissed.

So be it.

He turned and strode down the street, eyes sharp, gaze straight, doing his job, but he'd left a portion of his heart back there in front of Macy's. He hurt her feelings by dismissing midwives. That was the last thing he wanted to do. Still, she'd offered him useful information, and he'd be able to find help for Mary Lynn. Knowing that eased a small part of his dented ego.

He stopped by Arnie's at the end of his beat. Stan appeared busy in the back kitchen, doing the daily wash-down. Arnie repeated the process at the display case. "You are done this day?" Arnie straightened to face Mike, and even though Arnie wasn't old, fatigue weighted his eyes.

Mike moved closer, concerned. "Arnie, are you feeling all right?"

The older man waved his question off. "These days I begin in the dark and end in the dark. I miss the longer days of summer. The light."

Mike nodded, understanding. "I think the Christmas lights shine brighter because of those long, dark nights."

"And our eight nights do as well," Arnie agreed. "Did you want something, Mike?"

"Three bagels for supper. Plain ones."

"I've got them right here." Arnie rinsed his hands and reached for a waxed paper bag. He chose three bagels, put them in a small sack, and handed them over. "Here you go. And did our little bell ringer enjoy her coffee today? And her bagel?" Mike's slow reaction hiked the baker's brow. "She didn't?"

"I'm sure she did. I think I insulted her without meaning to."

"Men should talk less," Arnie scolded. "Nod more. My father taught me this."

Mike couldn't find fault with the theory. "My father would have agreed."

"I miss your father, Mike."

An ache in Mike's gut rose up to choke him. "Me too."

"He was a good man, raised by a good man. And you know this, but did you know that your grandfather was a very bad boy?"

Mike frowned. "Jaja?"

Arnie smiled at the deliberate mispronunciation of *dziadzia*, the Polish word for *grandfather*. "Got himself in with a bunch of bad boys from the old neighborhood and landed in a mess of trouble. Of course he came over on his own, just him and his sister, to meet your great-grandfather here. And he was working all the time."

"Like everyone, I suppose."

Arnie nodded and shrugged. "But when kids are faced with so much change at once, they need extra time. With no mother around—"

Mike's great-grandmother feared water and change. She refused to get on the ship to America, but once his great-grandfather had settled in Brooklyn, she sent their oldest two children to be new Americans. "It had to be tough."

"Yes. But your jaja got straightened out by a cop who saw the good in him. Became his *mensch*. His advisor."

"And that's what drew him to the force later."

Arnie nodded. "It was rare to have a Polish cop in those days. But he married his mensch's Irish daughter and that gave him an inside track."

"Which led to a family tradition, it seems."

"Leadership. Kindness. Understanding. Fearlessness." Arnie accepted Mike's money and tucked it into his back pocket. "These are Wolzak qualities. Yours were refined in war, early, much like your father's."

Mike heaved a sigh. "He didn't have to go back, Arnie. If he hadn't . . . "

His father had served in World War I. He'd survived the war, the great flu outbreak, the crazy twenties, and the Great Depression. Why had he felt the need to return to the front while he had a wife and daughter back home?

"A man does what he must, always. For your father, there was never a question, Mike. You are like him."

Mike wasn't convinced that was a good thing. Sometimes he felt too much, worried too long, tried too hard. He wanted goodness and righteousness to rule the world, but he surrounded himself with crime and greed. What did that say about him?

"You take those bagels home and relax tonight," Arnie instructed him. "Then tomorrow you bring something nice for our bell ringer. Make amends. She looked tired today when she walked by."

She had looked tired, and her words about working all night struck Mike hard.

She worked all night, cared for a child, then came to Midtown to raise money for the poor? When did she sleep? The shadows under her eyes answered that question: not as often as she should.

Protectiveness welled within Mike, a consummate warmth that made him long to protect and defend the industrious bell ringer. An idea sprang to mind, a good idea. He smiled at Arnie, went home, cooked bland scrambled eggs and plain bagels for dinner, a supper that might be easy on Mary Lynn's stomach, and planned what he'd do on his next day off.

His mother always said the best gifts cost no money but employ heart and time.

He'd be giving one of those gifts to Karen tomorrow.

* * * * *

"Mommy?"

"Hmm?" Laurie's voice pricked Karen's sleep, a small entreaty that didn't sound quite right. "What's up, Sweet Cheeks?"

"I don't feel good."

Karen sat up quickly. She reached out a hand to the precious child, felt the heat of fever against her palm, and scrambled up from her couch-bed. "What hurts?"

"Everything." Tears slid down Laurie's cheeks, one after another, silent tears, far more worrisome than their noisy counterparts. "My head. My tummy. And my boo-boo." She held out the hand she'd scraped in a tumble on the sidewalk the day before.

Karen kissed the hand, picked the child up, and moved to the small bathroom. "I'm going to pour you a nice tub of cool water and give you some medicine to help that fever. The medicine will make you more comfortable."

"But I can still go to school, right?" Sadness and anticipation warred for Laurie's voice. "We are putting up our stable today, and Mary and Joseph and their donkey friend will start walking. I promised I would help them."

Laurie loved school, much as Karen had. She enjoyed the interaction, the learning, the grace of the sweet Sisters who taught her. But there would be no school today, and that would cause an argument. The child came by her work ethic honestly, so Karen knew she'd have a quarrel on her hands. "Not with a fever, Laurie."

"Then the medicine can make it go away. Maybe I should take extra?"

Karen shook her head firmly. "Too much medicine makes the body more ill. And you must never touch medicines, all right?"

"Yes." Too sick to argue, Laurie's head lolled against Karen's chest. Karen checked her temperature, then cringed when the mercury finally paused above 103 degrees. She settled Laurie into a shallow, cool bath with a few of her favorite floating toys. She crushed half an aspirin into a small dish of applesauce, sweetened it lightly, and offered it to Laurie.

"It tastes yucky."

Karen didn't argue. "The medicine isn't sweet, but it's helpful. The applesauce is sweet. Focus on that. Getting your fever down is important, Laurie."

Glassy-eyed, the little girl eyed the applesauce, frowned, then pinched her nose and opened her mouth, but not any too wide. "Okay."

"Thank you." Karen fed her the applesauce, then offered her a cup of ginger water. "This will help your tummy stay settled."

"I like this."

Laurie's sincerity made Karen smile. "I'm glad, honey. And then I'm going to tuck you back into bed so you can sleep some more, okay?"

Laurie's yawn was answer enough. Karen lifted her from the claw-foot tub once the fever had broken, dried her off, and tucked her into lightweight pajamas.

"I like my fuzzy jammies," Laurie protested.

Karen nodded. "I know. But if the fever comes back, those

jammies are too warm. These are just right for keeping little girls comfy-cozy when they have a fever."

"Really?"

Karen smiled. "Cross my heart."

"Well, okay then." Laurie knew if her mother crossed her heart, she was being totally honest. It was a measure they'd begun once Laurie was old enough to understand the pledge, a building of trust in a world that sometimes didn't welcome a single mother with a child. But the war had made many women single mothers, and most assumed Karen was like so many others: a war widow.

Her lie of omission saved Laurie no small amount of grief.

And you, as well. Admit it, you seek no censure. But someday she'll find out, and that lack of honesty might trip you up, no matter how often you've crossed your heart in the past. One lie of omission about something so important . . . Are you willing to continue that risk?

Was she? For now, yes. Her day of reckoning would come, she sensed it. But for this moment, caring for her sick child was the most important thing.

She hunted up Major Flora in the early hours of the morning. "Laurie is sick. I can't ring today."

"How bad is she? Is it flu? They've had an outbreak of cases all around the city, but it's not a real bad sort."

"It could be anything," Karen told her. "I'll keep her away from the mothers, but we need someone to ring at Macy's."

The major might have shrugged off another assignment, but the foot traffic to and from the shopping district fed their kettles and their outreach each year. "I'll find someone for today. And then I'll see about tomorrow, too."

Karen began to protest, but Major Flora would hear none of it. "We'll take each day as it comes." Firm, she met Karen's gaze. "Laurie comes first."

"Yes." Karen knew that, but she'd pledged her time as gratitude for the help she'd found in these walls. Mental, spiritual, physical . . . the army came through when family shoved her out the door. She had so much to be grateful for.

* * * * *

Mike had Arnie make a sandwich with plenty of meat and cheese. Bagels were well and good, but a hearty sandwich would put some meat on Karen's bones. And maybe give her added energy. He took the mug of coffee and the sandwich and walked to her spot, determined to make things right after his gaffe the previous day.

A heavyset man with a dark beard was ringing the bell on Karen's corner.

Mike's anticipation nosedived. Had he insulted her so much that she wouldn't come back? Had she taken ill? Been hurt? He crossed the street and headed for the bell ringer. "Where's Karen O'Leary?"

The man eyed him, suspicious. "Don't know no Karen anybody, copper."

Ah. Obviously this guy didn't think too highly of police. Mike swallowed a sigh and met the man's gaze. "Karen's been ringing here since Thanksgiving. And she was supposed to be here today."

"But she ain't." The old man offered a gap-toothed smile. "I'll tell you what. If you call the army, they can help you."

"Call them?"

The old man made a face of disbelief. "On the phone, you know?"

"I know phones." Mike couldn't believe he'd been that dense. Would a call to the Salvation Army headquarters in the Meatpacking District help his cause? Maybe. "You hungry?"

The old man's eyes went wide in appreciation. "Always."

Mike's heart melted.

This old fellow might not dress up the corner like Karen's beauty had done, but he was part of the body of Christ. Mike handed over the coffee and the sandwich. "Here you go. For when you're off duty."

The man's gaze brightened at the sight of the sandwich. His jaw worked left and right. His throat convulsed. But then he nodded, put his hunger on hold, and tucked the sandwich behind the kettle. "That's as good as a Christmas dinner, right there."

His words humbled Mike.

A gentle, inner nudge advised him to stop looking back at war . . . at choices made and unmade . . . at loss.

Instead he needed to press on and look forward. That had never been hard before the war, but evil and loss had taken a toll on his faith. His heart.

This old man's gaze said Mike should speed up his adjustment to a rapidly changing world. And Mike knew the old guy was right. "God bless you, my friend."

The man saluted him, and it was then Mike realized he was missing his right hand. "And you, copper."

Had the First World War taken his hand?

Or an industrial accident, too common in this age of bigger and better machines?

Either way, the man's grace taught a valuable lesson of appreciation. When Mike finished his shift midafternoon, he stopped at a station phone, called the operator, and asked her to connect him to the Salvation Army on West Fourteenth.

She made the connection faster than he expected, and when a woman's voice came on the line, he fumbled his words. "I, ummm . . . I'm looking for Karen O'Leary."

"For whom?"

"Karen O'Leary." He drew a breath, suddenly inspired. "This is Officer Michael Wolzak of the NYPD. Ms. O'Leary was mugged last week while bell ringing in front of Macy's."

"Yes, yes, she was!" the woman exclaimed. "Have you caught the muggers, Officer?"

"Not as yet, but I need to talk to Mrs. O'Leary. I went to her bell-ringing site and she wasn't there today."

"I'll give you the number to the Booth Home. That's where she works," the woman explained.

Mike was thrilled to get the information but dismayed that he uncovered it so easily.

What if he *hadn't* been a cop?

What if he was up to no good, tracking Karen? He'd make sure to speak to the army directors about safe protocol . . . now that he had the information he sought.

He took down the address and the phone number, thanked the woman, and hung up.

Mary Lynn would already be home from school. He tried their phone to tell her he'd be late, but the line was busy. No surprise there. Fast-talking neighbors rarely left the eight-party line open. He called his aunt, asked her to keep trying Mary Lynn to explain his delay, then headed for the downtown train.

Chapter Eight

. . . .

"May I help you, sir?"

Mike approached the front desk and decided honesty was the best policy. "I'm Mike Wolzak of the NYPD. I'm here to see Karen O'Leary. She's a nurse here, I believe. If she's not on shift now, I can come back later when she is."

"The police." The woman's left brow shot up, then lowered. "Oh, you're probably here about that nasty business last week."

"Yes." Mike hoped they were discussing the same nasty business. Either way, he wanted to see Karen. Check on her. Make sure she was all right.

"June?"

A heavyset teenage girl came forward from where she'd been stringing bright-toned Christmas balls in the front window with festive ribbon. "Yes?"

"Can you go 'round to Karen O'Leary's apartment and tell her we have an officer here to see her?"

June made a face of regret. "I can but it won't do any good. Laurie's sick and Karen won't leave her with a fever."

"I could follow you." Mike made the offer as if it was the most natural thing in the world to do, but his brain wrapped around this new piece of information. Karen lived on-site. Convenient and cost-effective. Add smart and frugal to his ever-growing list of reasons to like her.

Although, the way his heart skipped a beat every time he saw Karen O'Leary said his list didn't need to be lengthened. Something about her called to him. Protector, friend, confidant, partner . . . There had to be a reason he couldn't get her out of his mind, even when they were apart. Which was silly since they'd just met.

"Destiny. Your dad used to say that about your mother, that he knew right off she was his destiny, even though he fought the idea of settling down for nearly a year."

Arnie had shared that with Mike when he first came home from the front and was trying to wrap his brain around his new lot in life. His father gone, his mother dying. But neither one would have traded their years together despite the pain of loss. That knowledge spurred Mike on.

As the girl led him around a ninety-degree corner, a door ahead of them opened. Karen stepped into the hall, and as he searched her face, he saw only one expression: joy. "They buzzed me and said someone was coming down, but I never thought it was you, Mike."

He held out the cord-handled bag he carried. "For you."

"For me?" Wonder lifted her tone and her eyes after she peeked into the bag. "A Merry Christmas wreath for my door. Oh, Mike, how lovely."

"I thought Laurie would enjoy it, but now I hear she's sick."

"She is but doing better, which means I can work tonight. We've had a baby boom around here. . . . "

"As you mentioned the other day."

She nodded, swung the door wide, and called Laurie's name.

The little girl popped up from the couch, where a crew of stuffed animals and books surrounded her. "Officer Mike!"

"Hey." He crossed the room and bent to give her a hug. "Don't get me sick, okay?"

"I won't!" She giggled up at him and sent her mother a look of mischief. "Mommy said I can't go to school tomorrow, but I'm trying my best to talk her into it. It's December and we're learning so many marvelous things about Baby Jesus and the stable. How Mary and Joseph walked and walked and walked. And we're practicing for our Christmas play, and I get to be a singer but a singer must learn songs." Her overdone sigh was aimed straight at her mother.

"If your fever stays gone tomorrow, you may go back the next day. And cajoling will do you no good."

"So you need to be home with her tomorrow?" Mike watched as Karen withdrew the festive wreath he'd bought from a street vendor near the Midtown subway station. "Here, let me help." He spotted the nail on her door and worked the loop of aluminum wire over the nail's broad end. "There."

"It's just perfect!" Delight filled her voice and her eyes, and if Mike wasn't making a big thing out of nothing much, she looked happier to see him than he probably deserved. And that made him feel good.

"Yes." She answered his question as Laurie called her name. "It seems the healthier the child, the more trouble the care."

Her pretend scolding made Laurie laugh. Karen's sigh of relief told Mike she'd been worried about the girl not that long ago. "She was pretty sick, huh?"

Karen kept her voice low. "It's common with kids, but worrisome still. While the aspirin's working, she thinks she's fine. As its effects wear off, the fever rises. But the school nurse said there's a bug going around, nothing major, just a couple of days of congestion and fever."

"So. Tomorrow. I have off, and I'd like to step in and do your bell ringing for you."

"Bell ringing? I . . . um . . . "

"A simple 'Yes, Mike' will suffice. And then you and the major don't have to worry about a fill-in. And you can catch up on some sleep. May I?" He asked the question as he dropped his gaze to where Laurie was holding up a children's book about Christmas, her look imploring.

"But Mike, surely you have other things to do on your day off."

"I don't, not tomorrow anyway, so it's a done deal. I take it this book is a favorite?" He settled into the worn sofa. Laurie scrambled to snuggle in beside him, and it was the most natural and wonderful thing in the world to brace his arm around the sick child and draw her close.

"I've read it five times already, and that's just the afternoon count."

Mike laughed at her bemused expression, but her admission struck a chord within him. He used to read the same stories to Mary Lynn repeatedly when she was little. Their ten-year age difference kept them miles apart from playing together, but he'd been a good older brother in other ways. Reading and helping with homework . . . he'd done all right then.

A knock at the door drew his attention up as he started the story softly. Laurie cuddled into his side, ready to be swept into a land of fairy tales and make-believe.

"Louise." Karen crossed the room and grasped the hands of a very pregnant young woman. "Did you enjoy your shopping day?"

The young woman's face brightened. "Even without money, it's a thrill to walk the streets of Midtown."

Karen's emphatic nod said she agreed. "The lights themselves are enough of a treat, aren't they?"

"Amazing." Louise sent a look toward Mike and Laurie. "Is she better?"

"Getting better, I think," Karen replied. "But this is just part of motherhood. Dealing with the unexpected."

"And the worry," Louise answered softly. "I'm not sure I'm ready for any of that. I'm already worried enough about keeping *me* going. A baby?" She dropped a look of concern to her swollen figure. "I can't even imagine doing it."

Karen squeezed her hands and shook her head, confident. "Worry is not of God. We are in His hands, at His time. He wants us to not just believe that, but to *know* it. In our hearts, our souls."

"I want to." Mike could barely hear Louise's soft response over his storytelling, but the concern that shadowed her face said more than words ever could. "I want to believe that God's there, watching over us."

"He is." Karen's smile said she lived her faith, heart and soul. "But He gave us free will. All of us." She waved a hand indicating a big, wide world beyond their doors. "Our job is to make the best decisions possible from this point forward. But no one said it would be easy, Louise. Big decisions rarely are. Have you been to see Susan?"

Louise nodded. "She's not having any labor pains right now, and she said to tell you thank you for sitting with her. Talking to her."

Karen waved the thanks off. "Just doing my job."

"Oh, Karen." Louise reached out and gave Karen a big hug.

"You do so much more than that. You're such a good example to us all. I hope you know that."

Karen's face went still.

Louise didn't appear to notice.

Mike couldn't help but notice.

She made a little face of chagrin, stepped back, and waved Louise off. "Go, now. Stay away from the germs in here. I feel fine now, but I could be incubating whatever that one's got." She hooked a thumb toward Laurie. "And Mike, you should think of that too. We don't want to get everyone sick."

"I can handle a little bug," Mike informed her as Louise walked away. "A friend?"

"Oh, Mike"—she clapped a hand to her mouth as she crossed the room—"I'm sorry, I didn't introduce you. Yes, that's Louise, one of our expectant mothers."

Mike drew his brows together, finished the last page of the current story, then faced Karen. "One of them? They wander the halls of the hospital?"

She faced him, puzzled, but then her face changed as awareness dawned. "You don't know what this is."

"The hospital?"

She nodded but shrugged as well. "We're a hospital but also a home for unwed mothers. Our girls are in various stages of pregnancy. They need a safe place to learn, to live, to be loved while their babies grow. They've got some big decisions to make, and society doesn't always embrace them warmly."

"A home for . . . " He paused, not sure he should say more in front of Laurie, but then the child lived here, so she must have heard the phrasing before. "The Booth Home helps expectant mothers?"

"Those in need of faith, hope, food, love, and a roof, yes." She got up, crossed the room, and filled a small aluminum percolator with water, then spooned careful measures of coffee into the small, metal basket. "Coffee?"

"Yes, thank you."

"It will take a few minutes." She resettled herself in the only chair in the room, then dipped her chin toward Laurie. "We're losing her."

"Ah." Mike smiled as the little girl's eyelids drifted closed. Dark lashes lay against pale cheeks, but shadows darkened the hollow beneath her eyes. "She doesn't look as healthy as she did last week."

"She will. Children have amazing recuperative powers. I thank God for that all the time, because they catch anything and everything, and it's not easy being a parent on your own. But I wouldn't trade her for anything. She is my delight."

He wanted to ask more about this place. About a home for unwed mothers, but would Karen read too much into his questions? Worse, would he put his foot in his mouth again?

Most likely.

"Have you worked here long?"

"Since I graduated from nursing school at St. Joe's. I'd actually gotten into the Cadet Nurse Corps, but by the time I graduated, the war had just come to an end. So I'm here, doing what I love. Delivering babies. Helping young mothers. And the Salvation Army had this little apartment for rent, so that's a huge advantage."

"And the disadvantages?" Mike adjusted his seat slightly, tucking Laurie's head beneath his shoulder, against his heart. The scent of soap-and-water clean triggered memories of Mary Lynn, freshly scrubbed and in need of a story or a nighttime game. It was a good memory, all in all.

Karen rose and crossed to the two-burner as she pondered his question. "We're not as equipped as some places. We don't have special beds for preemies, those new incubators that help ease their breathing when they're born too soon."

"Do you send those babies to other hospitals?"

"We have, but it's so hard on the mother, Mike." She brought him his coffee, set it down, and then reclaimed her seat. "For a mother to be separated from her newborn is a grievous act. Some of our young moms are releasing their babies for adoption. In that case, the separation is twofold. They're giving up a child who is in a fragile state and that multiplies the loss. And the guilt."

"Will some of the girls keep their babies?"

She nodded. "Some, but not too many. Society bears unwed fathers no ill will. For unwed mothers it's a different story."

Mike was living that reality. The two-fold sword cut deep. "So the home helps place children?"

"Through private means or the Children's Aid Society. Would you like me to tuck her into bed?" Karen swept Laurie a look so sweet, so maternal, that Mike saw his future in her eyes, a glimpse of the family they could have together. A future he hadn't considered since coming home from the front, sad and resigned, jumping from one responsibility straight into another.

"I kind of like holding her. If you don't mind."

Karen's smile softened, as if she read his loss, his pain, his questions and knew the warmth of a child could heal. "She seems most content and that's never a bad thing."

"When she's better . . . " Mike swept Laurie a quick glance. "I'd like you two to visit us in Brooklyn. My sister and me. And I'd like to show Laurie the lights of Midtown at night, if that's okay."

"We have planned on doing that, but it's tricky," Karen admitted. "I only have two days off per week, and sometimes they're on nights when she must get into bed early for school."

"Then let's plan on this Saturday if she's better," Mike decided. "I can have you back here in time for your nursing shift. Who watches Laurie while you work the overnight?"

"The girls take turns sleeping here. They do it as a service to me, no fee required."

"So no babysitting expenses and low rent."

Karen tipped her gaze up. "Nursing pay isn't huge, but it's better than industrial wages right now and I love it. And isn't that the important thing, Mike? To love what we do?"

Mike couldn't argue the wisdom in that. "I love police work."

Her smile deepened. "It shows. But I expect your parents worried every time you went to work."

Mike shook his head. "They didn't, really. We bleed New York blue in our family. My father. My grandfather. He was one of the first Polish American officers in New York City and that was because he married a police captain's daughter. Lucy Carmichael."

"A tight society."

"A brotherhood," he corrected her. "Although that isn't always a good thing. But mostly, yes. We work together. But, sadly"— he glanced at his watch, grimaced, eased Laurie's head onto the pillow, and stood—"I must go. Mary Lynn will be wondering what's happened to me."

"Mike, thank you for coming."

"For finding you?" He stepped closer as she rose and was

pretty sure the mix of emotions said his pursuit earned him points in the "nice" column. "I kind of pretended I was here on official police business."

She laughed, then scolded. "I don't think that's allowed."

"When a girl doesn't give out her number . . . "

Karen blushed and dipped her chin.

"Or her address."

She made a face that said he'd caught her out.

"And barely lets a guy buy her coffee . . . "

"Mike, I—"

"It's okay." He smiled down at her and tipped her gaze up with one strong finger beneath her chin, and the touch of her skin to the pad of his finger . . .

That single connection flooded his heart and brain with possibilities he hadn't expected and now longed for. "Now that I've found you, I'd like to visit now and again. And have you visit me."

"Mike—"

* * * * *

His hand cradled her chin. The touch sent warmth spiraling through her, but she understood the danger of believing too much, too soon. And this was much too soon in Karen's book. She took a firm step back, toward the door, knowing she should waylay his entreaty.

She didn't need more complications in her life.

Laurie's existence shouldn't be clouded with adult choices that would most likely fall through. Wasn't it better all around for Karen to stay on her own? Less confusing for mother and daughter? If one didn't open one's heart, there was no chance for someone to break it, and Karen was pretty sure she couldn't bear to see the disappointment in Mike's gaze when he realized she wasn't a war widow but an unwed mother like the girls she served.

She turned back, square into Mike's broad chest. His strong arms braced her, kept her from falling, and that single moment pushed her to meet his gaze. "Yes."

His grin widened. His eyes dropped to her mouth once more, then he glanced around. The sleeping child, the open door, the possibility of others coming down the hall . . . she read his expression, that this wasn't the best place for a first kiss.

He made a face of chagrin and tweaked her nose. "I'll do the bell ringing tomorrow. Can you let me know if Laurie is doing better?"

She walked to the door with him and frowned. "Probably not. It's rare to get a phone line to use here. With so many people . . . " She shrugged her shoulders. "Really early in the morning or very late at night are the best options."

He laughed. "Well, our party line is no different, so I understand. Then I'll walk by Macy's to see you the day after. Or I'll call you here late in the evening." He turned and went through the door, then swung back. "I'm glad you like the wreath."

"I love it, Mike."

Was it her words or her tone that softened his gaze? Brightened his eyes? She didn't know, but as he walked away, she remembered her manners. "And thank you for ringing the bell tomorrow."

"My pleasure, Karen."

He disappeared around the corner, but for long seconds she stood and listened to the sound of his footsteps fading on the tile floor. She couldn't hear them once the connecting door clicked shut, but she stood there anyway, fingering the pretty wreath, imagining she could still hear him. See him.

Common sense tried to rein her emotions in.

Mike's kindness tempted them out of hiding.

Which was the right way to go? Which was in Laurie's best interest? And would Mike's opinion change when he realized that she not only worked at Booth Memorial Home, she'd been a client here five years ago?

What would he think? Would he be as attracted to a fallen woman? Would he want his younger sister around her?

Probably not. Worse, she couldn't blame him, a young man, old before his time, charged with raising a teenager in the thick of postwar opportunities.

She'd think and pray and ask God's guidance. She'd begun this new friendship, determined to guard Laurie's heart. But in reality, she was choosing to guard her own and that made her feel like a coward.

"She's doing better?" Major Flora approached Karen from the opposite end of the hall.

"Yes. The aspirin is keeping her comfortable."

"And we've added something new, I see." Major Flora's hiked a brow of interest to the wreath adorning Karen's door. "Your police officer visited."

"He's not mine, but yes. He stopped by."

"To talk about the mugging?"

Karen made a face. "No."

"Ah."

"He's interested in me. I see that clearly."

"And the interest is returned." Major Flora raised her shoulders. "Then what would be the problem with that?"

"He believes I'm a war widow."

"So do the girls."

"I know." Karen waved Major Flora into the apartment and

shut the door gently. "I'm living a lie and I don't know how to fix it."

Major Flora's gentle expression argued that point. "There is only one way, of course. The truth."

"But Laurie . . . " Karen sent the sleeping child a look of dismay. "I don't want to embarrass her. Or have her labeled. Her father made it clear that he had no interest in her or responsibility for us once he knew of my pregnancy. Should she have to live with that rejection as a small child? Is a white lie so bad when it protects her?"

"Is it the child we're protecting? Or the mother?" Major Flora wondered. When Karen began to answer, Major Flora held up a hand. "I don't need an answer, it is just something to think about. I think there is truth in both, and protection of one's self and one's child is what keeps us safe from danger. But you must decide if the omission is doing more harm than good. And then face the answer head on."

"I should examine my conscience."

"And your choices." Major Flora moved back to the door. She wasn't a demonstrative woman. She didn't freely hug or embrace, but her steady determination showed her love. "God places the paths before us. We choose the ones we travel."

"Blessed be the name of the Lord," Karen replied.

Major Flora was right. She'd put up walls to barricade herself and Laurie from hurt, but was it time to bring those walls tumbling down? Was this her Jericho?

She'd lived her childhood with her chin down, embarrassed by the drunken squalor that surrounded her life. She understood the scornful looks, the mean asides, the darkness of hopelessness when she was home.

She'd clung to school, her lifeline to new and wondrous choices. She'd excelled, not for her parents' sake, but to open new doors of achievement and possibility for herself as she matured.

And then she'd fallen for a glib-talking soldier, a man who saw her youthful naïveté and played it well.

Her fault, she knew. And she'd worked so hard to mend the broken pieces of her life. Her past, her shame, her choices.

And here they were, staring her in the face again.

Maybe there was no escape from past sin. Maybe that was the penance, meted out year by year.

She turned, half-hopeful, part-despairing, and her gaze fell on the small sampler she'd stitched while carrying Laurie in the womb. *"As far as the east is from the west, so far hath he removed our transgressions from us."* The psalm promised forgiveness. Christ's sacrifice guaranteed it. Why did she find it so hard to absorb? Why did she find it so easy to comfort others, yet impossible to forgive herself?

Laurie stirred on the couch. Karen moved to the counter, prepared another dose of crushed aspirin, and kept her hands busy tidying things that needed no attention. If she couldn't straighten out her soul, she could at least keep a neat-as-a-pin apartment.

Chapter Nine

Karen worked at a home for unwed mothers.

How could that be a coincidence? Was this an answer to prayer? His *and* Mary Lynn's? She dreaded having the neighbors know what she'd done. And he hated to see her go through any more suffering or consternation.

She hadn't been as sick these past few days. He took comfort in that. But he longed for her to be able to move on from this experience in six months' time.

For her to move on? Or you? How will you explain a new baby in the house? Think, man. There are no secrets in the neighborhood. You know that.

It didn't hurt to talk to her, though. To offer the option if it was truly available. He'd check further, but this would solve so many problems. She wouldn't be alone. She could study at the home, maybe even complete her senior year. And if she offered the baby for adoption, her college plans wouldn't have to go on hold. Their mother's dream for her daughter would come true, no thanks to Mike.

He broached the subject after supper that night. "Mary Lynn, have you ever thought of going to a home for expectant mothers to complete your pregnancy?"

Her face washed pale. Quick tears smarted her eyes. "You want me to go away."

Chagrined, Mike shook his head. "No, no, it's just something that popped into my head," he protested, but too late.

She sank further into the overstuffed chair. Tears slipped down her cheeks in rapid-fire fashion. She didn't sob or cry out, she just looked wretchedly helpless and lost, and that was worse. He crossed the room but she drew her knees up, wrapped her arms around them, and buried her face.

"Mary Lynn, I didn't mean you have to go away. I just wondered if you've given it any thought. If it might be easier on you. You told me you were worried about facing the neighbors. Going to school. Having people find out. I just thought—"

He wasn't sure what he thought, but her reaction said he hadn't thought enough. Or offered the option with proper care. Befuddled, he ran a hand through his hair. "Talk to me, Mare."

"No." She sniffled, head down, face hidden, and he couldn't feel worse than he did right then. Could he possibly mess up this situation any more than he already had?

Most likely not.

"Mary, I . . . "

She darted up, gaze down, and raced for her room. The slamming of her door punctuated the emotions of the night.

He stood there, staring at the staircase, wondering what to do. Should he go to her? Try to explain?

Thoughts of Maggie came to mind. She'd been extremely emotional during her pregnancy with little Joe. And the two miscarriages had put her in a mental tailspin, his mother said.

Karen told him that pregnancy wasn't a disease but a normal state of being.

Right now he didn't see one thing normal about any of it.

* * * * *

Mary Lynn refused to speak to Mike the following morning. Gaze averted, she ignored his questions and marched off to school, leaving him more frustrated than he thought possible.

Questions mentally flogged him as he trudged toward the subway station earlier than necessary. He'd be ahead of time at the bell-ringing site, but better there than mulling in the house, wondering how one man could possibly mess up so badly. The dark day reflected his mood, cold and gray, a leaden sky promising heavy rain by noon.

How could he fix this? He didn't know a thing about pregnancy or pregnant teens or being a dad in place of his father. He couldn't confide in family and break Mary Lynn's trust. That would come soon enough. Where could he turn?

He noticed a wooden sign as he passed the church of his youth, a beautiful stone building decked with tall, stained glass windows in pastel tones. He stared up, eyeing the poignant Biblical scenes portrayed, window by window.

His mother thought the colors pale and lifeless compared to Polish art, but Mike had always loved the muted scale the original glass artist employed.

The small sign graced the concrete walk leading to the narthex door. *Come unto me, all ye that labour and are heavy laden, and I will give you rest.*

Mike felt weary. Laden. Burdened. But he'd felt that way since hearing of his father's death, mid-war. Caught on the battlefield in a major game of life and death, he had no option to come home and offer comfort to the women of the family. Duty commanded he stay the course, and he had, but his mother and sister had paid a price in his absence.

He'd gone to church as a child. And he'd believed in the holiness of God, the Father, the Son, and the Holy Ghost.

But maturity and war turned him away. What form of God allows the callous inhumanity of battle? Of concentration camps and gas chambers, millions of sad souls cast aside by one man's crusade to "cleanse" the world?

The thought of Hitler's evil made his heart lurch.

But the sound of an infant squalling pulled his attention closer to the top step just beyond the sign. Drawn, he moved forward, senses reeling.

A round vegetable basket sat tucked behind the stone outcropping. There, nestled in the folds of a worn but clean blanket, a tiny child cried out to him, hands fisted, eyes pinched tight, a lusty cry taking hold as the baby begged his help. A scrap of paper with the name "David" was pinned to the top of the basket.

A baby here? On the church step? Who heard of such a thing?

He swallowed hard but didn't hesitate. He reached in, lifted the child with little finesse, and brought the baby to his chest. "There, there, little one. There, there."

"Another one?"

Mike turned.

The elderly rector approached Mike, his gaze gentle, his expression knowing. Reverend O'Krepky, Mike remembered, though he hadn't seen the parish leader in years. A younger reverend had offered his mother's funeral celebration. "Michael, isn't it?"

"Yes, Reverend. It's been awhile."

The wizened reverend acknowledged his words with an accepting shrug, and in the wisdom of his aged smile Mike saw the boy he'd once been. "In so many ways, Michael." The reverend noted the basket on the stoop with a glance. "We had a drop-off last week as well. Come here, little one."

He reached for the infant, but Mike dipped his chin toward the rectory. "I'll bring him in, Reverend."

"Ah." A look of acceptance softened the other man's gaze. "Follow me."

"Pieter! Another? So soon?" The middle-aged housekeeper, Mrs. Janas, bustled toward Mike. "Michael, how are you? And your sister, how is she doing? I pray for you both, daily. Your parents were such a gift to our parish, our congregation. They will never be forgotten here, Michael. Nor will you."

Her words warmed him. She reached out and took the small child from him, and there was no putting off a middle-aged woman reaching to soothe a small child. Mike wisely released the tiny boy to her capable arms.

Cool air swept in where the baby had cuddled against his chest. "This has happened before, Reverend?"

"Often enough." The reverend followed the baby's progress with gentle eyes. "During the war, soldiers would come in on leave or before they shipped out. As a result, we had many young women with child before their time. Now the war is over, but it seems the temptation to celebrate comes with consequences."

"He's beautiful."

"You know it's a boy?" The rector raised a quizzical glance his way.

"There was a note." He pulled the folded sheet of scrap paper from his pocket and handed it over. "His name is David."

The reverend took the note, eyed it, and sighed. "And no way of knowing who or where he came from."

"What will happen to him?" Mike knew he should be catching the subway, he was pushing the time frame, but he couldn't walk away from this abandoned child and not know something about the baby's fate. "Are there homes?"

"We have no legal papers and no information, so he'll go to a foundling home until they clear him for adoption."

Mike had passed a foundling home on his walk to the Booth Memorial Home the previous day. "How long will he be there?"

"There's no way of knowing. Sometimes months. Sometimes years."

Years?

Impossible.

A look in the older man's direction said it wasn't. "Can we keep him here, perhaps? For a day or two? See if the young mother comes back?"

The rector looked uncomfortable. So did Mrs. Janas. They exchanged guilty looks, and then the woman shrugged. "We have done that. Twice the young mother has quietly come back to recover her child."

"God bless you." Never had Mike meant a blessing so well. He grasped the reverend's shoulders. "You are a godly man."

The reverend's gaze brightened. His eyes twinkled. "You'd know this if you came around more often, Michael. He lives, He reigns, forever." He swept the cross a look of piety. "No matter what evil man conveys, God's love covers us."

Mrs. Janas had already changed the baby's diaper from a stash not far from her desk. She patted his bottom as she moved to the kitchen, humming a bright Christmas hymn.

"We keep a box of formula on hand. Just in case."

A new reality dawned on Mike. "If this happens here on a regular basis, how often does it happen in all of Brooklyn? Manhattan? The other boroughs?"

The reverend's gaze told him it was a regular occurrence.

An idea came to Mike, an idea that seemed God-given in its timing and simplicity. "Father, if no one comes for the child, I have a cousin who has lost two babies. Would it be possible for them to adopt David?"

Reverend O'Krepky frowned, but a spark of interest challenged the frown, as if Mike was brilliant beyond words. "If we follow certain procedures, then, yes . . . possibly. They'd have to do a home study, where a social worker would come and check out their home. Talk with them. Make sure they were suitable for raising a child."

"Of course."

"But with a recommendation of the church, the child could be placed with them for the duration."

Mike felt half-sick, half-empowered. What if Maggie hated him for suggesting an alternative to her own natural child? What if her husband Ben scoffed at the idea, and she loved it? What if . . . ?

"There is a time for every purpose under the heavens," the rector paraphrased.

A time to reap, a time to sow. A time for war, a time for peace.

Was it as simple as Ecclesiastes suggested? Could it be that evident? "I can contact Maggie and Ben. Talk to them. And then I'll come see you again."

"I'll be here."

Mike turned to go.

The older man stopped him with a hand to his sleeve.

Mike swung back.

"Welcome home, son." The old reverend wasn't a big man, nor was he in the strength of his years, but the vigor of his embrace heartened Mike. "You are always part of us, Michael Wolzak."

Part of the church. Part of God's people. Though he'd walked through the valley of the shadow, he'd come home. Now it was his job to do his best as a survivor. "Thank you, Reverend."

The reverend walked him to the door as the baby's squeals abated in the room beyond. "You're off to work?"

"No." Mike smiled, despite the rain that now fell in earnest. He pulled his cap down over his head and shrugged deeper into his coat. "I'm off to ring the bell for the Salvation Army outside Macy's."

"Pick an overhang to stand under," the reverend directed in a no-nonsense voice as he stepped inside to avoid the pesky drip of a leaky gutter. "God's work comes under many banners. Peace be with you."

"And with you. I'll be in touch."

He ran the four blocks to the subway, caught the train to Midtown, then hurried the three blocks to Karen's post outside the sprawling department store.

The kettle was in position, under a broad, green-and-ivory-striped awning to the left of the doors. A bell sat alongside, and as Mike began to toll the bell, he realized that although he'd been home for over a year, he'd been immersed in his mother's illness and care. His work. His emotions. Until this morning, seeing the reverend and housekeeper exchange glances, he had no idea how prevalent Mary Lynn's predicament had become.

But his sister wouldn't bear her child in a dark tenement to leave on a church step. Her child would be born in a clean, antiseptic environment. Homey. Loving. A place like the Booth Memorial Home, surrounded by clean sheets, kind folk, and tender-loving care. He'd see to it, one way or another.

Chapter Ten

. . . .

"Where are we going, Mommy?" Laurie wondered late Saturday afternoon.

Karen had done a poor job of hiding her excitement if the child's gleam was any indication. "We're taking the train to Midtown to see the lights."

"In the dark?" Laurie breathed the words as if the thought of walking the dark city streets bordered on disbelief. "Alone?"

There was the question of the hour. Karen fought to control an internal surge of sheer joy and shook her head. "Actually, no. Officer Mike and his sister are meeting us there."

"Really?" Laurie jumped up and down, which made buttoning her blue coat an impossible task. "We're meeting Officer Mike? Oh, yay! He's so wonderful, Mommy!"

He was.

Laurie's tender heart was already opening a special spot for the rugged policeman. As was Karen's.

But widened hearts equated risk. Too much, perhaps. Her mother had called earlier that day, wanting to meet with Karen. Longing to see Laurie. She'd put her off, unsure. She'd be glad to meet her mother alone and make inroads toward peace. But with Laurie?

Not until she saw a gentler, more sober side to her parents. "Hold still, Laurie. We can't leave until you're bundled up, and I can't do these buttons with you jumping like a jack-in-the-box."

Laurie laughed, held as still as she could, and then managed to inform three people of their mission as they strode toward the door. Major Flora waved them off from behind the front desk, and her smile offered quiet approval.

The familiar jingle of bells rang out from Macy's storefront, but Karen's attention was drawn left of the kettle.

Mike stood there, looking handsome and strong in his thick, wool coat and hat. A teenage girl stood alongside him. Their resemblance to each other was negligible, but the girl's winsome look reflected the sadness Karen had read behind Mike's gaze since meeting him. The current holiday season was bittersweet for both. Karen empathized completely.

"Karen!" Mike hurried forward, smiling. He reached out and grabbed her into a spontaneous hug, an embrace that felt like she'd come home at long last. "I was scanning the crowd for your cloak."

"Ah." She stepped back, smiled, and nodded. "I wondered why your gaze wandered past me twice."

"Foolishness on my part." He exchanged smiles with her, bent and hugged Laurie, then stood, gathering the little girl up into his arms. "Karen and Laurie O'Leary, this is my sister, Mary Lynn."

"Mary Lynn." Karen extended her hand and grasped the girl's gloved fingers. "What a pleasure to meet you. And you are every bit as lovely as your brother implied."

Mary Lynn's face softened with pleased surprise. "He said that?" She slanted a quick look to her brother as if doubting Karen's word.

"I believe beautiful, smart, and talented sums up his praise," Karen assured her.

"And Mary Lynn, this is Laurie."

"Hello." Laurie smiled down at Mary Lynn from her perch in Mike's arms. "I'm five."

"And I'm seventeen," Mary Lynn replied. "It's nice to meet you."

Laurie leaned down, clearly secure with Mike's grasp. "Officer Mike is taking us walking to see the Christmas lights."

Mary Lynn pretended surprise. "Really?"

Laurie nodded wisely. "Oh, yes. I think it was s'posed to be a surprise, but I could tell because my mommy was so happy. I knew something wonderful was going to happen!"

"Was she now?" Mike leveled a look at Karen that made her blush. Her deeper color inspired his broader smile. "That's good to know, kid."

"The joy of the season is contagious, it seems."

Mike's gaze softened, but his eyes held more hope than she should ever deserve. "I like bringing you joy, Karen."

Her cheeks warmed.

Mary Lynn studied the pair of them wistfully, as if her teenage heart longed for that romantic connection. Karen understood that look far too well. "Shall we walk?"

"Oh, yes!" Laurie clapped her gloved hands in a muted show of support. "And may we peek at Santa Claus later, perhaps?"

Karen wavered. Her budget allowed so little. A visit to Santa might set up impossible hopes and dreams, but one look at Laurie's sweet face said she couldn't refuse the child. "If it is all right with Mike and Mary Lynn, then yes."

"I'd love it," Mary Lynn told Karen. She smiled up at Laurie and patted the little girl's hand. "My mom and dad used to bring me to see Santa every year when I was little."

"Why just when you were little?" Laurie wondered, aghast. "Why don't you come see him tonight? With me? Have you been naughty?"

Mary Lynn paled.

"I, uh . . . " Mike groped for words and came up empty.

"Well . . . " Karen wasn't sure what to say, how to respond. Soon enough Laurie would leave make-believe behind, but Karen wanted her warmth and innocence to remain as long as possible. Born in the midst of a world war, there had been little fancy in Laurie's life before now.

The teenager recovered first. "I think that's a brilliant idea," Mary Lynn told her. "I would love to go see Santa with you, Laurie O'Leary."

Laurie's shout of glee drew attention their way, and the sight of them, looking like a family on a holiday outing, made others smile.

"Then it's settled," Mike agreed. He took Mary Lynn's hand in his and grinned down at her. "We'll walk and see the lights, then visit Santa, then get a bite to eat."

"Like a real date," Laurie informed them.

Mary Lynn turned, surprised but smiling.

Karen blushed, full-tilt.

Mike redirected his gaze down. "Is this a date, Karen? Because I do believe it fits the definition."

"Louise said that when a man invites you to go walking with him, it sure sounds like a date in her book!" Laurie announced her verdict with all the five-year-old emphasis she could muster.

"I'll be sure to thank Louise," Mike mused as they rounded the first corner.

"Or strangle her," Karen whispered, but the sight of the familiar street, awash in Christmas lights, made her pause. She'd respected the simplicity of the wartime windows three years before, and a part of her embraced that sensibility.

But the array of lights, trees, and panoramic window displays captured her gaze and her heart. Reindeer pulled Santa's sleigh across the face of one building while below, a dimly lit crèche showed the true meaning of Christmas, a child. A baby, born to the poor.

Light unto the world . . .

"You like it."

Mike's voice brought her gaze up. "It's amazing, Mike. Simply . . . amazing."

His smile warmed her. Laurie scrambled down to see the windows from the lower level. Mary Lynn grasped her hand as if it was the most natural thing in the world, and Mike did the same to Karen's.

Her heart melted. This was her dream, from so long ago. To be loved and cherished, to feel the joy of Christmas as God intended, a beloved child, cared for and loved despite the circumstances of birth. Mike's hand, strong and firm, made hers feel small. Safe. Secure.

She'd never known such a feeling with her parents. Her aunt and uncle, yes. They'd nurtured and loved her as time allowed, until her father ordered them to stay away in an angry exchange of words.

She never saw them again, but she carried their love with her wherever she went. They told her she was special.

She chose to believe them, despite her ragged circumstances at the time.

"How about this?" Mike asked as they turned up Fifth Avenue.

"Oh, Officer Mike!" Laurie danced in front of a Santa's Toy Shop window, enchanted by the sight. "I bet this is just what the North Pole looks like!"

"I'm sure you're right." Mary Lynn stooped low and pointed out tiny stuffed mice, peeking from the corners of the room, watching in awe as the elves worked tiny tools.

"Why are actual mice in the house not quite as cute?" Karen whispered to Mike.

"You mean you don't outfit yours in tiny striped pajamas with mob caps?" Mike matched his voice to hers but laughed.

"Pesky things. I don't like mice and I don't like trapping them. But better to trap them than coexist."

"You know the NYPD specializes in removing trapped mice, don't you?"

She started to send him a dubious look, but their eyes met and suddenly all she could picture was the big, brave policeman striding through her door to take care of the mouse trap under the kitchen sink. "Do they?"

Their gazes locked. For a long moment, neither spoke, caught in a vision of what could be. Puffs of breath mingled beneath the department store lights, while strains of Bing Crosby's "White Christmas" trickled their way from a block above.

Mike smiled when Laurie straightened to resume their walk, but his hand tucked Karen's deep into his left-hand pocket. "Perhaps not as a general rule, but this cop would do it. For you."

She smiled. "My hero."

Mike's smile faded. His jaw tightened. The gleam in his eyes went dark. "I'm nobody's hero, Karen. Just a guy doing his job."

Karen couldn't miss the change in face and posture. Should she ask how she'd offended him?

Not now. It was enough to know that he recoiled at the thought of being called a hero. She'd seen that anxiety in many returning veterans, men called to do a job of necessity to regain world peace. But that job had entailed battle. Killing. These choices were not shrugged off easily, but tonight wasn't a night to rehash war wounds, hers or his. This time together was for the girls, letting them see and feel the joy of Midtown at Christmas.

Silent, she squeezed his hand lightly.

He tipped his gaze down, read the empathy in her look, and his face softened. "Thank you."

She met his gratitude with a small smile. "You are most welcome, kind sir. I do believe we are about to be dragged in to see the train display."

"I've always loved model trains." He pushed through the large door, then held it open as they entered. "My father and I would set them up, and then Mary Lynn would come through and in five short seconds have the entire track and pieces knocked over."

"I was little," she protested. She held up Laurie's gloved hand. "Laurie's age."

"You improved with time," Mike agreed with a smile. He reached over and chucked the tip of her chin in a friendly gesture, but Karen caught Mary Lynn's expression as Mike turned toward the elaborate train displays. Embarrassment and chagrin tainted the teenager's features as she averted her face. Engrossed in lifting Laurie high to see the upper level trains, Mike missed the look.

Not Karen. And Mary Lynn's expression told her that no matter how nice a family seemed, they most likely had some problems. But after the rigors of World War II, who didn't?

"Have you ever been to the Christmas Spectacular?" Mike asked when they turned into Rockefeller Center.

Karen shook her head but kept her gaze ahead. "I haven't." Making eye contact with Mike right now would be like begging an invitation to the pricey production. Going to the theater required a great deal more thought than walking the free streets of Christmas Manhattan.

"Oh, Mommy. Have you ever seen anything so beautiful in your life?" Laurie breathed the words on a gasp as the great tree rose before them. Skaters circled the recessed courtyard ice below, while lights and decorations guided the path to the glorious Norway Spruce.

Mary Lynn reached for Mike's free hand. "I'm amazed every time I see this."

"And you're not alone." He squeezed her hand, then reached down and picked Laurie up high. "I know the odds of you getting lost in this crowd are slim, but they're slimmer yet if I'm carrying you, kid."

She laughed and cupped his face between two tiny gloved hands. "Thank you, Officer Mike."

He bumped foreheads with her gently. "You're welcome."

"It's huge," Karen breathed. She'd seen the tree twice before. Once as a child with her aunt and uncle, then again as a teen with her high school choir. But tonight the tree seemed even more splendorous. Was it the tree itself or the company she kept?

The company, she decided as Mike moved forward. "I'm always amazed when I come here," she told them.

Mary Lynn turned and nodded. "Me too. My dad patrolled this area when they were doing construction."

A family of tradition. Worth. Substance. Faith. Those were the things of Karen's childhood dreams. Parents, treasuring a child. A clean place to come home to. "What a wonderful heritage."

"Dad got to see the first tree here," Mike went on. "It was a scruffy little thing decorated with cranberries and foil. The workers put it up as a way to remember Christmas and better times."

"The Great Depression." Karen considered the lack of that decade, the drinking and anxiety that went along with joblessness, homelessness, and little hope. "I didn't know they did a tree then."

"It started the tradition," Mary Lynn added. "Dad said people laughed at the idea of putting such a grand building here during hard times."

"But that construction brought a lot of jobs," Mike added. "And those laborers were grateful for the chance to work again."

"From humble beginnings," Karen breathed, seeing the Biblical analogy clearly.

"Born in a manger." Mike smiled at her. "God with us."

"May we go closer?" Laurie wondered, because while history lessons were all well and good, what a five-year-old wanted was to draw close to the majestic spruce and gaze upon the lights surrounding her.

"Yes!" Mike laughed and led the way up the steps to the closer viewing area. "How's this?"

"It is so very beautiful," Laurie whispered, eyes wide.

"I agree," said Mike, but he wasn't looking at the tree, or the spectacle of the skaters below, or the lights channeling people into the well-lit square. His gaze was on Karen, as if willing her to read beyond the words.

She smiled and lowered her gaze, but he tipped it back up with the edge of one gloved finger, just enough to smile down at her briefly. "Absolutely lovely."

She fell completely at that moment, the gaze, the touch, the words a perfect blend of romance and timing.

Mary Lynn drew their attention to Laurie's yawn. "I think we'd better head back toward the station if we're going to be awake enough to see Santa."

"Yes."

They made it back to Macy's just in time for the girls to stop by Santa's chair, then stopped for food at a nearby diner. By the time they walked through Penn Station, Laurie was half-asleep in Mike's arms. They boarded the downtown train, but as it rumbled to Karen's stop, Mike frowned, protective. He stood as the train slowed for her station, and Karen waved him off.

"This is nothing I haven't done many times over," she scolded him as she took Laurie into her arms. "Being a single mother isn't easy, but Laurie and I have had a great deal of practice, haven't we?"

Laurie cuddled into Karen's coat. "Will we be home soon?"

"Very soon."

Laurie's elongated yawn spurred Mike to action. "We'll walk you, then catch the next train to Brooklyn."

"Mike, it's late."

Karen's protest fell on deaf ears. "Exactly why we're walking you home. It's only a few blocks and I'll feel better."

Mary Lynn hopped off the train as the doors slid open. "There's no use arguing with him, Karen."

"I see that." Karen scolded him with a look, but the dark streets of Union Square would feel better with Mike and Mary Lynn at her side. A woman alone with a child was not exactly an ideal circumstance at this hour.

"And here we are," Karen announced a few minutes later. She pointed to the steps leading into the home. "Home and safe."

"You live in a hospital?" Mary Lynn's quizzical look said that was an odd circumstance.

"I'm a nurse, and I work here, but they have a few tiny apartments they rent to employees. And that makes life more affordable."

"A widow's pension isn't enough to live on," Mike agreed, and his sympathetic words held up a mirror Karen didn't want to see. She was living a lie, a falsehood he accepted easily. As did others. Knowing how many were deceived drove the guilt deeper.

"It's good to have a career," she added, not agreeing with Mike but not telling the truth, either. "Thank you, Mike, for this night. And you too, Mary Lynn."

"It was fun." Mary Lynn reached down and hugged Laurie.

Mike did the same to Karen, and in the warm embrace of his arms, the feel of his breath along her hair, against the sensitive skin of her neck, she knew a moment of wondrous assent. She belonged there, in this man's arms. By his side. It couldn't possibly feel so right and be wrong. Could it?

Would he hate her for being an unwed mother? Would he decry her lack of morals? Laugh at her naïveté?

He will do what any man of good moral sense would do: run in the opposite direction. And that would leave her and Laurie high and dry, hopes dashed. Risking her own grief was one thing. Laurie's? Quite another.

The internal scolding refused to abate as she tucked Laurie into bed a few minutes later. In the darkened apartment, the tiny Christmas bulb that lit her manger scene reminded her of the true meaning of Christmas. Lights and pageantry were wonderful, but the season of gifts lay before her in the poverty of a stable.

A knock on her door surprised her. She hurried to the door, sure she was being called on duty for an emergency. Louise stood there and gestured down the hall. "A phone call for you."

At this hour?

Karen hurried down the cool hall and lifted the phone. "Hello."

"I just wanted to thank you again for tonight."

Mike's voice, thoughtful and rich. Deep and commanding. Thanking her, welcoming her. Embracing her.

Embracing a lie.

She sighed and smiled while emotions struggled within her. "Thanks should be coming from my side. It was a lovely night, Mike."

"Are you working tomorrow?"

"Yes."

"So am I, but I was wondering if you and Laurie would like to take the train out here some night this week. When are you off duty?"

"Not until Wednesday."

"I'm done at three on Wednesday. How about if I meet you and Laurie and we take the train to Brooklyn? We can watch the lights of Manhattan come on together."

Her aunt had spoken of this tradition, as if she never grew tired of watching the nighttime island come to life. When one lived in Manhattan, the tall buildings blocked vantage points to see the array.

Off the island?

The beauty of the Manhattan skyline at night was world famous. But should they go? Should she accept the invitation? "Yes."

She committed before common sense could talk her out of it, and Louise's smile of approval said the teen agreed. "We'd like that, Mike."

"Me too."

She said good-bye, re-cradled the phone, and stood silent, staring, for just a moment.

She had to tell him. She knew that.

But was it wrong to dream a little while longer? To elongate this attraction a few days more? A week?

A lifetime. That is your wish, admit it. You have fallen for this warm, loving man and want a lifetime with him.

She walked back to her room, torn. Once again her eye was drawn to the manger, the tiny image of Mary, arms out, waiting for the promised child.

She'd been alone.

God had provided.

Most likely scared.

God offered comfort and protection in Joseph.

She'd been tired and worn, her long journey to Bethlehem accomplished while great with child.

The Lord welcomed their son with angels and stars and a gathering of shepherds. Isaiah's prophecy, God's fulfillment. Emmanuel, God with us.

God had sheltered her this far, giving her a wondrous child, friendships, and a career she loved. She had much to be grateful for, she knew that. But she fell asleep thinking of Mike.

Chapter Eleven

Mike put in a call to Reverend O'Krepky early on Sunday. "Reverend, I know you're busy, but I wanted to call and check on little David. Is he still with us? With the church, I mean."

"He is." The older man's voice went soft. "I will have to call in the authorities, Michael. We can't wait longer for the mother to return. Already they will have my head for keeping him this long."

"Then I'll contact my cousin," Mike promised. "I'll call you right back."

"I will be in church," the reverend replied. "But Mrs. Janas is here, caring for the boy. She'll answer your call."

Mike bit back a sigh. Of course the reverend would be in church. It was Sunday morning, after all.

He grabbed the phone line while he could and called Maggie. Luckily most of his neighbors were churchgoers, so getting the party line on Sunday morning wasn't too long a wait. "Maggie? It's Mike. I need to talk to you and Ben. Can I come out there today?"

"We're actually coming to Brooklyn," she told him. "Mom and I are baking kuchens while Dad and Ben take Joey to Billy Carmichael's birthday party."

"Can I see you guys alone before Ben heads out? It's important."

"Of course," Maggie replied. "We'll stop over after we drop Joe off. That will give Mom some time to spoil him."

"Perfect." Mike hung up the phone. Was it perfect? Or was he butting in where he had no business going, and would his idea cause more pain?

"Are you coming, Mike?" Mary Lynn came down the stairs half an hour later with her coat buttoned, ready for church.

He should go. He knew it. What was the harm in walking her to church? Going inside? Pretending?

Honorable men don't pretend.

He shook his head and motioned to the back room. "I'm cleaning out that old pantry today. You go ahead."

She left, but not before he sensed her disappointment. In him? Probably. And that made two of them these days.

* * * * *

"So." Maggie and Ben stepped into the Wolzak brownstone a short while later. "Joey's eating apple pancakes with Mom and Dad. What's going on, Mike?"

Feeling awkward, Mike motioned them in. "Sit down, okay?"

"Sit down?" Ben eyed him. "What's wrong with you, Mike? Spit it out. I promised your uncle I'd help him fix a leaky faucet while the kids play at Billy's party. What's up?"

"A baby."

"A . . . ? What?"

Maggie frowned. So did Ben.

"I found a baby."

Maggie's cautious scan of the house questioned his sanity. "Where is it, Mike?" She rendered the question softly, as if ready to phone mental health services.

"At the church with Reverend O'Krepky."

That tidbit of information drew Maggie's brows closer. "You're serious."

Mike stopped pacing and stared at her. "Of course I'm serious. Would I bring you over here if I wasn't serious?"

"I, umm . . . " She grimaced and raised her shoulders. "You're right, of course. I thought . . . "

Her rueful gaze said what she thought, that Mike was losing it. But he wasn't, not about this at any rate. He sank into the seat opposite them. "I was walking to the train the other day and heard a sound. Someone had abandoned a baby in a basket outside the church."

"Oh, Mike." Shock and sorrow filled Maggie's face. "How sad. Who could do that?"

"Someone wanting her child to have a better chance at a solid future," Ben told her. "That's a pretty amazing sacrifice right there."

Mike couldn't think of a way to make this easier, so he waded in. "I wondered if you and Ben ever thought of adopting a baby. This baby, actually. His name is David."

"David?" Maggie's eyes softened. "My grandfather's name."

"And my brother's," Ben added.

"It probably sounds stupid," Mike went on. He ran his hand through his hair and clasped the nape of his neck. "It's just, I kind of felt like it was meant to be. That I was walking by right then, the baby cried, and there we were, together, right after you and I talked at Thanksgiving."

"This is a big conversation to be having right now," Ben said.

Maggie looked straight at him. "Will it grow less big for waiting?"

Ben gazed at his wife, and in that look Mike read the pain and sorrow of those lost babies. The nights of weeping, days of waiting, weeks of nothing.

"Is it of God?" Ben wondered. "Or our sadness?"

"Can't it be both?" Maggie replied. "Can we see him, Michael?"

"Yes. Reverend O'Krepky said it would be fine to bring you over after church today."

Ben reached for the phone. "I'll call your father, Maggie. He can get Joey to the party without us."

The line was open again, and Mike counted that as a small miracle. They walked down the street together, and he'd have been foolish not to read the anticipation in Maggie's expression. Her footsteps, pushing the pace. When they arrived at the rectory, Mike pushed the doorbell and prayed.

And when he realized he was praying, a hint of warmth stole through him, as if a light that had been quenched in the trenches of war flickered to life again. The door opened and the aging rector aimed a smile at them. "Reverend O'Krepky, you remember my cousin Maggie, don't you?"

"Of course!" He swept the door wide. "And your husband, Ben. Reverend Tomer married you."

"Yes."

"And you have a son, Michael tells me." The reverend led the way into the rectory office. Mrs. Janas smiled a greeting and stood, then moved to the small room beyond her desk. "And some sadness."

"Yes, again." Ben acknowledged the words with a grimace, but his gaze changed as Mrs. Janas reentered the room. A look of awe took the place of sorrow in his reply, but it was Maggie's face that struck Mike's heart.

Blessed.

His cousin looked blessed.

Mrs. Janas brought the baby toward them and held him out. "Would you like to hold him?"

Maggie paused. She turned to Ben, and the question in her eyes said that if she held that baby, she would not want to give him back. Ever.

Ben's gaze offered encouragement and acceptance.

Maggie reached out her arms and the older woman settled the sleeping newborn into Maggie's embrace.

"Oh. Oh. Oh." Tears slipped down her cheeks, one after the other, quick tears, a mix of happiness and wonder.

Maggie sank into the chair the reverend offered. Ben sat beside her, and the way his big hand dwarfed the infant's tiny fingers showed Mike the power of love and life: the gift of a child.

"Would you like me to contact my friends at the Children's Aid Society?" The reverend leaned forward in question, but his look said he knew the answer already. "I think they will accept my recommendation for you to take little David home."

"Reverend, would they really?" Maggie turned surprised eyes to his. "They'd let us keep him now? Care for him while the legalities are straightened out?"

The rector's gaze tightened. "Foundling resources are strained at present. The homes are bursting. And we gave the mother several days to come back, and she hasn't."

"Yes. Call, Reverend." Ben nodded, then palmed the newborn's head with a big, gentle hand, a benediction. "We want him home, with us."

"And if God does send another child to you, in the old-"fashioned way?" the reverend inquired, solicitous but firm. "What will become of young David here?"

Maggie smiled up at the rector and held the baby tighter. "He will become a big brother. Just as it should be."

Reverend O'Krepky smiled and stood. "I will make the call."

"And you better call Uncle Reggie," Mike reminded Ben. "Because I think you're going to be a little too busy today to fix anyone's sink."

Reality hit Ben. "We have nothing ready. We'll have to find Joey's old clothes. . . . "

"Clean and stored in the attic," Maggie told him.

"The crib . . . "

"The cradle will do for a month or so," she went on. "It's wrapped in sheets, also in the attic. We will wash the bedding and the clothing when we get home. But we will need more rubber pants." Her knowing gaze met Mrs. Janas's. "Those don't stand the test of time well. And formula."

"You have a Woolworth's nearby?" the older woman asked.

Ben smiled in relief. "Of course, we can get it all there. I can't . . . " He reached down and ran a finger across the baby's palm. Instinctively, the baby grabbed hold and held on tight. " . . . quite believe this."

"Me, either."

Maggie smiled up at him. Ben bent low to kiss her cheek. "Congratulations, Mom. It's a boy."

She giggled, and in that joyous sound more of Mike's heart sprang to life.

"It seems it is."

"And the name?" The reverend reentered the room and tapped his watch. "They'll be here in a couple of hours. The emergency weekend crew is on call, and they're busy elsewhere. Will you keep his name? It was pinned to his blanket when Mike found him." He handed over the scrap of paper and Maggie touched it, reverently.

"He will be David," she decided. "It's a beautiful name. He is her gift to us. The name is her gift to him. He will grow up knowing his mother loved him enough to ensure his future and give him a godly name."

Mike glanced at his watch and whistled. "I've got to work. A lot of flu going around, and we're shorthanded. You guys are okay here?"

Mrs. Janas shooed him out the door. "You go to work. I'll stay with Ben and Maggie. We've got a nice soup going for the reverends and there's plenty for all."

"Should we call Mom and Dad?" Maggie asked as he approached the entry to the rectory. "And Joey? Or just walk in later with David?"

Mike laughed because this was a problem his cousin hadn't envisioned two hours ago. "I'd walk in. But bring hankies along."

Maggie's voice hailed him as he swung open the door. "Mike. There's no possible way we can repay you for this. Thank you."

He saw her face, warm and maternal. Ben's, fatherly and strong. He lifted one shoulder in understanding. "My pleasure."

Chapter Twelve

....

On Monday, Mike brought Karen a small box of chocolates from San Francisco, a mix of dark and sweet, even though it was his day off and he had no other reason to take the train into Manhattan.

Karen was reason enough.

On Tuesday, he just happened to have a treasure he found at the neighborhood bookstore, a children's book of verses with full-color illustrations, the kind of book that fed a child's imagination.

And on Wednesday, he got off the train two blocks east of the Booth Memorial Home and walked, palms damp, to pick up his girls.

Was he silly to feel this way after so short a time?

Yes.

And it felt good to be silly after so many years of serious. If all went well, he'd talk to Karen about Mary Lynn's condition this week. Share the confidence. If she could secure Mary Lynn a clean place at the home to have this baby, he'd sleep better at night, knowing she was in the best hands available. Karen's.

"Officer Mike!"

"Hey." He reached out and caught Laurie up into his arms, her red knit stockings and blue wool coat making her look like an all-American girl, precious and beloved. "You were watching for me."

"Mommy said if we want to see the lights blink on, we have to be quick because it gets dark so early."

"Mommy's smart."

"And thank you so much for my book!" The little girl's voice tipped high, then low. "I wanted to bring it, but Mommy said I'd get tired of carrying it, although I don't think I could ever get tired of carrying it, Officer Mike! It's so very wonderful and"—she leaned in, sharing a secret, just for him—"it has pictures of beautiful princesses in it. I would like to be a beautiful princess one day. With a magic horse."

Mike touched his forehead to hers as Karen approached, and the sight of Karen . . .

Young and lovely, the red scarf snug around her neck . . .

Went against any past images he had of Salvation Army bell ringers.

Karen smiled as she drew up to his side, and it seemed the most natural thing in the world to turn and swipe a gentle kiss to her mouth, a touch fleeting and sweet but filled with promise. A feeling he hoped she shared.

She met his gaze. He refused to acknowledge the thoughtful side of her look, grasped her hand, and started walking back the way he came. "You girls ready for an adventure?"

"Yes!"

"Good."

Dusk was falling by the time the train let them off in Brooklyn. "This way," Mike said. He led them to a higher vantage point, facing the East River. The clear sky streaked oblique light above the dark harbor water, gold-tipped shades of pink and purple. He stood there, Laurie snug in his left arm, while his right arm drew Karen in. "Standing close keeps us warmer," he explained when she sidled a look his way, but her smile said she understood.

And approved.

"Oh, Officer Mike, it's happening!"

"So beautiful." Karen leaned her head against his chest, and the soft scent made him think of springtime flowers. Warm, lazy sunsets. Romps in the park with Laurie and the dog.

"It always amazes me." When the cold chased them to the lower sidewalk and the six-block walk to Mike's home, Karen indicated Manhattan with a sweep of her hand. "The lights, the busyness, the people, the majesty. Living in it, you don't get the full effect. From here? Manhattan is a showcase."

"It pales in comparison to some things," Mike replied. His smile finished the thought.

Karen's glance of wry appreciation said she got his drift. And was the heightened color of her cheeks from the cold or her proximity to him?

"Here we are." He led them up the steps of the brownstone, plied the key, then held the door wide as they stepped through.

"Laurie!" Mary Lynn's greeting made Mike feel better about his decision to have Mary Lynn stay at the Booth Home. She clearly liked Karen and Laurie. At the home there would be no censure. No condemnation.

"We came to your house!" Laurie exclaimed. "And it is so big and pretty! And I saw people lights outside, and I loved them so much."

Mike hung her coat and Karen's on the wall hooks behind him and frowned. "People lights?"

"People lights, yes." Laurie hugged Mary Lynn, then tugged her to the window and pointed. "We saw the store lights last week. And Officer Mike took us to see the city lights come on. But you guys are so lucky because you live where there are people lights." Her crinkled expression disparaged their lack of understanding.

"Because people live here, so these are real lights. People lights. Where people live."

"People live by us, Laurie." Karen bent low and met Laurie's gaze. "A lot of people."

Laurie nodded. Clearly she'd thought this through. "But we live in a hospital, not a house," she explained. "And someday I want to live in a house, a big house like this, with so many rooms and neighbors. I want to play stick ball and have people lights all around me."

Mike tousled her hair and met Karen's gaze. "The kid's on my side."

Karen's smile said that might be so, but the smile didn't chase that hesitation in her gaze. Not fully. As if part of her longed to step forward, but something held her back.

"Are you any good in the kitchen?" He directed his question to Karen and hooked a thumb up the two steps. "Come help me while Mary Lynn amuses Laurie."

"You cook?" She followed him up the two steps into a well-outfitted kitchen as Mary Lynn took Laurie upstairs to see the rest of the house. "Really?"

He shrugged as he started to brown small chunks of meat. "I make do, mostly. But my mother showed me a thing or two. Then the army had their go at it. I get by. How about you?"

* * * * *

In a kitchen like this? A dream come true? I could cook anything, Karen thought. She swept the pretty kitchen a look of approval. "I can hold my own, but I've never had a setup like this to test my talents. Mike, this is charming."

"My mother loved to cook," he told her, easy. "And my father loved to eat. A smart man does not argue cost when outfitting a woman's kitchen, so he made sure Mom's setup was wonderful."

Karen took an apron from a hook and put it on. "I like how the Wolzak men think."

"Do you?" Mike stepped closer. He glanced through the doorway leading to the living area, but footsteps above said Mary Lynn was still showing Laurie the house. "Do you know what I'm thinking right now?" He slipped an arm around her. His gaze went from her eyes to her mouth and lingered there, wondering.

"I do. Yes," she whispered, and this time she couldn't and wouldn't step back. She stepped into the kiss, into his embrace, and let herself revel in the feel of his hard, muscled back, the buzzed hairs along the nape of his neck, the warmth of his embrace, and the beauty of the kiss.

The clatter of footsteps ended the moment too soon. Way too soon. "Mommy, they have four bedrooms! And a real big bathroom upstairs, and a washline that goes back and forth to the neighbors three times. And Mary Lynn let me hold her baby doll, see?"

"I do see!" Karen exclaimed. She offered a smile of approval. "This is a beautiful doll. Be careful with her, okay?"

"I will!"

Karen stood and faced Mary Lynn, but as she began to thank the girl, Mary Lynn's face grayed. She inhaled once, paled more, and headed for the stairs, looking like she was about to be sick.

In that moment Karen knew why Mike had been checking out obstetricians in early December.

Her heart broke for the girl. The sight of Mary Lynn's face, her demeanor, her bad color . . . Karen remembered all too well. But at least Mary Lynn had family to love her. Cherish her. Forgive her.

Once dinner was over and the kitchen cleaned, Mary Lynn disappeared upstairs. Laurie lay sleeping on the sofa, curled up, a ripple-stitch afghan keeping her warm. Mike took a seat in a big easy chair and motioned for Karen to do the same. She glanced at Laurie and shook her head. "I've got to get her home, Mike. It's late and a school night."

He took her hand and brought it to his mouth for a soft kiss. "Ten minutes. Please?"

She read the need in his eyes. Heard the plea in his voice, and there was no way she could refuse his urge to talk. This man had lost so much. He'd *done* so much. He'd sacrificed years of his life to maintain her freedom. He'd lost his father, and his mother. And now, Mary Lynn . . . She sat and faced him directly. "I'm aware of Mary Lynn's condition."

Relief washed angst from his features. "She told you?"

Karen shook her head. "No, but when you've seen the symptoms as often as I have . . . "

Lived them, you mean, in a similar fashion . . .

She ignored the thrust of conscience and shrugged one shoulder. "It was easy to figure out."

He ran a hand through his hair, then hunched forward. "My mother's single dying wish was for me to take care of Mary Lynn. Look out for her. And I messed up, big time."

"Mike, no, it's—"

His raised hand stopped her protest. "I know what you're going to say, but I'm not afraid to accept my share of the blame."

A warning ping sounded in Karen's brain. She took a small breath, then exhaled. "Blame? Surely what's done is done, right? And then you move on?"

His face said it wasn't that easy. Karen's heart wrenched further. "We already have a nosy neighbor who suspects."

Karen had no trouble recalling her father's tirade. How she brought shame to them and the neighborhood. As a teen she'd been devastated, thinking that. Now? Washed clean in the beauty of a Savior, a forgiving God? She shrugged. "Who cares?"

His raised expression said everyone cared, and more internal red flags popped up inside Karen.

"She'll be embarrassed. Ostracized. Made fun of. I can't stand by and let that happen."

"We had this discussion before," she reminded him. "That women bear the brunt of unwed pregnancy and men go blithely on with their lives."

"Exactly." He nodded. "But if she comes to live at the Booth Home, she'll be among other young mothers. Good examples like you and the major. People of peace and goodwill who can ease her through this."

Karen's hopes plummeted.

Despite Mike's warm and caring ways, he longed to send his sister away to bear her out-of-wedlock child. He claimed it was to save her embarrassment, but Karen understood that two-edged sword too well. If Mary Lynn was tucked out of sight, Mike would be saved a great deal of chagrin as well.

Her heart tightened. Her lungs followed suit. She knew she couldn't talk of this here and now. Not and keep herself calm and impartial. She stood.

So did Mike.

She faced him square, knowing this would be the last time she'd see him, hating that truth, but knowing it would be best for all. Because if Mike Wolzak couldn't understand and forgive his younger sister's sin after the trauma of losing her father and mother, he'd never forgive hers. So be it. "Mike, the Booth Home is a wonderful place."

He nodded, but his face showed uncertainty as he read her mixed emotions.

"But Mary Lynn has family who love her. You, her aunts and uncles, her cousins. And she has a lovely home here, with you. The girls that come to Booth are generally cast-offs. Young women who've been thrown out of homes and jobs because of their condition. Mary Lynn doesn't need us. She needs you."

His jaw tightened in surprise. "You won't take her?"

She shrugged into her coat. "That isn't for me to say. The majors decide each case. But I'm telling you for Mary Lynn's own good, sending her away isn't the answer. Loving her is. And now . . . " She turned to gather her child. "I must get Laurie home."

A sorrowful subway ride seemed much longer than the cheerful one of late afternoon. When they got to the home's door, Karen reached out for Laurie once she'd released the latch.

"I'll bring her in," Mike offered.

Karen shook her head and raised her chin. Heartbroken, she faced him one last time. "I'll take her, Mike. And I want you to know I had a lovely time these past weeks, but I can't see you again."

"Karen, I—"

He looked shell-shocked.

She felt the same, but how could she pursue a relationship with a man who turned his back on his younger sister? Karen's sin was easily as grievous. Would he hold that against her as well?

She wouldn't and couldn't take that chance. Not for her sake or Laurie's. She stepped through the door.

Mike started to follow.

She turned and shook her head at him.

He hesitated, then stopped, allowing the door to fall into place. Karen moved toward the hallway leading to her room. At the right angle, she turned back, just to see.

He was gone. And with him went the foolish hopes and dreams she'd harbored these beautiful, light-filled weeks.

Chapter Thirteen

He'd talk to her tomorrow, Mike decided. Karen was clearly upset tonight, but was that his fault? All he wanted was a safe place for Mary Lynn and her child.

Thoughts of the abandoned baby filled his mind. A child, born to the poor, left on a cold, wet step. Mary Lynn deserved better, and what was wrong with conserving propriety? His mother had loved a proper upbringing. His father, too.

Was he wrong to want the best for Mary Lynn?

No. Finally, at long last, he was being the big brother he should have been months ago. He raised the subject to her the next morning.

Mary Lynn stared at him. Her lower lip quivered. "I thought we stopped talking about this. You made me a doctor's appointment."

"Yes." Mike didn't see what one had to do with the other.

"I thought that meant I'd stay here. Have the baby. Decide what to do."

"You'd still do all that, just on East Fifteenth Street. You could take classes there and stay on course for college. Just like Mom wanted."

"But what about what I want, Mike?" She stared at him, tears slipping down her cheeks. "How come you get to make decisions and it doesn't matter what I want?"

Because you're a kid, he wanted to say. *Because you've already messed up, and I'm trying to help you save face. Because . . .*

"You're ashamed of me." Sorrow and humiliation fought for her features. "Okay, then. I don't want to make things worse than they are. You'll make the arrangements?"

He nodded, feeling like he just got kicked in the head. And the heart.

She hadn't harangued him. Guilt had pushed her to agree, a guilt he fostered in her.

He went to work, conflicted. He walked his beat the same way, and when he turned the corner toward Macy's, a grizzled older man stood on the corner, ringing the bell.

Not Karen.

He paused at the kettle, dropped in some change, and faced the man. "Is Karen sick?"

The man frowned.

"The woman who usually rings the bell here in the morning. Is she sick? Is her daughter ill?"

The man shrugged. "Alls I know is I'm s'posed to ring here every mornin' the rest of the week. Till Christmas Eve."

Realization struck.

Karen was avoiding him. She said she wouldn't see him anymore and then took steps to ensure it.

Why? Because he wanted to send Mary Lynn into Karen's care? That made no sense.

Did it?

He finished his shift, took the train to Brooklyn, passed the sweet Polish church, and longed to kick something. He'd felt so good a few days ago, watching Maggie hold that baby, the child of her dreams.

Now?

He felt wronged. In trying to do his best, he'd caused the worst, but why?

The old church door invited him in. He ignored the silent call and trudged by. Years of prayer had led to nothing. His parents gone, his sister's predicament, so many hurt or killed. He thought he'd cast bitter thoughts aside, but they rose this day, reminding him of all he'd lost.

And now he'd lost Karen too. And Laurie.

He refused to look up and see the "people lights" the child embraced. He'd get through Christmas, somehow, someway, and then face the future with his sister. A future that suddenly seemed bleak and sad all over again.

* * * * *

"I'm not a war widow." Karen faced the gathering of girls after their evening meal that night and let her gaze meet theirs, one at a time. "I am an unwed mother, just like you."

Most looked surprised. A few didn't.

"I met a soldier when I was eighteen, just out of high school," she explained. "I fell in love with him. I believed his promises. I let the needs of my life dictate the choices I made then." She made a face, acknowledging her mistake. "My parents threw me out. They cast me onto the streets where I lived for weeks until Major Flora found me. She brought me here. Taught me. Helped me. And when Laurie was born, she made sure I had help while attending nursing school. With the army's help, my poor choices turned into great hope. I know many of you thought I was widowed, and I let that go on for Laurie's sake. And mine," she admitted. "But I need to be honest with you and myself. God has forgiven my iniquity. I hope you will, too."

The girls gathered to console her. Empathize with her. Relief mixed with pain as she began her shift that night. She may have gained the girl's trust with her honesty, but she'd lost a man who touched her, heart and soul. For knowing him so short a time, she was amazed how much that hurt.

* * * * *

Karen didn't return to her bell-ringing post on Thirty-Fourth Street.

Arnie looked saddened by the news, as if he bore some weight in her decision. But that was ridiculous, Mike decided. What would an elderly Jewish baker have in common with a Salvation Army bell ringer?

A shared love of good bread. That's all.

Mary Lynn faced him on Christmas Eve. It had been a long, silent stretch of days, but now she met his gaze with a firm look. "I've been thinking this week."

He nodded, listening.

"Thinking and praying," she went on, and her pointed use of the second verb caught Mike up short. "I've decided I'll do whatever you think is best after Christmas. I know I've made bad decisions in the past, and I'm trying to learn from them. So yes, if you want me to go to a home like where Karen works, I'll do that because it's time for me to take responsibility for my actions. I won't fight you on it. But on one condition."

Mike raised a brow. "And that is?"

She picked up his coat off the hook inside the door. "You come to church with me."

"Now?"

"It's Christmas Eve. Yes. And every Sunday thereafter."

"Because?" He faced her square, half-proud, half-miffed that she called him on the carpet.

She thrust the coat at him and kept his gaze locked with hers. "Because it's the right thing to do. Mom and Dad would have expected you to go with me. Even though I've messed up."

She was right on all accounts. Walking the two blocks to the church, he wished his father were still here to talk to. Mike Sr. held a wisdom and grace that inspired those around him. His inner strength called to others, and his helpful nature welcomed everyone to their table.

How he'd love to talk to his father one last time.

They walked into the church. Twin wreaths decorated the broad, wooden doors. Candlelight brightened the deepest corners of the oak-trimmed sanctuary. Tall, thin, short, and wide, the gift of light shimmered around them. And in the middle of the sanctuary stood a crèche, lovingly cast and painted, the Holy Family celebrating the gift of a child.

As the service began, Mike's gaze strayed back to the manger. The loving mother, solicitous, bent over her child. The Jewish father, caring for a son not his own. He'd protected Mary from shame and possibly death by marrying the young woman who carried God's Son.

Joseph had gone the distance to protect his betrothed. A simple man who worked with his hands, a protector, he sheltered God's son from evil and mayhem.

Mike recalled the feeling of holding little David in his arms, the newborn's warmth and trust a thing of beauty.

He pictured Mary Lynn's face as she confronted him earlier, ready to do as he asked to protect her child.

He raised his gaze to the wooden cross. God had given His
all, His Son, to live and die for the sins of the world. A Father,
loving and beloved.

Arnie's words flooded back to him. "If the army helps you,
you help them. It is a payback."

Karen's profile, rocking the bell, the young child tucked in
the safety of the overhang.

Karen who worked in a home for unwed mothers . . .

A woman whose angry father treated her poorly.

Light dawned. Awareness awakened within him.

Karen hadn't shied away from him because he wanted Mary
Lynn safe. She'd backed away because she feared the truth of
her situation would shame him.

What a fool he was. A stupid, silly, sanctimonious heel, and
when church drew to a joyous, music-filled close an hour later,
he caught Mary Lynn up in a full hug outside. "You're not going
anywhere, Mare."

She pulled back, not understanding.

"Not to some home or anywhere else. We're family. We
stick together through thick and thin. Just like Mom and Dad
taught us."

"Oh, Mike." She hugged him back, and when she finally
pulled away, tears of joy brightened her light blue eyes. "Thank
you. Thank you so much."

"Don't thank me. Thank Him." Mike hooked a thumb back
to the sanctuary behind them. "God told me I was being stupid.
And I couldn't deny it. But tomorrow morning we're not going
to Aunt Frannie's like we planned."

"No?"

"Nope." He looped an arm around her shoulders and headed up the street, "people lights" shining around them as a light snow began to fall. "We're going to the Booth Home to celebrate with Karen and Laurie. If they'll have us."

Mary Lynn hugged his arm. "I'd love that, Mike."

Chapter Fourteen

. . . .

"Mommy, can we go down to the tree now? Please?"

"May we."

Laurie sighed. Clearly the ten minutes Karen had used to get dressed tested the child's Christmas morning patience. "May we?"

Karen glanced at her watch. The home's morning celebration was scheduled for ten o'clock, with a midday dinner at one. Surely a few minutes early to see the tree wasn't a bad idea. "Okay. Let's go."

Halfway there, Karen stopped, surprised.

Her mother was coming down the hall from the opposite direction.

Trudy O'Leary here. On Christmas.

A blend of dismay and caution filled her. Why had her mother come? In the five years since Laurie's birth, her mother hadn't come to see the child once.

A part of Karen longed to turn. Take the opposite hall into the hospital gathering area. She didn't want Laurie's Christmas to be tainted by anger or caustic words of reprisal. She wanted . . .

"Karen." Her mother spotted them and proceeded at a quicker pace. "I found you."

"Right where we've been for over five years," Karen replied.

Her mother accepted the retort with unexpected ease. "I know that. When Laurie was smaller, I used to sit in the park across the way and watch for you to bring her out in her stroller. That way I could see her grow."

"You did that?" Karen thought back, wondering if the claim was true. Would she have noticed someone watching from afar? Probably not.

"You watched me?" Laurie's upraised brows said she thought being watched was quite special.

Trudy squatted low and handed Laurie a gift. "For you."

"From you and Dad?" Karen asked.

Trudy looked up and there was no mistaking the added firmness to her expression. "From me. For my beautiful granddaughter."

"May I open it?" Laurie asked.

"Please do."

Laurie's hands fumbled the wrapping, but once she got it undone, she sighed and smiled as she held up the framed photo. "Look, Mommy! It's a picture of me!"

Karen looked at the old print and sighed. "It looks like you, doesn't it? But that's actually a picture of me in kindergarten."

"So beautiful." Laurie touched the glass covering the old photograph with a gentle reverence. "I love it, Mommy. I look like you."

"You do. Beautiful. Kind and good," answered Trudy. She turned and handed a similar-sized package to Karen. "This one is for you."

The gift held a framed photograph of Karen with her aunt and uncle, a picture they'd had taken at Yankee Stadium. The bright summer's day was reflected in their smiles for the camera. Karen's eyes filled. She held the picture up. "Thank you. I had no pictures of them to show Laurie. Just stories in my head."

"Well." Her mother raised her shoulders and settled a softer expression on Karen than she'd ever known growing up. "They were good to you. And us. Until . . . "

Karen understood "until."

She motioned to her right. "They're having a Christmas celebration out by the big tree in the gathering area. Would you like to stay, Mom? Celebrate with us?"

Her mother shook her head. "Not this time. But perhaps another? Right now I'm doing things day by day. And it's getting better."

Karen understood what her mother didn't say. She had entered some sort of program, something that offered help for her drinking problem one day at a time. She reached out and gave her mother a quick hug. "I'll pray for you."

"As will I." Trudy reached down and touched Laurie's cheek briefly. "God bless you, child."

"Thank you, Grandma. Merry Christmas!"

They walked down the hall with Trudy O'Leary. At the "T," she turned left, out into the snow-covered walks. Karen and Laurie moved to the right, but as Trudy passed along the front wall of windows, she turned and waved to her daughter and granddaughter.

"Did you know she was coming, Mommy?"

Karen shook her head. "No."

Laurie held up the wooden frame surrounding the only picture they had of Karen as a child. "I'm glad she did."

Poignant emotions swirled within Karen, but the overwhelming one she felt seeing her mother sober and clean was joy. That alone felt wonderful. "So am I."

Half the young mothers had already arrived in the gathering room. Staff members mingled with the girls, drinking coffee and juice, laughing and talking. Obviously Laurie wasn't the only one anxious for the festivities to begin. And outside, thick snow fell softly to the ground, the clean white coating a cleansing of heart and soul.

"Mommy, look! Isn't the snow the most beautiful snow you've ever seen?"

Christmas snow. Karen smiled and nodded. "That's a gift right there, Laurie."

"Oh, it is!"

But as wonderful as snow was, Laurie's attention was pulled to the big, centered tree. She peeked around the semicircle, sounding out names, and when she got to the largest pile of all, her eyes grew round. "Mommy! These all say my name!"

Karen skirted the growing crowd of girls, then stopped.

Each of the young mothers had found something to give Laurie for Christmas. From the size of Laurie's pile, they might have to put dinner off a while.

Tears pricked the back of her eyes. These girls gave from their need, and that blessing was Spirit-filled.

Her thoughts ran to Mike, but that was no surprise. She hadn't stopped thinking of him since the night she sent him on his way. For five days she'd rung her bell in the financial district, surrounded by suit-clad men. There was no bagel maker looking out for her on Maiden Lane. No Officer Mike patrolling the Federal Reserve or Wall Street, and the smaller shop windows didn't hold a candle to Thirty-Fourth Street.

"Karen?" Major Flora's voice tugged her attention away from what might have been.

She turned, determined to move forward because there was no other place to go. "Yes, Major?"

"I'd like you to meet someone." Major Flora shifted her attention to the tall, well-dressed man at her side. "Mr. Cooper, this is Karen O'Leary, the young woman you asked about."

Karen wasn't sure why this man had asked about her, but she stuck out her hand in greeting. "Pleased to meet you, sir. Merry Christmas."

He shook her hand with hearty intent. "You took care of my daughter last year. She told me about you."

Karen waited, one brow arched.

"She said you stayed with her in her moments of joy and sadness."

Karen accepted the praise with a quiet dip of her chin. "That's my job, sir."

"It's not, you went far beyond your job, young woman, and my daughter and I wanted to find a way to thank you. Repay you. Those acts of kindness meant a great deal to Genevieve."

Genevieve.

The young mother whose premature son passed away eighteen months ago. They'd cried together, her and Gen, as tiny Samuel's life slipped through their fingers.

"I was stupid then," the man confessed. "I don't know what got into me, and I'm ashamed of myself, but I've come back here to make amends."

Amends?

How could he amend the lost life of a small child?

Major Flora slid her gaze to the far left. There, wrapped with a big, red bow, was an Isolette, the new enclosed, oxygen-enriched baby beds that helped support premature babies. "You bought us an Isolette? A preemie bed?"

"Six of them," he explained. "And my people are going to build a separate unit to house them upstairs. By spring, there will be a small Intensive Care Unit for struggling newborns."

Tears threatened again. "I don't know what to say. Thank you seems inadequate."

The man reached out and grabbed her in a hug. "The thanks come from us. The army's kindness helped Genevieve through a time when her family didn't stand by her. I'll never forgive myself for that. But my shortcomings then will help others now."

Major Flora motioned to a sign suspended above the Isolette. "Samuel R. Cooper Intensive Care Unit."

Karen smiled through her tears. "This is a dream come true."

"And could there be more dreams coming true this day?" the major wondered out loud.

Karen followed the direction of her gaze.

Mike.

He and Mary Lynn were crossing the snow-covered sidewalk. In one hand he gripped a cord-handled bag. His other arm embraced his kid sister's shoulders, a silent message of love and protection.

Karen stood rooted to the spot until Major Flora nudged her forward. "I expect you'll want to let them in."

Did she?

Absolutely.

But their days apart made her steps unsure. Why had they come? Hadn't she made herself clear? And how could she make Mike understand her firm stand, with all these people gathered in celebration of Christmas? She crossed to the main foyer entrance and pushed through the heavy door, uncertain.

Mike looked up. Saw her. Smiled.

The warmth of his look made her long to move forward, into

his arms. Lay her head against his snow-dotted coat and rest there, the beat of a true heart strong beneath her ear. But she couldn't, so she swung the door behind her wide and motioned them in. "Merry Christmas, Mike. Merry Christmas, Mary Lynn. We're gathering for a little Christmas party here in the waiting area."

Mike swept the busy foyer a quick look of decision. "Mary Lynn, can you take these over by the tree while I talk to Karen a minute, please?"

"Yes." She smiled up at her big brother, leaned in, and gave him a kiss on the cheek. She turned back toward Karen. "Is it okay if we put these under the tree?"

Karen thought Mary Lynn's sweet face showed less consternation. More peace. Just as she'd hoped. "That would be lovely."

Mary Lynn moved into the waiting area as Karen redirected her attention to Mike. "Mike, I—"

"Me first." He moved closer as the door swung shut, until the breadth and solidity of him blocked her view of the party commencing inside. "I went to church last night with Mary Lynn."

Karen sent him a soft smile. "I'm glad, Mike."

He made a face of regret. "Well, I should have done it sooner, but I'm a stubborn cop sometimes."

She would have said sweet and amazing, but stubborn probably fit as well. She nodded. "I'm a little stubborn myself."

His gaze went past her, to the gathering inside, and the hospital entry itself. He waved a hand in that direction. "I remember thinking how sensible it was that you worked here and lived here. A nice, safe setting, the little park across the road. Helping these young mothers is a wonderful thing."

Just repaying a favor, Karen thought. She opened her mouth to tell him exactly that, but he shushed her with a gentle shake of his head. "I sat there in church, surrounded by soul-stirring music and candlelight, thinking about what Arnie told me."

Karen frowned, confused.

Mike saw her expression. He paused, inhaled deeply, and motioned to the hospital again. "About how people repay the army by volunteering their time. Ringing the bells. Thinking about you living here with Laurie, all I could see was Mary, facing Joseph, trying to explain a baby that wasn't his. A baby conceived without marriage."

Karen's heart chugged to a stop within her chest.

"That had to be so hard for her. For him," Mike went on. He reached out a hand to Karen's face, her cheek, and the rugged touch of his hand made her long to step closer. "You sent me away because I wanted to avoid embarrassment by tucking Mary Lynn away. I was putting reputation ahead of brotherly love."

"I don't find fault with a good reputation," Karen told him softly. "But if God is willing to wipe a slate clean of sin, why do people have such a difficult time doing likewise?"

"We're human. He's God."

The simple truth made her sigh inside. "Yes."

"I don't want to be sent away, Karen."

Her heartbeat spiked at his words. His look. "You don't?"

He shook his head and halved the already narrow distance between them. "No. Not ever. And you know what else?" He drew her into his arms for a big hug, a warm embrace, the kind she'd love to treasure forever. "I'm glad the army helped you. No matter what the circumstances were, I'm so glad that they were here, helping take care of you in your time of need."

"I'm not a war widow, Mike." She pushed back and faced him square. "And I shouldn't have pretended I was, because it wasn't fair to you." She shifted her gaze to the girls clustering around the tree inside. "Or to them. And while I don't want Laurie bearing the brunt of my mistakes, I can't live a lie any longer."

"Would you be open to a new truth, then?"

A new truth? She met his gaze, and her heart did a silly dance in her chest. "What do you mean?"

"I mean this." He took a knee before her and grasped her hands in his. "Will you marry me, Karen? Share the people lights of my neighborhood? Spend your life with me and maybe give Laurie some little brothers and sisters?"

Mike's move had drawn the attention of those gathered within. Karen couldn't hear them through the thick glass doors, but she felt them watching. "Mike, I—"

"If I throw in the great kitchen, does that help?" he interrupted her with a smile. "Because this floor is rather cold and hard."

"Yes." She laughed and threw her arms around him as he stood. "Yes, I'll marry you. I'd be delighted to marry you, Mike."

His arms surrounded her.

A cheer erupted in the room beyond, loud enough to be heard through the solid doors.

"I love you, Karen. And Laurie, too. And I will bless God all the days of my life for bringing you into my life. Into my heart. Showing me the way to truly come home."

Home.

The thing she'd longed for all her life, a sweet, clean place, filled with love. A dream come true, a place to call home. She laid her head against his chest, his strong heart muffled beneath thick wool. The steady beat was a beacon of hope, not unlike the soft chime of a little bell on a dark, city street.

She'd come full circle, from God's forgiveness to forgiving herself. And now . . .

The door burst open and a caroling of good wishes surrounded them.

Now began the first day of her new life. A life with Mike and Mary Lynn and Laurie, a life renewed and anew.

Church bells chimed nearby, the melodic call to worship reminding Karen of the reason behind this blessed holy day. "For unto us a child is born, unto us a Son is given. . . . " Isaiah's prophecy, fulfilled in a manger, a child of the poor born to redeem mankind.

She gripped Mike's hand, not for strength but for solidarity. Together they would face the challenges of life, a family bound by faith and love, the family she'd always longed for. Through God's love and grace, it now was hers.

About the Author

....

 RUTH LOGAN HERNE loves to write about small towns, big cities, and the family and folks inhabiting both. Born into poverty, she embraces the opportunity to spread warmth and cheer by living Mother Teresa's sweet quote, "Peace begins with a smile. . . . " Married to a very patient man, and a mother of ~~six~~ *seven* children (she may or may not have stolen a niece, who became a daughter of her heart), Ruthy lives in a big old farmhouse in upstate New York surrounded by small children, cats, dogs, chickens, and delightful young families.

Since publishing her Carol Award finalist and Holt Medallion finalist debut novel in 2009, Ruthy has published thirteen "4-Star" and "4½-Star" novels (RT Book Reviews), with more under contract. You can e-mail her at ruthy@ruthloganherne.com, visit her at ruthloganherne.com, cook with her and a bunch of great authors at the www.yankeebellecafe.blogspot.com, or chat with her and dozens of author friends in "Seekerville" www.seekerville.blogspot.com.

Manhattan Miracle

ANNA SCHMIDT

Dedication
....

To the city of New York: I consider you my second home in spite of the fact I have never lived there. More times than I can count, it has been your diversity and energy that have helped me meet some of the biggest challenges of my life. Thank you!

Every time you smile at someone, it is an act of love,
a gift to that person, a beautiful thing.

MOTHER TERESA

Chapter One

....

New York City, Upper West Side, Thanksgiving Eve
Present day

Parades were not exactly Max Wolzak's thing. And in his opinion,
any parade that featured giant cartoon character balloons making their way down Broadway was the height of absurdity. Having
received his discharge after serving his third tour of duty in the
chaos that passed for normal life in the Middle East, he was hardly
in the mood for crowds, a giant balloon turkey, or Santa Claus. It
was impossible for him to reconcile such frivolity with the reality
of life in the villages he'd just left. For most people there, simply
getting home safely in broad daylight was an adventure in survival.

"Where's your Christmas spirit, Scrooge?" His sister, Grace,
delivered her question with a teasing tone, but her eyes reflected
her concern. She had stopped by to check on him, as she had
several times a day since he'd come home. *"Just to see how you're
settling in,"* as she liked to say.

Max reminded himself that it was only because she cared so
much that Grace kept pushing him. "Hey, it's only Thanksgiving,"
he reminded her. "I've got a month to find my Christmas spirit.
And stop looking at me like you think I might go postal on you
any minute. I'm fine—just need some time."

"You're so quiet these days. When you came over to our place the other night to watch the game with Jack, he told me you hardly said two words. I'm worried. We all are."

"Well, don't be. All I'm asking is a little space to figure out my next step."

Her eyes widened in horror. "You aren't thinking about going back for a fourth time, are you? Because Gramma Karen would—"

"Hey, I just got home less than a week ago. I'm still half in that world and half in this, okay?" He forced a grin and tweaked her nose the way she'd hated when they were kids. It worked. She ducked away as she had hundreds of times before.

"Stop that." But she was giggling and for the moment seemed to have forgotten that she'd been about to remind him—*again*—of how everyone had worried and prayed and finally released a long breath of relief when they heard that Max would be home for the holidays.

"I've got to shave," he said as he ran his hand over the five o'clock shadow that had arrived an hour early. He headed for the stairway that curved itself up to the top two floors of the brownstone mansion where he and Grace had grown up. He took the stairs two at a time, as he had throughout his youth to his mother's dismay, then walked toward his room, down the hall lined with one of the expensive Oriental rugs his father had collected over the years, past the modern paintings his mother preferred. Any one of those rugs or paintings could feed a family in Afghanistan for years.

Actually the lavish home was a far cry from the little house in Brooklyn that generations of his father's family had called home. Their old neighborhood was one where most women, including his grandmother, had raised the children and kept the home fires burning as they waited each day for their men to return safely from their jobs as officers in the New York Police or Fire Department. "Soldiers for the city," Grampa Mike had called them, proudly pointing to the framed photographs of generations of Wolzak men in blue that lined the wall along the narrow stairway in that house.

But Max's father had broken that mold when he fell for an uptown socialite and set out to prove himself worthy of marrying her. By working two jobs while getting a master's in business at Columbia University, he had succeeded in impressing not only the girl but also her very wealthy family. Her father had taken him into the commercial real estate business—a sign that he had finally accepted his daughter's choice in husbands. In those days, the young family had lived in Brooklyn, just blocks away from Max's grandparents. Then on Christmas Eve when Max was twelve, his dad had driven them to the impressive brownstone on the upper west side of Manhattan and told Max and Grace that this was to be the family's new home. Max remembered how proud his dad had been that day and how thrilled his mom had been. Even Grace had been excited at the idea of this new life. Only Max had seemed to realize that this was more than a change in address. This was a change that would affect his whole life—school, friends, everything.

He'd had little choice but to move, but he made sure he spent every spare minute in Brooklyn. He had sat with Grampa Mike, listening to stories of the older man's years on the police force. He had dreamed of the day when he would join the force and continue a family tradition. He was determined to make up for the breach in family tradition that his father—also named Mike and for years referred to as "Mikey" to distinguish him from his dad—had caused.

And then Grampa Mike had died—struck down by a massive heart attack while doing the job that he loved. Max had just started high school when his world changed yet again.

After the funeral—complete with a long line of police cars with their lights flashing and dozens of NYPD men and women marching solemnly behind the hearse—Max's parents had insisted that his grandmother sell the Brooklyn house and come live with them. And because Max and Grace had pleaded with her to do just that, Karen Wolzak had agreed. Life had improved after that. With Gramma Karen in residence to stay with Max and Grace, Max's parents had begun to travel more often and for longer periods. More often than not, it was Gramma Karen who showed up for parent-teacher conferences or school plays and sporting events. It was with Gramma Karen that he and Grace shared the highlights and lowlights of their lives. And, since once again his parents were out of the country, it had been Gramma Karen who was the first family member to learn that Max had enlisted in the military the day after the planes crashed into the World Trade Center. For Max, enlisting seemed so very right. Once his parents were finally able to get a flight home and were told of his plans, his mother warned him that he'd just made an enormous mistake—one that could change his life forever. As for Gramma Karen . . . well, he was never really sure, but he thought perhaps she was proud of him. He knew that his father was.

Now, as he wiped away the last residue of shaving cream with a towel, he studied his face in the mirror. He looked older than thirty-two. His eyes held that weary, seen-too-much-suffering, haunted look so common to those who had served in war zones. Max ran his fingers lightly over the scar that remained from when the doctors at the field hospital had removed a piece of shrapnel from his shoulder. There were other scars as well. He'd been wounded at least once on each tour of duty. But it was not the outer scars that troubled him. It was the emptiness he felt inside.

* * * * *

Sarah Peterson loved Thanksgiving, and she especially loved the parade that wound its way from Central Park down Broadway to Macy's Department Store and Herald Square every year. During high school and college, her part-time job at Macy's had given her a front-row seat to all the preparations for the big parade. And every one of those years, she had marched in the parade holding tightly to the guide wire for one of the incredible balloons. For the last several years, her job heading up relief missions for the United Nations had kept her in other parts of the world during the holidays, but this year when she'd called her former supervisor and now chair of the parade committee to volunteer, Roger Evans had been delighted.

"Absolutely," he had replied. His familiar gravelly voice triggered memories of the days when she'd first started at Macy's in the toy department, when Roger was far from convinced that she could manage a full course load at New York University plus the demands of extended holiday hours at the store. But she had proved him wrong.

Now, as excited as a little kid about to meet Santa in person, Sarah prepared to attend the pre-parade party in Central Park. She was assigned to the Snoopy balloon—her favorite. The handlers were to be dressed as various other characters from the beloved cartoon family. As Charlie Brown's nemesis—Lucy—Sarah would be dressed in a jumpsuit designed to resemble a blue dress with short puffed sleeves, a ruffle at the hem, and a round collar. But tonight—when thousands of volunteers as well as out-of-towners gathered near the Museum of Natural History on the west side of Central Park to watch the gigantic balloon figures come to life— she would dress for comfort and warmth. Jeans, a thick turtle-neck, boots, and her puffy purple down vest.

She was just pulling her long brown hair into a ponytail when the buzzer rang, announcing the arrival of her longtime friends, Mary and Ned Sinclair. Together, the three of them would take the subway uptown from her Chelsea loft to Central Park. She punched the intercom. "Be right down." She grabbed her keys, then pocketed her phone, subway pass, and other essentials and waited impatiently for the freight elevator that served the tenants of the former factory to lumber its way up to her floor. When she finally reached ground level and hefted the heavy elevator door and gate open, she started to laugh. Standing outside the secured door to the building, peering in through the glass was none other than Charlie Brown himself. And standing next to him, clutching a raggedy blue blanket, was Linus.

It was obvious that her friends had concocted their own unique version of the characters since the actual costumes they would wear in the parade would not be handed out until the fol-lowing day, but they had certainly done a great job of getting the costumes right. "You two look wonderful," she said as the three of them headed for the subway station.

Mary and Ned were two of her family's oldest and dearest friends. They had actually been friends with her parents, and when Mom and Dad left New York, the Sinclairs had assumed the role of surrogate parents for Sarah. Whenever she returned from one of the relief missions, the two of them would have already been to her loft, cleaned it, and stocked the refrigerator with food. Mary would meet her plane and drive her back to Chelsea, where Ned would be busy preparing a feast to welcome her home. "But aren't you—as they say—rushing the season?"

"We are simply getting into character," Ned announced. "Is this what you're wearing?" He surveyed her tight jeans, knee-high boots, down vest, and white mittens.

"I think Lucy requires a bit of mystery, and I plan to keep her under wraps until tomorrow."

He shrugged. "As you wish, my dear." He clutched his blanket tighter and stroked it fondly. "But there is something to be said for allowing time to get fully into the character."

Ned and Mary were the very successful owners of a popular home decor boutique in Chelsea. Originally they had come to New York with Broadway on their minds. They had each gotten a couple of small parts in those early years but soon decided that earning a living in the theater was not in their future.

"I guess I'll just have to wing it," Sarah admitted as she linked arms with her friends and began to hum the theme from the Peanuts musical.

By the time they exited the subway at Columbus Circle and started walking along the west side of the park, Sarah could practically smell the excitement. Those in the know were well aware that this event was definitely on a par with the parade itself when it came to a good time. Sarah gratefully accepted the cup of hot chocolate Ned bought for her as they passed a row of vendors selling souvenirs, hot beverages, and snacks. Then the three of them wandered through the crowds sharing memories of past parades as they repeated the ritual they had begun years earlier of moving from the staging area for balloon after balloon until they reached the all-time favorite—the beloved Snoopy.

Sarah sighed with pure happiness. "Don't you just love this whole scene?"

"They say the weather promises to be perfect—clear, sunny skies with temperatures reaching the midforties by parade time." Mary delivered this news with the wide-eyed wonder of a child.

"Gotta love this global warming thing," Ned said. "Remember that year when it snowed?"

"Remember the year it poured?" Sarah replied.

"That would be plural, as in the *years* that it poured," Ned said.

"Well, we count our blessings." Sarah glanced up at the sky, where a full moon shone brighter than any spotlight on Broadway. How she loved this city!

A child near them broke away from her parents and headed across the park. "There's Snoopy!" Her high-pitched squeal resonated with unadulterated excitement.

Something about the little girl's mother looked familiar, and Sarah hurried to catch up to the couple, who were now calling after the girl to wait for them.

"Grace? Grace Wolzak?" As girls, Sarah and Grace had spent hours playing and gossiping and planning their lives together whenever Grace visited her grandparents in Brooklyn. Sarah and her family had lived next door to the Wolzaks.

The woman turned at the sound of her name and then broke into a grin. "Oh my stars!" she exclaimed. "Sarah Peterson! I haven't seen you in a hundred years. How are you?"

The man had corralled the little girl and was kneeling next to her, his back to them, evidently explaining the importance of not taking off on her own in the crowded park.

Grace turned her attention to Ned with his blanket and Mary. "Are you guys working Snoopy?"

"Lucy, Linus, and Charlie Brown himself at your service," Sarah said with a grin as Mary and Ned caught up to them.

"And with this mop," Grace replied, running her hand through her tangle of golden curls, "who else would I be but Sally?" She turned to where the man and child were waiting and motioned them forward. "This is my daughter Molly."

"I get to be Woodstock!" Molly announced. "And I get to just walk along with Mom. This is my first time actually being in the parade. I'm still too little to hold one of the wires. Daddy says the balloon would lift me right up into the sky."

"And, Sarah, you must remember my brother Max," Grace continued. "As I recall, once upon a time you two had a bit of a thing going."

Sarah felt her cheeks flame as she met the gaze of the tall man she had assumed was Grace's husband. Now she saw the boy she had once thought beyond good looking, all grown up and more handsome than ever in a dark, brooding, fictional hero kind of way. He was wearing jeans and a desert camouflage jacket. His hair was dark and close-cropped in the military style. He acknowledged the introduction with a polite nod but did not smile.

Mary cleared her throat as she studied Max closely and then glanced at Sarah, eyebrows raised as if expecting a more complete explanation. Later she would want to know all about this past crush since she spent a good deal of the time they were together these days bemoaning Sarah's need to find a "significant other."

Sarah hurried to make introductions, and as the group continued on their way across the park to where the Snoopy balloon was being covered with netting that would anchor it to the ground through the night, she found herself walking with Max. Ahead of them Grace, Mary, and Ned kept pace with Molly—the child chattering away about the parade, the party that would follow at her great-grandmother's house, and her certainty that the Santa Claus whose arrival would be the grand finale of the parade was the real deal. "My great-grandmother told me so herself," she announced in a tone that dared anyone to disagree. "A long time ago she used to collect money for the Salvation Army outside Macy's, and she knows Santa personally."

"How is your grandmother?" Sarah asked Max, desperate to find some topic of conversation that might break the man's silence. He didn't appear to be angry, and he certainly did not give off the vibes of a man who was shy. Shyness would not be at all in keeping with the confident, popular teenager she'd known. But there was something. He moved through the park with all the reluctance of someone about to face a firing squad.

"She's well. Thank you for asking." He shoved his hands deeper into the pockets of his jacket. "My grandfather died and . . . "

"I remember," Sarah said softly. "Mrs. Wolzak moved in with your parents after that."

"My aunt Laurie offered her a place with her out in California, but Gramma Karen said she could never leave New York."

"We were so very sad to see the house sold after all that time that our families had been neighbors. And of course, I missed running in and out and talking to your grandmother and the times that Grace would stay over and we could be together. And then when I started college at NYU and was working at Macy's, imagine my surprise to run into your grandmother and . . . "

She was babbling like a teenager who had suddenly found herself walking alongside the football quarterback. She forced herself to be silent for at least ten seconds then asked, "So, what's your costume?"

He grimaced. "Schroeder."

Sarah couldn't help it—she burst out laughing. The image of this tall, muscular man with his military posture and buzz-cut hair as the piano-playing Schroeder was ludicrous. "Whose idea was that?"

The suggestion of a smile tugged at the corners of his mouth, and for the first time his features softened. "Gramma Karen volunteered me for the part," he admitted. "She thinks I'm too serious."

"Like Schroeder?"

She saw a flicker of surprise and realized the irony of his grandmother's choice had not yet hit him. But she could almost see the image of the popular cartoon character sitting at his piano, a scowl on his face as he practiced and tried to ignore Lucy's chatter. "Yeah, like that," he murmured.

He seemed to really look at her for the first time. "And you are?"

She grinned mischievously. "I am your worst nightmare, Schroeder. I am Lucy."

He groaned, and this time the smile that definitely struggled to break free of his more serious demeanor nevertheless was in full bloom in his eyes. The corners crinkled into lines that proved he had once smiled often. She couldn't help wondering why that might have changed.

Chapter Two

. . . .

Thanksgiving Day—parade day—came earlier than Max remembered. It was still dark as they all made their way to the park, but
Max was unwavering in his resolve to do whatever was required of
him. He was that determined not to disappoint his grandmother—
or Molly. His niece was so excited about what she kept referring
to as the "magical season" that it was hard to hang on to his usual
cynicism. Finally, after what seemed like hours—and was—
the signal sounded and the parade began to move forward. Molly
was instantly in constant motion, bouncing from her mother to
Sarah Peterson to him as they made their way along the parade
route, past crowds of smiling adults and wide-eyed children. At
seven years old, she still was a firm believer in the tale of Santa Claus.
Max wondered if she would still believe by this time next year.

He looked ridiculous, of course. He was dressed in a kind of
jumpsuit that made him look like an exaggerated version of the
cartoon character—striped T-shirt over black pants, and on his
head a blond wig. He glanced over to where his sister and Sarah
Peterson were walking along together. Sarah looked twenty
years younger than her age in the dark Lucy wig that framed her
face and highlighted her best feature—large blue eyes that had
always seemed to Max to reflect what was good and decent in the
world. At the moment, she was listening intently to his niece's

chatter—giving the child her undivided attention. At one point he saw Molly slip her hand into Sarah's, and something about that seemed so very natural. He had a sudden vision of Sarah with children of her own. She had always had a knack for nurturing and would no doubt be a fabulous parent.

Max shook off the thought and focused on holding onto the guide wire in his hands. In a couple of hours they would reach Macy's, and soon after that he could ditch the ridiculous Schroeder jumpsuit costume and wig and lose himself in the masses of people still buzzing about the parade. He would reverse the parade route on his way back to the house and some of his grandmother's renowned cooking. By now he knew the turkey was in the oven, and she was up to her elbows in flour and sugar preparing at least three different kinds of pies for the party she traditionally hosted following the parade. The door to the brownstone would be open to anyone who had no other place to be on this Thanksgiving Day, just as it always had been at that small house in Brooklyn all those years ago.

He heard Molly let out a shrill cry and saw her take off running ahead toward the crowd of people straining to snap photos of the Snoopy balloon. Instinctively he went on alert as he assessed the facts—he could not release his guide wire to go after her without upsetting the careful balance that was keeping Snoopy upright and safe. He saw his sister and Sarah calling out to the child, urging her to stay with them. And then he saw where she was headed. Grace's husband, Jack Watson, stood with his back to the passing parade as he and other NYPD patrolmen scanned the crowd, watching for trouble.

Molly reached her father and tugged on his uniform jacket. Jack turned, his wide smile making his pleasure at seeing his daughter obvious to everyone around. He hoisted Molly high in his arms and returned her to Grace. Then he placed a quick kiss on his wife's cheek, gave Sarah a wave, and returned to duty.

Duty.

It had been Max's mantra most of his adult life. And now he faced a decision that he wasn't prepared to make. Grace had asked if he planned to return for a fourth tour of duty. That was one option. He could also apply to the police academy as he'd intended before 9/11. But then maybe he was too old. . . . He felt too old. Most mornings he felt a hundred and five, so battered was his mind and body after years of the physical and mental stress of his job in special forces, working behind enemy lines, trying to end whatever conflict was the focus of the government's latest plan to thwart terrorism.

Of course he could always go back to college and get his degree, then go into business with his father—his mother had mentioned that several times when the family had visited via Skype over the last few months while he was overseas. He did have a start on a degree in business. But the idea of sitting in an office or in front of a computer screen for hours every day was not a career move that held the slightest appeal for Max—no matter how much money he could make doing it.

No, he would not work for his father. He was sure about that. He was less sure about whether or not he might make the military his permanent career. It was the life he knew best, but there had to be something else.

"Maxie!" His sister's childhood name for him rang out above the din of the crowd as they reached Times Square. When he glanced her way, she gave him an exaggerated grin. "Smile," she instructed.

"I'm Schroeder," he shouted back. "Remember?"

But when Molly danced over and grinned up at him with a gap-toothed smile, showing off her latest tribute to the tooth fairy, he couldn't help laughing.

"Are you sad, Uncle Max?" Her smile morphed into a frown of concern.

He rallied for this child he loved. "Now, how could anybody be sad on a day like this? Just look at that blue sky."

She looked up past the towering skyscrapers to the patch of clear blue above them. "It's magical, isn't it? I think Santa Claus is going to be more jollier than ever when he sees what a beautiful day it is." She skipped along at his side. "I'll tell Mom you're okay," she announced. "She told Sarah that you were sad. I like Sarah. Mom invited her and her two friends to come to Gramma Karen's for turkey dinner after the parade."

Max glanced at Sarah. Like Molly, she was practically dancing down the avenue, her eyes glowing almost as brightly as Molly's were, looking all around like she wanted to memorize every detail of the experience.

Molly was still talking. ". . . really nice, and did you know that Sarah was like Mama's very bestest friend when they were my age? But I don't think Daddy knew her because when Mama was telling him about her last night he didn't seem to 'member her at all."

I remember her, Max thought.

Molly's slender shoulders rose and fell as she released an exaggerated huff. "Well, I should get back to Mama," she said almost apologetically as if she needed to keep track of the grown-ups in her life and the task could be exhausting. "We're almost to Macy's and Mama said . . . "

He didn't hear the end of her sentence as she headed back toward Grace, but he was pretty sure she had been about to remind him they would be done with their part of the parade in plenty of time for them to double back and see Santa arrive.

Santa Claus. For a kid like Molly, that character—like many of the characters represented in the parade—represented an American childhood. Whatever happened to celebrating the birth of the Christ child? On the other hand, Max couldn't help thinking about the kids he'd seen as he traveled throughout the war-torn lands of the Middle East. Those kids had no illusions about what was real and what was fantasy. He couldn't help but believe that a kid from Afghanistan or Gaza would have serious doubts about the concept of a jolly old elf running around the world handing out gifts. For that matter, Max couldn't imagine those children buying into the whole birth of a Savior idea—not in the world they knew.

* * * * *

Sarah was having such a good time that their unit reached Times Square almost before she realized it. Between chatting with Grace and exchanging observations with Mary and Ned, she had lost track of time and just how far they'd come along the route. Grace's daughter was a delight—a little chatterbox who skipped from one subject to the next with lightning speed.

"Well, he's not sad," Molly reported as soon as she returned from walking part of the route with her uncle. "I think he's just worried." Molly had the self-assurance of a child born and raised in one of the world's most sophisticated cities, and yet there was an innocence about her that was so very touching.

"Worried about what?" Grace asked.

Molly appeared to consider the question. "I think probably he's worried that Santa might not remember him. He's been gone away for a very long time," she said. "And he is a grown-up, but Gramma Karen says that where he was all those Christmases, life was really, really hard, and sometimes even Santa couldn't make it all better."

Sarah glanced at Max, who was trudging along with eyes straight ahead, not looking at the crowds of happy people lining the route or at the glorious sight of a beautiful autumn day in New York City. He wasn't exactly scowling. It was more an expression of determination, as if he would see his current task through, no matter what. Grace had mentioned that he'd only come back from his service in the Middle East a few days earlier. Having been in that area of the world more than once, Sarah could certainly understand how it would take some time to adjust to a world where people laughed and cheered and seemed to have no worries.

"He's doing this for Gramma Karen—and Molly," Grace explained when Max had deliberately taken his position with the balloon unit at a distance away from family and friends. "But he has what he likes to refer to as his 'ground rules,' and apparently they include marching along without looking left or right or engaging in any conversation with his fellow balloon wranglers."

"But if he dislikes being in the parade so much, then why do it?"

"Oh, he used to love the parade as much as anyone—more, actually. But lately, not so much. I think all the hoopla surrounding Christmas gets to him. He's seen far too much misery."

"I can certainly understand that. Perhaps in time he'll find a way to embrace the season," Sarah said. "Not the materialistic side of things—although it's hard to deny the charm of at least some of that. But the feeling of hope—that peace on earth is possible . . . "

Grace smiled at her. "You always were intent on saving the world, Sarah. How's that working out for you?"

"Step by step," Sarah replied and illustrated the point with an exaggerated marching step.

When they had passed Macy's and the crowds of people packed into bleachers there, they moved on to the de-staging area, where the balloon was deflated and packed up for storage until the following year, along with the costumes. Knowing that Ned and Mary would expect to follow their Thanksgiving tradition of meeting friends in the Village for a potluck meal, Sarah declined Grace's invitation to come for Thanksgiving dinner with her grandmother. "Besides, yours is a family thing, and as you mentioned Max just got home, and—"

"Okay, here's the deal. This thing goes well into the evening, and by the time we put out the turkey sandwiches and leftover pie around seven, we are pretty well talked out. New blood counteracts the turkey's nodding-off effect. So bring Mary and Ned and come whenever."

"I'll try," she promised.

Their role as balloon handlers complete, they stepped out of the jumpsuits depicting their characters and straightened the regular clothes they'd worn underneath. As Sarah turned in her costume and waited for Mary and Ned to do the same, she caught a glimpse of Max in street clothes walking away, his shoulders hunched although the day was mild, and his hands thrust deep into the pockets of his jacket.

"So, tell me more about this teenage crush on the hunk," Mary said as she followed Sarah's gaze to where Max was jaywalking across the street, dodging traffic the way he had once threaded his way through oncoming defensive players on the football field.

"It was one date," she assured him as Ned joined them. "A kid's fascination with her best friend's older brother."

"Right," Mary murmured, and Sarah knew that she didn't believe her.

"I'm telling you there was nothing to it. Our date was on September the tenth, and the next day the planes hit the towers and by that night Max had enlisted," she continued. "I haven't seen either Grace or him for years."

Ned and Mary exchanged a look. "And he went off to save the world and you pined for him," Ned said. "And now here he is—a soldier come home to be reunited with the girl he never forgot—the girl whose smile and kiss kept him going all those years . . . "

"Do not start with this," Sarah admonished them as the subway doors slammed shut and the train jerked into motion. "I am perfectly happy with my life. Right now at this stage of my life relationships like that are . . . "

Mary laughed. "I believe the word you are searching for is *nonexistent*."

Sarah grinned at the two of them. "I have both of you, don't I?"

"Not the same thing, my dear," Ned replied as the train reached their stop and they lined up at the doors. "Not the same thing at all." He gave Mary a kiss on the cheek and then interlocked his fingers with hers.

Of course her friends were right. Ever since she received her master's degree in social work, Sarah had dedicated herself to her job. She traveled overseas constantly, first as a team member and then lately as the leader of relief missions for various groups connected with the United Nations. She loved the work but had to admit that sometimes she longed for the kind of romantic companionship many of her friends had found—like Grace had with her husband Jack.

198

They certainly made a handsome couple, and in the brief encounter they'd had during the parade it was obvious that the two of them were crazy about each other. Stir in their daughter, Molly—a real charmer—and they were the picture of an all-American family. If Norman Rockwell were alive and still doing magazine covers, he would simply have to paint them.

Not that Sarah hadn't had her chances. There had even been one romance that came close enough to marriage that the man had given her a ring. George Hampton had appeared to be the perfect match for her, but she ended it when she realized he wanted her to leave her job—the same job he had—and stay at home with the half-dozen children he announced they would have while he continued to travel the world. She had been so certain that she loved him—and perhaps in one way she did. After all, love came in many guises—friendship, parental, romantic . . . But just in time, she had realized that what she felt for him was a deep respect and admiration for his courage and dedication. Any lingering doubt ended when, after she tried to explain why a marriage between them would not work, he had become angry and accused her of leading him on.

After that experience, Sarah had backed away from encouraging any man who seemed to have romance on his agenda. Soon after the breakup, she was able to get reassigned from overseeing missions in Africa to traveling to and from the Middle East for her work. George had been horrified and had warned her repeatedly that the Middle East was no place for a woman. That had only strengthened her determination to succeed in her new assignment.

And she had—beyond anything she could have dreamed. There was even talk of putting her in charge of the whole Middle East—a position that she did not want and would turn down if offered. She was not one to sit in an office and give assignments to others. She wanted to be out among the people her work served—see their faces, hold their babies, help them restore their communities and their lives.

"You're very quiet," Mary noted as they walked through the winding streets of Greenwich Village on their way to the small neighborhood café that traditionally hosted their Thanksgiving potluck. "You know I was only teasing you back there."

"I know," she said with what she hoped was a reassuring smile. "Holidays tend to bring out the ghosts of the past—memories."

Ned burst into the title song from the Robert Redford and Barbra Streisand classic film *The Way We Were,* and by the time they reached the restaurant all three of them were singing a little off-key but loud enough to turn the heads of normally seen-and-heard-it-all New Yorkers.

The buffet was set and the restaurant was already packed. The owners of the café provided the dishes and cutlery and ran a cash bar for those attending, while everyone else brought a dish to share. Sarah had sent over her contribution for the meal earlier—a special lemonade gelatin salad that had become her tradition. It was easy to make, although she wasn't much of a cook, and to her delight everyone came back for seconds and asked for the recipe. So it was pretty much a home run as potluck contributions went. The buffet setting made it easy for everyone to move around the room talking about the latest news or catching up on the lives of those they had not seen in a while.

Before Sarah realized it, she saw that it was nearly seven. If she was going to stop in at Grace's family gathering, she really needed to get going. "Coming?" she asked Mary and Ned as she shrugged into her down vest and pulled on her mittens.

"No, you go on. It will be easier for you to catch up without having to constantly fill Ned and me in on the old stories."

"Okay. If you're sure."

"We're sure." Mary gave her an air kiss and walked her to the door. "Oh, and Sarah? You just might want to consider taking a long second look at his hunkiness—something tells me the two of you have much in common." She winked and then went back inside the restaurant before Sarah could come up with a response.

"His hunkiness," she muttered as she hailed a cab. She got in and settled back for the ride uptown. Mary was such a tease—and such a romantic. Of course she did have to admit that Max was not exactly hard to look at. He had the kind of shoulders that looked as if they could easily handle the weight of the world. And there was that smile—so rare but bordering on heart-stopping when it appeared.

"Stop this," she grumbled, and to her surprise the cabbie squealed the vehicle to a jolting stop at the next intersection. "Not you," she protested, but the driver who spoke next to no English simply pointed to the meter.

Sarah craned her neck to see where they were. In front of the Plaza Hotel at the south end of Central Park. She could walk from here. She dug into the pocket of her jeans for cash—she never carried a purse. "Thank you," she said, speaking what she guessed to be the man's native language of Farsi, and when his brusque manner softened she knew she had guessed right. Then she was stunned to see tears coursing down his weathered cheeks. He gave her instructions—also in Farsi, of which she really only understood *please* and *thank you*—accompanied by hand gestures entreating her to stay put as he practically leapt from the car. Dodging the ire of other cabs and cars as they careened around him, he made his way to her side of the cab and held the door open for her. When she got out and handed him the fare plus tip, he actually bowed repeatedly, mumbling his thanks again and again until Sarah was safely on her way.

She glanced back once to see the driver getting into his cab even as he made a rude gesture to another cabbie honking his horn at him. And with a squeal of rubber on pavement, he was gone.

As Sarah walked along the avenue next to the park, she saw crews cleaning up the last of the debris from the staging area for the parade. It had been a wonderful day so far—the parade and turkey with all the trimmings with her friends, and now she was going to end the day not only with her childhood friend but also with her beloved former neighbor and Grace's grandmother, Karen Wolzak.

"Oh yeah," she whispered to herself with a giggle, "and let's not forget 'his hunkiness.'"

Chapter Three

....

Max was looking for an escape route. He loved his sister and his grandmother dearly, but the two of them never met a soul that they didn't eventually consider part of the family. People were stashed in every nook and cranny of the house—perched on the stairs, standing in corners balancing a plate of food and a punch cup filled with apple cider, and even spilling out into the back garden since the evening was so mild. Max had completely lost track of the names thrown at him in a steady stream of introductions almost from the minute they had returned from the parade and guests began arriving. Neighbors, coworkers of Jack's, parents of Molly's friends, his grandmother's church circle . . .

He carried a relish tray to the kitchen, where Gramma Karen and Grace were busy refilling the platters and side dishes that Jack and Molly brought them from the buffet set out on the fully extended dining room table.

"Oh, Max, dear, the doorbell—could you get that? I don't know why whoever it is doesn't just come on in." Gramma Karen brushed back a wisp of her gray hair with the back of one hand.

"Maybe it's Santa Claus," Molly suggested. "Gramma knows the real Santa," she reminded Max, "and she told me he might just show up today." She lowered her voice to a whisper. "Gramma says that if he comes, he won't be wearing his red suit or bringing his reindeer. She said he'll look just like anybody else because he'll be checking to see who's been naughty."

"Have you been a good little boy, Maxie?" Grace teased.

"I'll get the door," he replied, ignoring her question and accepting the obvious fact that as an escape route, the kitchen was out.

He threaded his way through clusters of people until he reached the front door. He swung it open and found Sarah Peterson standing on the front steps, her arms wrapped around her body like a shawl. "You look like you're freezing," he said as he stepped aside to allow her to pass.

"I walked from the Plaza."

"Why?" It seemed a logical question, but he saw a hint of laughter in her eyes as she stepped inside the front hallway and he closed the door.

"There was a miscommunication with the cabbie about the address." She stuffed her mittens in the pockets of her purple vest then offered him a handshake. "It's nice to see you again, Max. I enjoyed catching up some last night and . . . "

"I'll tell Grace you're here. She's in the kitchen." Sarah was taller than he'd first realized. She only had to tip her head up slightly to meet his eyes. Ah, those eyes—large, curious without being intrusive, and an astonishing shade of light blue. Warning bells sounded in his brain. There was something about Sarah— there always had been. But Sarah all grown up was far more confusing than the girl who had been his sister's friend. For one thing she exuded a kind of contentment with the world that he could not fathom. And when she looked at him—as she was now—he had the distinct impression that with very little effort she could get him to reveal every secret he'd ever held.

Okay, over the top. He glanced out the open door before closing it. "You came alone?"

"My friends couldn't make it," she said as she waited for him to close the front door and then lead the way down the hall past the curved staircase and on to the kitchen. He couldn't help noticing how she seemed instantly comfortable in these surroundings that had to be new to her as they moved through the crowds of guests. He didn't like crowds—they made him uneasy. As for strangers, they reminded him too much of the people he'd had to trust back at the front—people he could never really be sure of when it came to where their loyalties might truly lie.

"You're not much of a talker, are you?" she said when their way was blocked by a gathering of parents trying to corral their small children. "I get the impression that chatting with you is pretty much of the need-to-know variety. And yet as I recall, you used to be the one leading any conversation." She was looking at him again, those eyes bright with interest as if he were some fascinating specimen she needed to understand. More likely she—like Grace—was just trying to lighten the moment.

"Grace has always been the talker in our family," he replied, and to his surprise Sarah laughed.

"From what I've seen of Molly, it would appear the adage 'like mother, like daughter' might apply."

"Good observation." He pushed open the swinging door to the kitchen and stepped aside. "Grace? Company," he announced as Sarah stepped past him and went directly to his grandmother.

"Mrs. Wolzak," she said, taking both of Gramma Karen's hands in hers. "It's been far too long."

"Little Sarah Peterson," Gramma Karen replied with a wide smile and a hug. "Can this be that same little girl who used to sit at my kitchen table solving the problems of the world in exchange for a couple of my chocolate chip cookies and a tall glass of milk?"

"The very same," Sarah replied. She glanced around the kitchen. "Got any cookies and milk?" she asked with a mischievous wink that made Gramma Karen laugh. "How can I help?"

Max had meant to lead her to the kitchen and then make his escape. Instead he found himself rooted to the spot, half in and half out the door watching this exchange.

Grace hugged Sarah and then handed her an extra apron, and within no more than a minute she was slicing bread and sharing memories of the old neighborhood with both women.

"How are your parents?" Gramma Karen asked.

"Dad sold his business a year ago, and the two of them bought one of those enormous recreational vehicles and set out to tour the country—determined to make it to every single state. They're somewhere in Arizona now."

"And you? What do you do, Sarah?"

"I work for the United Nations."

"Don't be so modest," Grace said. "She's totally in charge of this huge relief program for the United Nations, Gramma, and she goes around the world saving lives."

Max's grandmother smiled. "So you're walking the talk as they say. All those hours spent solving the world's problems now put to concrete use?"

"Something like that. These days I work mostly in the Middle East."

"You know my grandson here has just returned from that part of the world. We can't get two words out of him about being over there, but clearly you two must have a great deal in common."

Gramma Karen glanced his way with clear instructions to

become part of the conversation. A five-star general with a chest full of medals could not top the power of his grandmother's silent order. He stepped fully into the kitchen and let the door swing shut behind him.

"What part of the Middle East?"

Sarah shrugged as she continued slicing loaves of the thick multigrain bread. "Afghanistan, Syria . . . wherever the need is greatest."

"Those are pretty dangerous places for a—"

His sister's head shot up. "Don't you dare finish that sentence, Max Wolzak," she ordered. Then she turned to Sarah. "My brother—the original male chauvinist—was about to say 'for a woman.'" Grace rolled her eyes and went back to filling a platter with fresh vegetables and a bowl of spinach dip.

"Those are dangerous places for all," Sarah said quietly, "especially for children."

As if on cue Molly burst through the swinging door. "The Kelly twins just spilled a whole bunch of cranberry sauce on the carpet," she announced.

"I'll go," Grace said, grabbing a roll of paper towels as she followed Molly to the scene of the accident.

Gramma Karen followed her, pausing to grab a bottle of club soda from the refrigerator. "Use some of this before the stain sets," she called out as she hurried after them.

And with the closing of the door blocking out the wails of the children apparently responsible for the accident and several adult voices trying to reassure them no real harm had been done, Max found himself alone with Sarah.

"Good thing my mother isn't here," Max said. "She'd be more upset than those kids." *Nice banter, Wolzak.*

Sarah gave him a curious glance and then wiped her hands on a towel while at the same time looking around for anything else she might do to help. "Where are your parents? I thought I might have a chance to—"

"Mom likes to make an annual trek to Paris at this time of year. She doesn't really care for the crowds and clamor of the parade and the shopping season." She had her back to him as she wiped bread crumbs from the counter so he couldn't read her reaction.

"And your father?"

Max shrugged. "He used to love the parade. But he does what Mother wants—in this case, an extended trip so they can go to the Christmas markets in Germany. Why she thinks the shopping there would be any better than it is right here, in the most . . . "

TMI, Wolzak. Way too much information.

"Maybe he loves her more than he used to love the parade," Sarah said softly. Then she turned and faced him. "Sorry. It's just your statement triggered a memory. It always seemed to me that you were somehow at odds with your mother."

Her directness surprised him. There was no malice in her comment, and he certainly couldn't deny the truth of it. "It works out to be a win-win for everyone. My parents get away and Gram gets the run of the house for one of her favorite holidays. My parents are good people," he hastened to add. "They just . . . "

Anyone else might have jumped in to finish his sentence, recognizing that he was searching for the right way to phrase things. Not Sarah. She simply waited. She had stopped wiping the counter and was watching him, listening—really listening to him in a way people rarely did these days.

He decided to change conversational paths. "You never really had a chance to know my parents."

"But I remember your grandmother talking about them. She was so very proud of your dad. He went into business, didn't he? Banking or something like that?"

"Real estate."

"And speaking of real estate, this is a beautiful home." She folded the dish towel and laid it across a towel rack. "Do I get the nickel tour?"

Talking about his parents always seemed to make Max tense—as if somehow he needed to explain or apologize for their success and wealth. But there was something about Sarah that put him more at ease. "Nickel tour? Did you not get the memo about inflation?" he teased.

"All right, a quarter, but that's my final offer." She hung the apron Grace had handed her on a hook and waited for him to lead her back into the main part of the lavish house.

Max did not miss the way his sister's eyes lit up, and she nudged Gramma Karen when she saw him with Sarah. Grace was an incurable romantic and no doubt already had devised an entire happily-ever-after scenario. Too bad he wasn't a happily-ever-after kind of guy.

* * * * *

If there was one thing that Sarah remembered about Grace, it was that her friend was a dyed-in-the-wool romantic. Grace also loved her brother very much, and during the parade she had confided to Sarah how worried she and her grandmother were about him. "Gramma Karen tells me that ever since he got back, he spends most of his time alone either holed up in his room or out for a long run or walk. He won't say if he plans on reenlisting, and that makes me think he just might."

"But if the military is what he loves—if that's where his heart lies . . . "

"His heart lies with the long tradition of service that has been our family's coat of arms for generations. With the single exception of our father, every Wolzak man has served as a policeman, fireman, or soldier."

"Well, there's your answer."

"But it's so dangerous over there," Grace had protested.

"It's dangerous here."

"Yeah, but at least here Gramma Karen and I can be there to take care of him."

"Max must know how those who love him worry." It had occurred to Sarah that nowhere in this conversation had there been mention of how his mother worried. She really wanted to ask Grace about that but felt it would be far too intrusive.

Now as she followed Max into the large front room of the house, she saw Grace watching them. She knew that look—it was Grace's matchmaking look.

"Ignore them," Max said.

"Excuse me?"

"My grandmother and my sister are convinced that what I need is a good woman to settle me down and keep me here at home. It appears that at least for the moment they have set their sights on you. Sorry about that."

"On the other hand it would definitely get you off the hook if they had reason to believe that you and I had . . . reconnected?" As soon as the words were out of her mouth she wished she could take them back. What was she thinking? From the expression on Max's face he clearly thought she had completely lost her mind—or more likely that she was some kind of desperate stalker. "Ignore me—I have no idea what—"

The man was grinning at her. "It could work. I mean if you really mean it."

Was that a dare? His eyes were practically twinkling. "I don't think it's necessary to make fun of me," she muttered and turned away from him, pretending to study a large abstract oil painting that dominated one wall.

"I'm not. I mean I wasn't thinking. Of course you must have someone—someone special in your life and . . . Hey, forgive me. I'm a little out of practice when it comes to the social graces."

"There's no one special." She turned to face him. "My work doesn't leave a lot of time for . . ."

"Mine either. Sounds like we're a perfect short-term match. What do you say? I mean, if you're going to be in town for a few weeks."

"I leave the day after Christmas for Syria."

"And you told Gramma Karen that your folks are in Arizona, right?"

"Yes, but . . . "

"Look, Sari, where's the harm? It's the holidays and no one likes to be alone and—"

"Who says I'm alone? I have friends—a lot of friends." She had not missed the way he'd called her by the nickname he'd tagged her with when they were kids. Oh, he still had some of those social skills.

"I'm sure you do. You always were surrounded by a crowd of admirers. Why do you think it took me so long to ask you out?"

She laughed. "You are something else, Max. You always were."

"It might be fun—hanging out for a few weeks."

She was actually considering this. Well, why not? After all, it had been her idea. "Okay, here are my ground rules. . . . "

Max groaned.

"Grace told me you always set ground rules."

"Yeah, but the key point there is that *I* set them—not somebody else. But go ahead."

"We do not lie about what's going on. We are friends who have decided to act as each other's . . . companion for holiday occasions requiring a date."

"Grace is never going to believe that."

"That can't be helped. The bottom line is that when we go our separate ways we can both honestly remind all concerned—including your grandmother—that we never pretended this was anything more than just friendship."

"Agreed. What else?"

"That's it, unless you have something."

"Nope. Let's keep things simple. So how about I get you home? You look exhausted."

"I am perfectly capable of finding my way home, Max."

"You'd actually leave me here stranded in a house filled with strangers—at least most of them are for me. What about our bargain?"

"You can leave any time—you don't have to see me home."

"Just say yes."

She *was* tired. And it was getting later. As much as she loved her city, she was not about to tempt fate. "I'll take a cab."

"That relief mission gig of yours must pay pretty well the way you keep riding around town in taxis."

He had a point—the cab ride would be expensive. "All right, if you insist, come take a subway ride with me."

"I'll get our coats—you go say good night to Grace and Gramma Karen."

"Aye, aye, sir." She gave him a mock salute.

"Sorry. Giving out orders is an occupational hazard, I'm afraid."

"No harm, no foul," she replied.

Max smiled. "Beautiful and a sports fan. This just keeps getting better."

She couldn't help feeling pleased that their encounter seemed to have lightened his mood considerably. He was sounding more and more like the Max she had known years earlier.

* * * * *

The train was so crowded that Max ended up standing while Sarah found a seat next to an elderly woman who looked as if she might burst into tears at any moment. He watched as Sarah engaged the woman in conversation. He saw the woman's expression shift from despair to hope, and when the train screeched to a stop and the woman edged toward the doors, he saw Sarah give her a parting hug.

"What was that all about?" he asked as he took the seat the woman had vacated.

"Oh, the poor dear. She was supposed to spend the day with her daughter, but that fell through, and then she got caught up in all the after-parade crowds and she was simply exhausted."

"And what did you say to her? Because whatever it was seems to have been a game changer for her."

Sarah shrugged. "Nothing really. I just told her that in spite of her disappointing day, I felt thankful to have had the chance to meet her and talk a little. That seemed to cheer her up some."

Max thought about the way the woman had walked off the train, her head high, her shoulders squared, and with a definite spring in her step. "I'd say you made her day."

"Way too much credit," Sarah protested, and he noticed that she was blushing. "This is my stop," she added as she pulled on her mittens.

They exited the train and climbed up to street level, emerging in a neighborhood of warehouses converted into art studios and lofts. They passed some restaurants and other businesses and then Sarah turned down a narrow alley. "This way," she said when he hesitated. She stopped at a doorway lit by a single bulb and inserted a key then turned to him. She pulled off a mitten and thrust her hand into the pocket of her jeans, then handed him a crumpled business card. "Well, thanks for seeing me home, Max. Here's my number—I mean if you really want to call. You don't have to. I get it that the idea of . . . "

"I'll call," he said, taking the card from her. "And thanks. You may have made that old lady on the train have a better day, but that was nothing compared to what you did for me, Sarah Peterson." Spontaneously he leaned in and kissed her forehead. "Good night."

"Good night," she murmured and then hurried inside, where she opened the heavy freight elevator gate. He was still standing in the doorway holding it open. "Does this thing lock automatically?"

"Yeah, you kind of have to let it close though."

"Got it. What floor are you on?"

"Third."

"I'll just wait to see the lights come on . . . just to make sure . . . "

"Mary and Ned are probably there already so I'll be fine."

Max frowned. "They live with you? Your friends from the parade?"

"They live down the block, but they have a key and they like to check in."

"I see."

"You could come up if you like," she suggested.

"No. It's getting late." He tapped the business card she'd given him. "I'll call you," he promised as he stepped away to let the exterior door close, then checked to be sure the lock had caught.

* * * * *

As she had suspected, Mary and Ned were waiting for her, anxious to hear all the details of her evening.

"So?" Mary demanded.

"It was a lovely evening. It's been years since I saw Mrs. Wolzak and—"

"Blah, blah, blah. What about Sir Hunkiness?"

"He has a name—Max."

"And?"

"And it's late and I have a full day tomorrow."

Ned sighed. "I will never understand the kick you seem to get out of waking up before the sun to hit the stores for Black Friday bargains."

"Ah, Ned, where's your Christmas spirit?" she teased as she herded her friends toward the door. "Besides, part of my shopping will be to find the perfect gift for the two of you."

Her cell phone started to ring.

"He's calling already?" Mary's eyebrows shot up.

"Go," Sarah instructed as she pulled her phone from her pocket and checked the caller ID. Unknown caller. She shooed her friends the rest of the way out the door as she answered the call and closed the door. "Hello?"

"Hi. It's me."

His voice was rich and deep, and she was surprised to hear it. "You're going to have to do better than that—I know a lot of 'me's' in this world."

"Max? Max Wolzak?" The confidence in his tone wavered slightly.

"Oh, that me."

"I said I'd call."

"So you did."

Neither of them seemed to know what to say next, so after a minute they both started talking at once.

"I meant to tell you how much—" she began.

"I was thinking and wondering if—"

They both laughed and stopped talking. "You first," she said.

"I was wondering if maybe you'd help me with some Christmas shopping tomorrow. I know the stores will be mobbed and all, but I haven't a clue what to get for Molly or Grace or Gramma Karen. Jack's easy—he's a guy. But . . . "

"How about I meet you at Macy's at seven?"

There was a pause. "As in seven AM?"

"Actually that's late, but we'll probably still qualify for the door-buster specials."

"Stores actually open at seven," he repeated. "In the morning."

"I'll bring coffee," she promised.

"Black, and none of that frou-frou-latte-chino stuff."

"Black it is . . . for Black Friday."

"Perfect."

Neither of them spoke for several seconds.

"Well, if we're going to get any sleep at all we'd best continue this conversation—fascinating as it is—tomorrow. Good night, Max."

She clicked off her phone and laid it on the kitchen counter next to her keys. Then she settled cross-legged onto the daybed and began making her list. She might be an only child, but her extended family of cousins, aunts, uncles, and special friends and coworkers stretched into the dozens, and nothing would do but that she find the perfect gift—within budget of course—for every single one of them. That was a full day of shopping in and of itself. Adding Max's list to hers . . . she'd better make that coffee doubly strong.

Chapter Four

In spite of the fuss he'd made about a seven o'clock meeting time with Sarah, Max's normal habit was to be up at five and out for his daily run through the park. It felt odd to be back in this country, doing the same things he'd done in the years before he'd enlisted. In junior high school, around the time they had moved away from the old Brooklyn neighborhood, he'd started a fitness routine of running five to seven miles every morning. He'd found it a good time to think, to work out problems he might be facing at school—or at home. He remembered the day after he'd dropped out of college and enlisted. He had spent those five miles trying to figure out how he was going to break the news to his family.

His parents were in Japan and trying to get home, so he had decided to start with his grandparents. He'd been right to assume that Gramma Karen would understand why he'd signed up, but his maternal grandparents were something else. They came from a long line of old money and a tradition of service at home, not on the battlefield. As he had anticipated, his mother's parents were shocked at the news.

"Why?" his grandfather had asked.

"Because we have been attacked on our own soil—innocent Americans have died right here in New York City." His logic made perfect sense to him. His grandfather had tried to pull strings in

Washington to assure that Max would be assigned to a desk job stateside. But Max had refused and reported for combat training.

Each time his stint ended he had taken this same run, had considered all the pros and cons of signing up for a second—and then a third tour. The way he saw it, there was still work to be done. They might have finally gotten Bin Laden, but that was not the end of it—not by a long shot. And yes, on this chilly November morning, he was actually contemplating the possibility of returning to the Middle East to stand alongside his buddies still over there—still trying to make sense of a culture that was so very different from everything they knew back home.

By the time he got back to the brownstone, he was no closer to a decision, and he had decided that for today he would put such thoughts aside in favor of spending time with Sarah Peterson. It would be an early Christmas present to himself. There was something about her that made him feel calmer, less tense about the future, more inclined to consider his options beyond reenlisting. The truth was that watching her that night in the park and then again the day before, especially with the woman on the train, he envied her the certainty with which she seemed to approach life. There was no cynicism in her, no hesitancy to reach out to other people. Somewhere along the way he had lost that trust factor. Maybe it had been not knowing who he could truly rely upon during his missions overseas—never knowing when choosing the wrong person might result in one of his troops being injured or killed.

"You're back from your run early." Gramma Karen was dressed and preparing dough that she and Molly would turn into dozens of holidays cookies. Another tradition—one that he and Grace had looked forward to as children.

"Got things to do, places to be." He kissed her cheek. "Nice party yesterday." He dipped a finger into the batter, and Gramma Karen swatted his hand away.

"You certainly seemed to enjoy yourself . . . for once." She continued stirring the batter then added, "Sarah Peterson is such a nice girl."

"She's a grown woman, Gramma, and if you think you're being subtle, think again." He stuck his finger in the batter once more and then laughed as he dodged his grandmother's raised hand. "Got to shower," he said.

"Do you want breakfast?" she called.

"I'll take care of it. Got to meet somebody at seven."

"Sarah?"

"Not subtle, Gramma." He couldn't help but smile when he heard his grandmother's knowing chuckle follow him up the stairs.

* * * * *

Sarah was nothing if not organized. She had perused all the ads—printed and online—listing promotional deals for Black Friday, and she had mapped out a plan of attack. They would start at Macy's, where she already had a list of suggestions for Max in terms of gifts for his sister and grandmother. The store had a terrific deal on the perfume that Grace had loved from the time they were teenagers. Back then her mother had vetoed her wearing the scent, saying that it was far too sophisticated for a girl of sixteen. But on Thanksgiving night, Sarah had caught the subtle fragrance of the expensive perfume when Grace welcomed her with a hug and then handed her an apron.

So perfume for Grace would be her suggestion. Of course Max might have something else in mind, and she certainly did not know his budget. Best to listen first and make suggestions later. She glanced at the clock. She was going to have to hurry if she was going to pick up coffee and make it to Macy's by seven.

As she might have guessed, the line for coffee was long no matter where she stopped. By the time she reached the ornate entrance to the world-famous department store, Max was already there. He stood in an at-ease position, his hands clasped loosely behind his back. He was wearing jeans, a heavy canvas jacket, and a bright red scarf.

"Sorry," she said as she handed him his cup of coffee. "Apparently everyone got the same memo about starting the morning with coffee."

He took a sip and sighed. "Perfect." Then, to her surprise, he drank down the rest of the scalding liquid and tossed the cup in a nearby trash container. "So, what's the plan of attack?"

Sarah juggled her coffee and her phone. "I started a list," she said. "But then I realized that beyond your immediate family, I had no idea who you might need gifts for. I thought we could get your shopping done first and then you could go on with your day."

"What about your list?"

"I'll get to that, but there's no reason that you—"

"I want to tag along with you, unless I'd be in the way."

"You want to? Seriously?"

"Why not? Like I said, I'm out of practice and it seems to me you're something of an expert when it comes to this holiday cheer thing." He indicated the front door, where people were flooding in. "Shall we join the masses?"

Sarah took a final swallow of her coffee and tossed the cup. Inside, she asked Max for his ideas on what to buy for his family members.

"Why do you think I asked to go shopping with you? I haven't a clue."

She suggested the perfume idea and led the way to the counter that sold Grace's preferred brand. When the woman behind the counter seemed inclined to regale them with the full range of choices, Max pointed to a bottle of perfume cradled in a blue velvet gift box. "That one."

"How much?" Sarah asked, wanting to make sure that Max understood that he had just selected the line's most expensive product. The clerk murmured a price. Max's eyebrows shot up.

"That includes the fancy box, right?"

"Of course, sir."

Max shrugged and pulled out his wallet. He handed the clerk his credit card, and while she processed the sale he turned to Sarah. "Gift wrapped and everything. Now for Gramma Karen, what were you thinking?"

And so the morning went. Max saw no reason to go to any other store. He bought a pair of down gloves for Jack and a pale rose-colored shawl for his grandmother. He took some time deliberating over a leather carrying case for his father's e-reader and a sterling silver cuff bracelet for his mother. "They can return these, right?" he asked the clerk three times.

So far, everything he'd purchased fit nicely in a single shopping bag.

"Finally we get to shop for someone who will truly appreciate whatever we choose—Molly loves presents. To the toy department," he announced and headed for the escalator.

But Sarah had another idea. "When it comes to shopping for children Molly's age in this city, there is no place like FAO Schwarz. Don't get me wrong—I love Macy's, but for toys . . . "

"Okay. That's in the neighborhood."

"I'm talking about the store on Fifth Avenue," Sarah said as she led the way to the exit. "It's so cool."

"It's also all the way uptown."

"And your point is?"

"Why waste time when you still have your shopping to do?"

"Oh, so when it comes to your very favorite niece, just any toy store will do?"

"Molly is my only niece," he reminded her as they cleared the revolving door and joined the crowds outside.

"Trust me. You're going to enjoy this," she replied as she took his hand and ran to make a blinking *Don't Walk* sign. "You know, I can see that you really have a lot to learn when it comes to this Christmas spirit thing, and since you gave me the assignment of teaching you, we're going to make a couple of stops along the way, okay?"

"You're the boss . . . teacher."

"Great." She checked her watch. "Come on. If we hurry we'll just make it." She picked up the pace as they walked east toward Fifth Avenue, but instead of continuing on to the toy store, Sarah stopped at Saks. "Their hours for early bird specials are a little later than Macy's, so hopefully . . ."

Inside the store were dozens of shoppers bobbing their heads in time to the music, even as clerks sang along to the city's namesake song, "New York, New York." Sarah looked at him and started singing along as well. "If I can make it there . . . " And Max had to admit that he couldn't get the lyrics out of his head even after they had walked through the store and out a side exit to continue their way uptown.

"Now that's better," she said as he continued to hum softly. "Next stop—Rock Center—have to see that tree, and I'll bet you haven't yet."

"Well, no, but Sarah, I do live here. Chances are sometime over the next few weeks I'll have the chance to get to Rockefeller Center and see the tree."

"No time like the present." They crossed at the light and then walked through the courtyard that led to the famous golden statue, the ice rink, and the huge decorated tree. "Now that's your basic Christmas tree," Sarah murmured as she gazed at it.

"Pretty special," Max agreed but he wasn't looking at the tree. He was looking at her. When she caught him staring, he cleared his throat and put on his grumpy voice. "Okay, so we've seen the tree. Can we go toy shopping now?"

"You can fight it all you want, Max Wolzak, but the spirit that is Christmastime will not be denied. I defy you not to get truly in the mood once we are inside FAO Schwarz."

"You're on," he replied, and this time he took the lead as together they walked the last blocks to the renowned toy store.

* * * * *

Sarah could not remember laughing more than she did in the next hour spent with Max. The minute they stepped inside he spotted an enormous Christmas stocking, and he gave her a mischievous smile. "Let's fill it up," he said as he chose a soft, stuffed, floppy-eared dog and pushed it deep inside the toe of the large stocking. Next came books and games, and finally he topped it off with a large doll that looked a lot like Molly. "What do you think?" he asked, surveying his handiwork, now placed carefully across a countertop. "It needs something, don't you think?" He began roaming around the department, his eyes laser sharp for anything he might have missed. "Music," he called out to Sarah, who had remained with the stocking, afraid that some overzealous clerk might decide to dismantle the whole thing.

"Music?"

He pointed to a wall filled with musical toys from keyboards to music boxes to harmonicas and drums and flutes. He took down a drum and banged out a rhythm, then looked to her for approval.

"Your sister will not be amused."

He replaced the drum and selected a wooden flute. "Better?"

"Perfect." She waited until he had made his way back to the counter. "Now, there is just one other tiny problem that I can see."

Max looked mystified. "What?"

"How in the world are you going to get this home?"

A clerk was waiting to ring up the sale, and he paused while Max considered his options.

"Delivery?"

"We can arrange for that, sir," the clerk assured him. "May I?" He indicated the need to unload the stocking so he could ring up the individual items. Max nodded.

"Of course, if they deliver it then there's always the risk that Molly will be home when it arrives."

"Oh, we would package everything in a plain box—a large box or perhaps even several," the clerk assured them. "You'd simply need to repack the stocking at home."

"Great! All taken care of then," Max said as once again he took out his credit card.

"We aim to please, sir," the clerk said as he scanned the bar-code for the doll and then all the other items and finally for the stocking.

Max stared at the clerk's name tag. "So, Greg, you'll personally take charge of this and see that it gets delivered?"

"You have my word, sir."

Max nodded as he put his card and wallet away and then glanced around. "I am seriously starving. It must be lunchtime."

"It's eleven o'clock, sir," the clerk replied.

"Late breakfast then, or brunch?" He glanced at Sarah. "You have got to be hungry after all this running around and fighting crowds."

Sarah handed him the shopping bag that held his other gifts. "This way," she said and led the way back to the escalator and out to the street. "I know a great little place."

She led the way down a side street toward Madison Avenue. "If you like breakfast at any time of the day or night, as I do, this place makes the best oatmeal in Manhattan," she promised as she pulled open the door that led into a narrow space just large enough for a counter with eight stools, two small booths, and a round table set for six in the rear.

"Sarah!" the woman behind the counter shouted, and she hurried around to greet Sarah with a hug. The three other patrons barely glanced up. "How long are you in town for?"

"I leave the day after Christmas."

"So soon?"

"Amal, this is my friend Max Wolzak. Max, Amal immigrated here from Iraq. She didn't speak a word of English and neither did her three children. Her husband was fluent because of his job as an interpreter." She turned back to Amal. "How are Samir and the kids?"

"They're fine." She turned her attention to Max. "Sarah is being far too modest. She was the one who got us out and set us up with connections here. Without her help, this place would not exist." She waved a hand to incorporate the entire restaurant. "Now come, sit. Let me feed you—it's what I do best."

"Two oatmeals," Sarah ordered. "With all the trimmings please."

"Coming right up," Amal announced as she headed back toward the kitchen. "Samir?" The rest of her words were spoken in her native tongue.

"What did she mean about you getting them out?"

"It was nothing really. On one of our missions, her husband, Samir, was our interpreter. Someone in the Iraqi government accused him of being a spy for the Americans. It became clear that he was a marked man, and as such his family was also in danger. We were able to arrange for them to escape."

"You make it sound like you made a phone call and it all came together."

"It was a little more difficult than that, but Amal insists on giving me far too much credit."

Max glanced around. "They own this place?"

"Well, not the building of course, but the restaurant has been here for a good five years now. They've made a real success of their new life. Can you imagine, Max? Leaving everything and everyone you've ever known or loved behind and starting from scratch?"

"The American dream," Max murmured.

Amal returned with their oatmeal and then went to ring up a customer's bill.

"What's your dream, Max?" Sarah asked.

He hesitated—spoon filled with oatmeal topped with nuts, dried cherries, and brown sugar poised in midair. Then he shrugged and shoveled the food into his mouth. But Sarah was not about to let the moment pass.

"You must have a dream—something you looked forward to doing once your service ended? Or maybe that's the dream—serving your country?"

"What's your dream?" he countered.

"Peace on earth." She took a bite of her oatmeal as she held his gaze. "And stop turning the tables on me."

"Does everyone have to have a dream?"

"No, but I find that most people do."

He focused on eating, and Sarah gave him the time he needed.

"I had a dream," he finally admitted. "To be a cop—like my grandfather."

"And?"

He scraped the last cherry from his empty bowl. "And nothing. It was another time. It wasn't realistic."

"Dreams rarely are," she said. "But that doesn't mean they aren't possible."

"Like peace on earth?"

"Impractical—definitely. Impossible? I refuse to accept that."

"Even in the face of all the evidence to the contrary?"

Sarah smiled and glanced at her friend Amal, who was busy taking orders and refilling coffee cups as the tiny restaurant filled with customers. "Look at her, Max. They came here with little more than the clothes on their backs, but they found a way just like millions of others who have come here over the years. They found a way to make their dream come true against all odds. Why wouldn't I believe that anything is possible?"

"You haven't changed much, have you? I seem to remember this skinny kid who thought she could do pretty much anything she set out to do—even try out for the football team as a kicker."

He was changing the subject, and she was inclined to let him. This was not a day for serious conversation. "I almost made it," she reminded him. "If you and your male chauvinist teammates hadn't—"

"Whoa! Why is this on me?" But he was laughing, and she really liked the way laughter made his entire body finally relax out of the military posture that she had noticed he adopted whenever he didn't want to discuss something. The man sitting across from her now was more like the charismatic Max she had once had such a crush on.

* * * * *

Over the next several days Max realized that spending time with Sarah was working out better than he could have imagined. For one thing it got him out of the house. For another, with Sarah in the picture Grace had let up on her constant attempts to manage his life. And for a third, Sarah was as good as her word—this was two people sharing time together, getting reacquainted, with no expectations that things needed to move to another level. No pressure.

So when he called Sarah the Wednesday after Thanksgiving anticipating that she would be up for some excursion followed by coffee or even dinner, he was surprised when she turned him down.

"I can't tonight."

For a moment he felt like a jealous boyfriend. *Why not?* was the first thing that sprang to mind. "Oh, well, maybe another time," he said and prepared to hang up.

"I have choir practice. Hey, here's an idea, why don't you come? It's a special choir for Christmas Eve services at the little church around the corner from my loft. Mary and Ned run the program, and I have a tradition of joining in if I'm in town."

"That's okay," he replied, already feeling better. "How about tomorrow? Dinner?"

"No, seriously. I'm remembering that you had the lead in your senior production of *South Pacific*. Grace invited me to come see it with her and your folks. You have a wonderful voice, and the choir can always use more male voices. Come on. It'll be fun."

The idea of spending time in a church was not all that appealing to Max. After everything he'd seen overseas, he was having a hard time justifying his faith in a loving God with a world that seemed to have gone insane. "I'm out of practice," he said, trying to keep things light.

She laughed. He really liked the sound of her laughter.

"Max, it's a little church choir, not Broadway—although please don't tell Mary that. Come on. Think how pleased your grandmother will be."

"Not fair, playing the Gramma Karen card."

"I do whatever it takes. Then you'll do it?"

She sounded like she really wanted him to say he would . . . so he did.

* * * * *

The church was old and held the familiar scents of candle wax, furniture polish, and fresh evergreens that decorated the deep window ledges and the low balustrade that separated the pulpit from the pews. Max liked the simplicity of the place. The pews were dark wood, lined with blue seat cushions. The floor was wooden and it creaked as he crossed the vestibule on his way to the stairs that led up to the choir loft. He was running late and apparently the others were already there, greeting each other as they settled into their places.

"Max! Over here."

Sarah stood at the far end of the crowded choir loft next to Ned, who was seated at the impressive organ. She looked the way she always looked—happy, fully engaged in the moment, and beautiful. Max edged his way past other choir members to reach her.

"Hi," he said, including Ned in the greeting. "Sorry I'm late."

"Bass, baritone, or tenor?" Ned waited for his answer, his fingers poised above the organ keys. "Sarah says you sang baritone in high school, but that was years ago and voices do change."

"Still a baritone," Max assured him.

Ned struck a note and waited. Max followed his cue and sang the note, finishing the scale without prompting. Ned grinned. "Baritone it is." He handed Max a loose-leaf binder filled with song sheets. "We're still working out the order of things, but this is the playbook."

Behind him someone rapped on the conductor's podium. Max turned to see Mary. "People, settle down and take your seats, please. We have a great deal of work to get through tonight."

Sarah pointed to a place between two older men where Max should sit, then took her seat on the other side of the semicircle of chairs. Mary called for one of the hymns, and everyone started turning to the correct page. As Ned played through the melody, there was a general clearing of throats and the rustle of bodies sitting up straight and focusing on Mary's uplifted baton.

The time passed quickly and Max realized that he was enjoying himself. It felt good to sing—to harmonize with the others, to follow Mary's direction, belting out some parts and almost whispering others. And of course looking across and seeing Sarah glance his way and smile from time to time wasn't bad at all.

"Okay, that's a wrap for tonight," Mary announced. "And remember I want everyone off book by next week."

"Off book?" Max asked after Sarah had made her way to the stairway where he was waiting for her.

"It's a theater term meaning learn your lines, or in this case the words to the songs."

"Thought you said this wasn't Broadway," he reminded her with a teasing grin.

"I also warned you that for Mary, everything is Broadway. She is always theatrical."

Downstairs they retrieved their coats, and outside the carved double wooden doors they said their good nights to the others.

"Where to?" Max asked.

"There's a tearoom some of us favor after rehearsal."

Put that way, it sounded like she might expect to meet up with others. Max couldn't help feeling a little disappointed. He had been imagining the two of them maybe taking a long walk or sitting at a coffeehouse and talking late into the night. He wasn't much for group socializing, even though he had to admit the mix of choir members and the way they had immediately accepted him in their midst had been nice. On the other hand, his only other option was a lonely train ride back uptown.

"Sounds like a plan," he said.

The tearoom was only a couple of blocks away. It was small and cozy with several bistro tables positioned around the room, walls lined with large framed posters featuring advertising for a variety of international teas, and a piano in one corner. Max recognized several members of the choir as Sarah led the way to a table for two tucked away near the piano.

A young woman in a long skirt, peasant blouse, and sandals took their order. "Green herbal house tea with honey," Sarah said.

"Make that two," Max added.

"I have something I want to tell you," Sarah said, her eyes glowing in the candlelight from the small lantern in the center of the table.

"Sounds serious."

"You know I have a mission that leaves the day after Christmas." The waitress brought their tea, and Sarah began pouring for both of them. "The thing is, one of our team has decided to take a position in Washington and he has to start immediately."

"And you need a replacement," Max guessed. In the time they had spent together and on the phone, they had talked a lot about their work—his on the front lines battling terrorism and hers on the front lines battling the ravages of war on ordinary citizens caught in the middle. "What's the job?" He assumed she was telling him this hoping he might know of someone who could fill the position on such short notice.

"Interpreter, guide—somebody who knows the region and knows the differences between the various factions. It's going to be a delicate assignment because it affects mostly the women and, well, sometimes the men can get . . . prickly about anything that seems to threaten their paternalistic traditions."

"Prickly?" Max lifted his eyebrows. "Sarah, in some parts of the Middle East women have been stoned to death for looking at someone the wrong way."

"I know, and that's what makes it so important that we have just the right people on our team for this mission." She took a long swallow of her tea, refilled her cup from the teapot, and added more honey. "I don't suppose you might consider taking on the job. . . . " Her voice was low and muffled by the fact that she was staring down at her tea cup as if reading the leaves or something.

"Me?"

She looked up at him, her eyes locking on his as she pleaded her case. "It's only for six months. Our main goal is to set up a school and a factory where the women can learn a trade and start earning enough to support their families. Do you have any idea how many households there are where the men have either been killed or have deserted their families in order to join the Taliban, Al Qaeda, or some other rebel group?" Her tone was passionate as it always was whenever she talked about the suffering she had witnessed.

"Sarah, I'm not sure I'm ready to go back. I'm not that sure that I ever will be. But if I did return, it would be to rejoin my bud-dies—the ones still there to continue the work I was doing before."

"But this is that work—it's just a different version of that work."

He took his time, wanting to get the words right. "I'm not wired for the work you do, Sarah. Don't get me wrong. What you and your team do out there is beyond important—every bit as important as what our armed forces are doing. Maybe more, but . . . "

"Just think about it, okay? Let me send you some information about the mission and the job."

It was impossible to refuse her anything when she looked at him with those wide eyes that mirrored her certainty that all things were possible in this world. "All right. Send me the information."

"Thank you," she said, and she squeezed his hand.

Before she could pull her hand away, he entwined his fingers with hers. "No promises, okay?"

"Got it." But there was that smile again—the one that seemed to say she was already sure he would not be able to resist the opportunity.

"What's going on with you two sitting back here all huddled together?" Mary asked as she slid onto the piano bench. "People are beginning to talk." She winked at them and then launched into the introduction for a current Broadway musical score.

Soon others had gathered 'round the piano and were singing along as Mary and Ned took turns playing show tunes both old and new. "How about something from *South Pacific*?" Mary suggested.

Sarah turned to Max as she began the song that had been one of his solos in the high school production. "'You've got to be taught to hate and fear . . . '"

She motioned for Max to join her as she continued. "'You've got to be taught from year to year . . . '"

"'It's got to be drummed in your dear little ear,'" Max sang, and then together they ended the verse. "'You've got to be carefully taught.'"

Others joined in on the remaining two verses, but Max kept his eyes on Sarah's face. He heard the words through her ears, and he knew that this woman did not have an ounce of prejudice in her entire body. He understood that she did not see color or gender or politics or religion when she met someone. All Sarah saw was goodness and potential.

Sarah clearly had never been "taught," but Max had. He had lived his life under the game plan of "us versus them." It had started innocently enough, first at home, where his grandfather and uncles were the "good guys" fighting crime in the city. Then in school the lesson had continued on the athletic field, where winning was everything. Then in the military, the lessons were really driven home—there were enemies that needed to be subdued.

But through his conversations with Sarah, he understood that she didn't think that way at all. For Sarah there was only "us." Everyone had value. Everyone could be saved. Max had never met anyone quite like her. She made him believe that maybe all was not lost—that maybe *he* wasn't as lost as he was feeling since coming home.

Mary and Ned had changed up the playlist once again as they launched into a duet of Scott Joplin's ragtime music. Max studied the laughing, joyful faces of the people surrounding the piano enjoying the music. No doubt these people had troubles of their own, but right now they were not thinking of those things. They were simply living in the moment. He thought about the times that he and other soldiers had shared similar occasions with their counterparts in Afghanistan—times when their differences in belief and tradition had not existed. Moments when they had simply been soldiers weary of the battle and sharing a rare moment of calm before the next firefight. And he understood that it was moments like this—moments like those shared over there—that made everything worthwhile.

His gaze settled on Sarah. She was watching him in return, her smile a little less certain than usual. She glanced toward the exit and he understood that she was asking if he wanted to leave. He nodded and edged toward the door, holding up his hand in a farewell gesture. He wished he could think of a reason why Sarah should leave with him, but this was her part of town. It would be silly to have her ride all the way uptown with him and then return alone.

Outside, the night had turned cold with a sharp wind that cut through the layers of Max's clothing. He turned up his collar, hunched his shoulders, and headed for the subway station.

"Hey, wait up."

He stopped and turned to see Sarah running toward him, her coat half on. And it was the most normal thing in the world to hold out his arms to her and fold her into his embrace the minute she reached him.

Chapter Five

Standing in the warmth of Max's embrace, Sarah felt as if she had come home. *Now that is simply crazy,* she thought as she eased away from him and finished zipping her jacket. They had a bargain— a bargain that was rooted in friendship and was firmly without romantic overtones. But when she looked up at him, he was staring at her as if seeing her for the first time.

"Sorry about that," she murmured, figuring that he was having his doubts that she could keep things on a platonic level.

"I'm not," he replied. "It was nice. It felt . . . right."

Okay, she was now officially confused, and as usual when she did not quite know how to read a situation, she made a joke. "Well, it certainly felt good to get out of that wind. Thanks for acting as a barrier." She concentrated on pulling on her mittens—an action that took no effort at all but one that she focused on as if she were performing some delicate operation.

Max took her hands in his. "Hey, I'm being serious here."

"I thought we'd agreed . . . "

He shrugged. "Yeah, well, sometimes things change." He ran his thumb over the fabric of her mitten. "Look, I don't want to make you uncomfortable, and if that's the case then maybe . . . "

She leaned in and kissed him lightly on the lips. "We're not teenagers, Max. I think we can both deal with whatever feelings might come out of this time we're spending together. The point is—"

He wrapped his arms around her and kissed her back—only this was no light peck on the lips. This was a kiss that spoke volumes—a kiss broken only by the sounds of laughter and conversation as others left the restaurant. Reluctantly Max took a step back and released her.

"Hey you two, it's warmer inside if you need to talk or whatever," Ned said as he and Mary caught up to them.

"Just making plans," Max said, and Sarah could not help but marvel at the casual way he wrapped one arm around her shoulder as they turned to face her friends. "I've been promising Molly that we'd go ice skating. How's tomorrow?"

"I'm in meetings all day."

"Next week then. How's Friday?"

Sarah mentally ran through her schedule. She had so much to do, and unless Max took the open spot on the team she was going to have to try to find someone else or go on the mission shorthanded. "I can't. I have to—"

"Another time then." He released her and turned his attention to Mary and Ned. "You'll see that Sarah gets safely home?"

"We usually do," Mary replied. "And we'll see you next week for choir practice?"

"I'll be there."

With a wave he started walking—no, practically jogging—to the subway entrance. Sarah's first thought was that he was having second thoughts about that kiss. Or did he think she was the one having doubts? Did he think she was making excuses not to be with him? As she fell into step between Mary and Ned, she tried hard not to overanalyze the situation. After all, she had been the one to point out that they were adult enough to handle whatever feelings might arise between them. Was she or not? At the moment she felt like a rejected sixteen-year-old.

She stewed about the situation for the duration of the walk back to her loft. Ned and Mary rode the elevator with her to make sure she was safely inside her apartment before heading down the block to their place. They didn't seem to notice how quiet she was. They were debating changes for the order of songs for the concert and who should do which solo.

"I think we ought to give that part to Max."

Mary shook her head. "Max? He's only just joined the group, and what if he decides it's not for him?"

As the elevator came to a creaky stop, they both turned to face Sarah. "Well?" Mary demanded. "Don't you agree?"

"What?"

Ned sighed. "That Max might not be the best choice for the solo on a number of fronts—for one thing, Frank Stover will have a hissy fit."

Mary rolled her eyes. "Frank Stover could not sing a note on key if his life—"

"I think Ned might have a point," Sarah said as she lifted the elevator's iron gate and stepped into the hall. "Max is . . . kind of in transition now. He's only just been discharged from the military, and I think he might be trying things to see if there's a fit." *Like that kiss.*

"So we should not ask him to do the solo?"

Sarah shrugged. "Ask him. Don't ask him. I'm beat, and I've still got a lot to do." She gave them a little wave as she closed her loft door, knowing they would wait for the sounds of three locks to slide into place. On the rest of their way home, no doubt, the couple would be wondering what was wrong with her. It was unusual for her to be so short with either of them.

Well, what *was* wrong with her? It was completely out of character for her to be so disinterested in anything that was clearly of utmost importance to her friends. She emptied her pockets, throwing her keys and wallet onto the small table in the entry hall that also held her book of daily devotions. The small dog-eared devotional fell to the floor at her feet.

"Okay, I get it." She was all too aware she'd been so busy that she often fell asleep with either her Bible or the devotional still in her hands and her prayers unfinished. No wonder she was feeling so confused and out of sorts. She took off her jacket and dropped it on the chair then sat cross-legged on the floor and opened the little book to the current date—the first of December.

The scripture passage for the day was from Luke 2. It was about the call for everyone to report to the place of their birth to pay taxes. It was about Joseph and Mary making the long journey to Bethlehem. The meditation focused on the fact that although surely God could have chosen any circumstance for the birth of His son, He chose to have the young expectant parents end up in a stable—destitute, hungry, and weary from their travels. The meditation went on to remind the reader that millions of people all over the world faced a similar plight every day.

Sarah thought about the people she'd worked with over the years. Fathers who could not find work or support their families. Mothers who were helpless to offer their newborn children milk because of their own malnutrition. Children—age seven or ten or thirteen—so riddled with disease and hunger that they looked years younger. And many of these people lived in countries with the resources to feed, clothe, and house them. Many lived in countries where there were riches beyond imagination.

Many of them live right here in America, Sarah thought, and a wave of guilt washed over her. Guilt that she had been so caught up in her happiness in spending time with Max, enjoying the traditions of the holidays that she had lost sight of how truly blessed she was. There were people probably within her very neighborhood who held no warm feelings for the season. Maybe that's what Max had meant when he'd talked about all the trappings of Christmas being a farce covering up the reality of daily life.

She picked up her cell and dialed Max's number.

"Hi," he said, answering on the first ring.

"This thing with Molly—ice-skating. I assume at Rockefeller Center?"

"Yeah."

"How about instead we take her with us to help out at a soup kitchen or food pantry?"

"She's kind of got her heart set on it."

"Couldn't we do both?" Ideas were flashing through Sarah's head the way they did when she found herself in a situation where things were not going according to the original plan. There was silence on the other end of the conversation. "Max? Are you there?"

"What's going on, Sarah?"

"I just think it's important that we don't forget to focus on those who are less fortunate."

"And you do that every day in your job. I think it's okay for you to take some time to enjoy the season."

"You were the one who described everything we've surrounded Christmas with as a Hollywood version of the perfect holiday," she reminded him.

"Don't pay any attention to me, Sari. I'm far too burnt out as a human being. I'm going to view everything through the eyes of a guy who has seen too much hate and anger and suffering in the world."

"Then let me show you the other side of that."

"You're talking about the job?"

"I'm talking about finding a way for Molly—and you—to experience the lessons of the true meaning of Christmas. I'm talking about the fact that maybe I've gotten far too caught up in parades and shopping and such myself. Maybe both of us need to take a step back and look at things through a child's eyes."

"We're not her parents, Sarah."

"I know that, but don't you think that Grace and Jack would agree that it's important for her to learn that Christmas is about so much more than Santa Claus?"

Again a long silence. She was beginning to get used to these. This time she waited for him to speak.

"I thought you had to work."

"I do tomorrow and I do next Friday. But there are several days in between when I can get things arranged so that I could take off early. We could go after Molly gets home from school—go first to the food pantry and then from there we could go ice-skating . . . Maybe Grace and Jack could meet us if Jack's schedule allows for him to be off."

"Do we get to eat anywhere in there?" His tone was lighter, and she was relieved to realize that he was seriously considering her plan.

"Sure."

"Let me run the idea past Grace and Jack, okay?"

"Absolutely, and in the meantime I'll see if I can find a pantry or soup kitchen that's not halfway across town from you." Sarah felt better—as if she had once again found her bearings. And at the same time she was reluctant to end the call. "Well . . . " she said and found she really had nowhere to go with that.

Max chuckled. "Me too. I could talk to you all night, but you have to go to work tomorrow and save the world, so hang up now and get some rest."

"Okay. Good night. And Max—thanks."

"Not sure for what, but you're welcome."

* * * * *

The texts started coming within ten minutes of ending the call with Sarah. She had found a listing for food pantries and soup kitchens in the Manhattan area.

This one is close to Central Park.

And then, *Oops! Looks like that one has really limited days and hours, none of which work for us. This one?*

Followed by, *This one does a brown bag thing and is also close to you. Maybe?*

There were half a dozen more messages over the next hour—each new place she found had something good and something not so good. But every message made Max smile, and he found himself checking his phone to see if there were any more that he might have missed. Each time he texted back with the same message. *You choose.*

I can't, was her reply. *There are so many and they all seem worthy.*

In the end they decided to let Grace choose. After all, Molly was her daughter and she might not want the child doing charity work around a bunch of homeless people.

"Are you nuts?" was Grace's succinct response when he called the next morning to tell her about Sarah's idea. "Jack and I have been racking our brains trying to come up with some way we could insert a little true Christmas spirit along with all the fantasy world stuff. This is brilliant."

"You and Jack are invited as well."

"I'll be there, but Jack's on duty all that week. It's day shift. I can see if he could meet us after for the skating part."

"Then it's a date."

Grace laughed. "Well, especially for you and Sarah—seems there have been several 'dates' over the last couple of weeks. What's the story?"

"Just friends, Gracie."

"Right. Gramma Karen says you've joined a choir—as in a church choir. It's been—what?—a dozen years since you darkened the door of a church?"

"It's a choir. I was in one when we were in high school, remember?"

"Okay. It's just that—"

"I'm trying a few things—dipping my toes in the real world again without jumping in head first."

"And Sarah?"

"She makes it easier to be out in the city. She knows me and . . . "

"Seriously? She knows you? You had one date in high school. You knew her pretty much as my friend until she blossomed into the beauty she is and then you took notice. She does not know you."

"Gracie, it is what it is. Don't make a federal case out of a simple friendship, okay?"

"If you say so."

But Max had no illusions that this was the end of it. As he and Sarah had both expected, Grace was going to see this as a romance whether they wanted her to or not. And after the kiss they had shared, Max had to admit that what he was feeling for Sarah went at least a couple of steps beyond simple friendship. Still, he had to try to give Grace a reality check.

"Need I remind you that the day after Christmas, Sarah's off to her new mission for the next six months?"

Grace's laugh was more of a hoot. "Did they brainwash you over there or what? Here's an idea: ask her not to go."

"What? I couldn't do that. I mean, her work is important— to her and to those she serves. She's not going to just throw that aside on the off chance that . . . " He had said way too much. He realized it the minute that Grace started laughing. "Okay, hanging up now."

"You know there's another option," Grace said.

"And that is?"

"Go with her. Sarah told me she had a vacancy on the team. She wondered if maybe you might be interested. I told her it would be perfectly okay to ask you. So, did she?"

"Say good night, Gracie."

Max clicked off his phone and set it to recharge. Sometimes his sister could be beyond ridiculous. Take the job after everything he'd experienced over there? Ask her not to go? "Yeah, that'll work," Max muttered.

But the more he thought about it, the more he wondered what Sarah would say if he asked her to stay. He'd never do it, of course. He respected her and the work she did too much to put his needs ahead of that. As for going with her, he had promised to keep an open mind, but he was pretty sure there wasn't a pamphlet in the universe that could persuade him to go back to that part of the world as anything other than the soldier he'd been. And that was highly unlikely because he was battle weary and burnt out, and there was nothing left to give.

Clearly he had allowed his sister to mess with his mind, creating images of things that would never be—could never be. Him with Sarah? Not likely. And yet . . .

* * * * *

To Max's surprise, Molly took the entire idea of volunteering very seriously. A few days later, on their way to the church soup kitchen they'd finally settled on, Molly peppered her mother with questions—questions that Grace kept directing at Max. "Yeah, Max, how come these people without homes don't go to a hotel like we do when we go away on vacation?"

He wished Jack were there—or better yet his grandfather. Now there was a man who had been a master at answering a kid's tough questions without giving them nightmares.

"Here's the thing, Molly. These folks don't have a lot of the things that we have. They don't have a job like your dad does, and that means nobody is paying them money for the work they do."

"Like sometimes I forget to do my chores, and then Mom won't give me my allowance till I do?"

"Sort of like that. Anyway, if they don't have money, they can't pay for things—like a place to stay or warm clothes or food."

"You see, sweetie," Grace chimed in, "they want to work and have all those things but . . . " She stopped talking, clearly at a loss to explain things further.

Max tried again. "You remember when the big hurricane came and lots and lots of people's houses got broken up and their stuff got wet and ruined and they had to start again?"

"Yeah. We brought cans of food to school. Gramma Karen said we would have to keep on doing what we could until everybody got back on their feet."

"Well, this is sort of like that. These people need our help and because we know that our friends and neighbors would help us if something bad happened like a hurricane or fire or something—"

"Not that anything is going to happen," Grace interrupted.

"Mom, it might. You just never know."

Max thought he had never in his life been happier to see Sarah walking toward them. For reasons he couldn't define, he was quite sure that Sarah would know exactly how to answer Molly's questions.

"Sarah!" Molly bounded forward to greet her. "Guess what? We're on our way to feed the hungry just like Jesus taught us to do."

"Out of the mouths of babes," Grace muttered, but Max saw tears of pride glistening in his sister's eyes.

"I know," Sarah was saying. "Could I come along and help?"

"Sure. Uncle Max says these are people like those ones we helped after the big hurricane. But"—Molly frowned—"if they really don't have a place to live, I don't suppose they even have a Christmas tree, and I know they don't have any presents."

"Well, maybe not, but tonight they are going to spend time in a warm place eating good hot food, and in a way, that's the best kind of a gift."

Sarah took Molly's hand as they walked down the outside steps that led to the church basement-turned-soup kitchen. Max and Grace followed. Max noticed that while he and Grace could not seem to meet the eyes of the men and women already lined up outside the church, Molly had no such reservations.

"Don't worry," she told one young man. "We're going to feed you good stuff."

The man looked a little taken aback, as if it had been too long since anyone even noticed him at all. And then he smiled at Molly, revealing a missing front tooth. "Thank you, miss."

Molly's eyes went wide with surprise as she stared at the man and then slowly she gave him a huge smile—revealing her own missing front tooth. "It'll grow back," she whispered as she hurried down the church steps and inside.

In the church's kitchen, there were large pots of soup steaming on top of the restaurant-style stove, while a woman removed several trays of rolls from the double ovens. Within minutes Grace, Max, Sarah, and even Molly had their assignments. They were to serve the food once the doors opened and the people began streaming in. Around the church hall there were card tables and chairs set up where their guests could sit down.

"Molly, you hand each person this napkin wrapped around a spoon," the lady in charge instructed. "Then, Grace, you can dish up the soup. Max, you give them a roll, and Sarah, you're on coffee." She moved toward the door. "Everybody set?"

"All set," they assured her.

Max kept a wary eye on Molly, prepared to rescue her if—as he expected—the crowd of people waiting in the cold should suddenly rush the doors in their zeal to be first in line. But to his surprise, they entered in an orderly fashion, nodding—if not smiling—at the church ladies and minister waiting to greet them. When they were all inside, the minister said a prayer, and then their guests began working their way down the line. First they accepted the napkin-wrapped spoon that Molly gave them and then the bowl of soup—barley thick with vegetables—and the roll before finding a place to sit. He saw Sarah moving among the tables offering coffee and hot water for tea. Each table was set with a cloth as well as with cream, sugar, and butter. They might have been at any church supper except for the fact that most of the people ate without speaking, their heads down, their eyes focused on their food.

As soon as Molly completed her assignment, she started working the room. Max saw Grace make a move to stop her, but he restrained her. "She'll be fine," he said.

And indeed she was. Along with Sarah, the little girl moved from table to table. At first she mimicked Sarah's questions about whether or not the person wanted more coffee or tea or perhaps another roll. But then Max noticed that both Molly and Sarah were engaging people in conversation—Sarah would kneel next to someone's chair and ask a question and gradually the people began to respond. Not in the monosyllables with which they had received their food but in sentences animated with hand gestures, smiles, and in one case tears.

After several minutes, Molly returned to her mother. "Well," she huffed, "they tell me they never, ever have dessert. We have to do something about that. I'm going to ask Gramma Karen to help me bake cookies for them. Sarah said she would help. And we need a tree, Uncle Max. That woman over there? She hasn't had a real Christmas tree in nine years. That's longer than I've even been alive. And Mom, there just have to be presents. Even baby Jesus in the stable got presents."

"Maybe we could arrange to do a special Christmas Day celebration," Sarah suggested. Her eyes shone with the same childlike enthusiasm with which Molly greeted new ideas that she liked.

"Pretty short notice," Max said and immediately regretted throwing a damper on the idea. "I mean, maybe we could get something together for New Year's."

Molly sighed and rolled her eyes. "One, New Year's is not about baby Jesus and trees and presents. And two, Sarah won't even be here."

Max had not yet gotten used to the way his niece could sometimes sound more adult than the grown-ups in the room.

"I'm sure that everyone in the choir would help if they are in town, and then they all have friends and well—if the church will permit us to use the space . . . "

Max was beginning to see why Sarah must be so very good at her job. Nothing fazed her when she set her mind to accomplish something. He spotted the pastor of the church moving among the people, offering words of comfort. "Let me talk to the minister about using this place. That's step one."

The truth was, at that moment he would have walked over hot coals the way Sarah looked at him as if he and he alone could move mountains. He was beginning to think that just maybe Grace was right—just maybe he should ask Sarah to stay, or at least come back to him as soon as possible.

* * * * *

Sarah had tried hard to keep her spirits up as Christmas Day approached, just a week away. She'd love to join her parents as they traveled the Southwest, but it wouldn't work with her leaving the day after Christmas for the Middle East. She was facing her first Christmas without any real plans—other than packing for the trip. Mary and Ned would spend Christmas Eve and part of the day itself with family and friends in Connecticut, and no doubt Max would be involved with family traditions as well—whether he liked the idea or not. She knew that he would not disappoint his grandmother.

So when Molly talked about a tree and presents and cookies for the homeless people gathered in the hall, Sarah simply took things to the next logical step—a celebration like the ones these folks might have known as children—or perhaps only just dreamed about as children. Why shouldn't they have the joy of the day with all its trimmings?

As the homeless people slowly—reluctantly—made their way back outside, she and Grace helped clear away the paper dishes and plasticware their guests had used. The church women scoured the soup pots and coffee urns and replaced them on the shelves in the large kitchen. Sarah kept her eye on Max and the minister. She was pleased to see that Max was clearly making a strong case for the cause. On the other hand, it was equally clear that the minister had some concerns.

Oh, please let him see the value of this, she prayed silently.

As she tied shut the last of the large garbage bags, she saw the minister and Max shaking hands—and both of them were smiling. The fact that Molly was hopping up and down and clapping her hands told Sarah the party was on.

"Be careful what you wish for," Grace warned, coming alongside Sarah and taking in the scene. "We have less than a week to pull this off."

Not to mention the choir concert on Christmas Eve, Sarah thought. But she refused to be rattled. "Well, maybe this is what people mean when they talk about the season's hustle and bustle."

Grace laughed. "You always did go looking for ways to complicate your life, Sarah. But in the end you always make it work," she added fondly. "Look at her." She pointed to where Molly was talking nonstop to Max as they crossed the large hall together holding hands. "You have absolutely made her day and in the process taught her the true meaning of Christmas. Thank you."

"As usual you are giving me way too much credit," Sarah replied as Max and Molly joined them. "Here's the person you should thank."

Max held up his hands. "Don't thank me yet. You've got one enormous project on your hands."

"We'll be fine, won't we, Sarah?" Molly asked. "We should probably make a list. When Gramma Karen has a party, she always makes a list."

"I thought we were going ice skating," Max reminded her.

Molly looked up at him. "Oh, Uncle Max, could we go another day? There's just so much we have to do for the party."

"Mission accomplished," Sarah murmured as she handed Max the garbage bag filled with trash and nodded toward the rear exit. "If you don't mind."

"We *are* going to eat," Max said firmly. "And Molly, what about your dad? He's planning to meet us for ice skating."

Molly reached into Grace's purse and pulled out the phone. "I can call him. Where are we eating? How about that pizza place Dad loves on Amsterdam? It's near the station house and he can meet us there."

Max glanced at Grace and Sarah.

"She seems to have us all organized," Sarah said with a grin.

"Yeah. I think maybe having her hang out with you might have created an organizational monster."

* * * * *

Even holding a large bag of garbage, Max couldn't help but smile. He was really proud of Molly and the way she had embraced the charity work. He carried out the garbage and then stopped in the kitchen to wash his hands and thank the church ladies before picking up Sarah's jacket. He held it while she shrugged into it. "Thank you," he said softly, allowing his hands to linger on her shoulders.

She looked back at him and smiled. "I'm glad it's all worked out. Molly is an incredible little girl. I think maybe she takes after her uncle a little."

Max couldn't believe it, but he was actually blushing. He hadn't blushed in front of a girl since his senior year. And come to think of it—that girl had been Sarah Peterson.

Chapter Six

With less than a week to go before she left for her next mission, Sarah's days began early and lasted well into the late night. But where only a few days earlier she had been melancholy, now she could not remember a Christmas season when she had felt more alive—more blessed. In truth, these days she was spending more time at the Wolzak house than she was at her own loft.

Each day she went there straight from her work at the United Nations for whatever Molly had scheduled—with her great-grandmother's help—as preparation for the party. Tonight they would decorate dozens of sugar and ginger cookies, and she looked forward to an evening spent with Karen Wolzak, Grace, and Molly. "A girl's night in," Grace had titled it.

"What about Max . . . and Jack?" Sarah asked.

"They're off to a Knicks game. We'll have the place to ourselves—hope you aren't disappointed," Grace teased.

"I'm looking forward to it—as I recall, your grandmother makes the best cookies in town."

"Come as soon as you're free. We'll decorate the cookies early so Molly can get to bed, and then we can have an old-fashioned gabfest."

So as soon as she could break away from the meetings and details that surrounded preparing for the coming mission, Sarah took a subway uptown and walked the last few blocks to the Wolzak home. Outside, a sleek town car was just pulling away, and a man and woman whom she recognized as Grace and Max's parents walked up the stone steps and entered the brownstone.

Neither Grace nor Max had mentioned that their parents would be back from their travels in Europe today. Sarah hoped they had decided to surprise everyone and at the same time wondered if she should call Grace and see if it would still be all right for her to stop by. After all, Max hadn't seen his parents at all since he got home from Afghanistan. Sarah was reluctant to interrupt a family reunion.

She called Grace's cell phone and was surprised when Max answered. "Hi," he said softly, obviously having seen her name pop up on caller ID. "Where are you? Please tell me you are not calling to cancel. Molly will be really disappointed."

"I'm actually across the street." She saw a curtain in the front window move, and then a minute later Max came outside, still holding the phone. "Come on," he said, motioning her forward and still speaking into the phone.

She crossed the street. Max was standing by the open front door waiting for her.

"I'm not sure this is a good idea," she began.

"Trust me, it's a wonderful idea," he said.

"Oh for goodness' sake, Michael, you left the front door open when you brought the luggage in," a woman called out, and Sarah heard the click of high heels on the tiled floor as she stepped inside. The woman was tall and willowy, tanned and beautifully dressed in a classic suit made in the Chanel style. Or perhaps it was a Chanel original, Sarah reminded herself.

"Honestly, Maxwell, your father would forget . . . " She looked at Sarah and then back at her son.

"Mother, you remember Sarah Peterson?" Max said as he closed the front door. "Her family lived next door to Gramma Karen. She and Grace were good friends."

It was clear that the woman had no memory of her whatsoever. Sarah stepped forward and offered her a handshake. "It's so very nice to see you again, Mrs. Wolzak."

"Marilyn—please," Max's mother replied. "My mother-in-law is Mrs. Wolzak in this house." She studied Sarah for a long moment and then turned to Max and arched one perfectly shaped eyebrow. Evidently she was waiting for further explanation for Sarah's presence.

Just then Molly raced in from the kitchen. "Sarah! Finally. Gramma Karen has made a bazillion cookies, but Nana is here now and that gives us an extra pair of hands—that's what Gramma Karen says anyway."

She looked at her grandmother with the critical eye of a seven-year-old. "You'd better put on an apron," she said, "and flat shoes. I'll get your slippers." She took off then, bounding up the curved stairway.

Sarah noticed that Max was having difficulty hiding a smile.

"Do not laugh at the child, Maxwell," his mother instructed. "It only encourages her rambunctious behavior."

A man—an older version of Max—stepped into the front hall. "Hello," he said, and Sarah immediately liked the way his eyes twinkled with interest and curiosity. He stuck out his hand. "I'm Mike Wolzak, and you are . . . "

"Sarah Peterson," she replied, accepting his firm, warm handshake. "My family lived—"

"Next door to my folks—I remember. You and Gracie used to play together before we moved. It's nice to see you again, Sarah."

"Michael, did you speak to your mother?"

"I did. I said, 'Hi Mom, we're home for Christmas,' and snatched a cookie." He actually winked at Sarah.

"Dad's going to the game with Jack and me, Mother," Max said. "Molly has apparently scheduled you and the rest of the females to decorate a bazillion Christmas cookies."

Marilyn Wolzak frowned. "I don't know why Karen is so late making her cookies this year. How on earth is she expecting to get them distributed by Christmas? I mean we have the Christmas Eve party for your father's partners to prepare, and Rosanna is going to need all the kitchen space just to put that together, never mind preparing for our open house on Christmas Day and . . . "

"We've given Rosanna the rest of the week off," Max said.

"We?"

"Me, Gracie, and Gramma Karen. And the plans for this year have changed, Mom."

"Grace was telling me all about Molly's party for the homeless people," Max's father said, ignoring the fact that not only did his wife seem to be speechless, she looked as if she might need to sit down.

"Are you all right, Mrs.—Marilyn?" Sarah asked, glancing around for a chair or bench just in case the woman actually felt faint.

Max's mother ignored her. "But people will expect . . . "

"We'll still have the open house. We'll just do it in a new venue. Instead of coming here for the open house, we'll tell them to go to the church."

"But—"

Mike Wolzak put his arm around his wife's shoulders. Gently and tenderly he spoke to her now as if they were alone. "Come on,

Marilyn. Molly has planned this whole thing. I, for one, am glad to see a kid thinking about something besides what she might find under the tree on Christmas morning. Let's get on board and give her our full support, okay?"

"I suppose one year won't matter."

"That's my girl," Mike said and gave her bottom a slight slap.

Marilyn blushed but she did not chastise him or pull away. Molly appeared at the top of the stairs. "Nana? I can't find your slippers. Will these do?" She held up a pair of lime green flip-flops with rhinestone flamingoes etched into the straps.

"Those will do just fine, darling girl," Mike said. "Bring them here." He led his wife to a bench upholstered in rich burgundy brocade. Once she was seated, he bent on one knee and carefully removed her high heels. Then, chuckling the whole time, he placed one ridiculous flip-flop and then the other on her bare feet. "Perfect fit," he murmured. "Just like Cinderella."

"Just like us," she murmured.

He kissed her then, and Sarah found the whole scene so very touching that she had to look away. She also had to wonder why Max was frowning.

* * * * *

On Christmas Eve morning, Max woke early. He was nervous— not about the concert but about the conversation he had decided to have with Sarah. Obviously he couldn't ask her at this late date to abandon her work and the trip overseas. But he had decided that what he could ask was if she felt as he did that there was a chance they might have a future together. If she agreed the possibility existed, then he would use all his time while she was away to get his life as a civilian back on track, so when she returned . . .

But what if she did not agree? Grace had confided that Sarah had once been badly burned in the romance department. He also knew that he'd never met anyone more dedicated to her work than Sarah. How could they build something together if she was always pulled away by work? Besides, she had been the one to lay out the ground rules—the boundaries—for their relationship. *"Just friendship."*

In the kitchen below his room, he heard sounds of cabinets opening and closing and water running. He checked the clock. Too early for Rosanna to arrive. Maybe Gramma Karen was the one making the coffee—the scent that now drifted up the back stairs to his room. Gramma Karen had always been the person he turned to at times like this, and with his parents still sleeping, this might be the perfect time to seek her advice. He got up, pulled on jeans and a T-shirt, and walked barefoot down to the kitchen.

To his surprise, it was his dad rustling around.

"Good morning," Max said.

"'Morning, son. Do you have any idea where we keep the sweetener?"

"I think it's the loose stuff in the sugar bowl." Max poured himself a cup of coffee and sat down at the table. "You still on Paris time?"

His dad chuckled. "That and I need to get to the office. Couple of projects that won't wait until after the holidays."

Max watched as his father added cream and sweetener to his mug of coffee. He was about to make some excuse and take his coffee back to his room when his dad surprised him by quietly asking, "So what's the plan, Max?"

"Well, the concert is at four and—"

"Not for the day. For your future—your civilian future, I hope."

"I'm not going back, Dad." He was a little taken aback to realize that indeed he was firm on his decision not to reenlist a fourth time.

"Good. Your mother and grandmother will both be relieved to hear that." He took a long time stirring his coffee before adding, "Where does Sarah fit into the picture?"

"She's . . . We . . . " Max shrugged. "I'm not exactly sure. We've been spending a lot of time together. It started out as just a way to get Grace and Gramma Karen off my back about how I was handling the holidays. But then . . . "

His dad grinned. "Yeah. That's kind of the way things went when your mother and I hooked up. She'd been getting some threats from a stalker and her dad wanted to hire your grandfather as her body guard. Dad offered me as the person for the job instead. I was just finishing up my degree, and the very last thing I was looking for was a relationship, but the money was great and I knew it would give me a head start on paying off those student loans."

"And the rest was history."

Dad laughed. "Well, eventually. Suffice it to say your mother was furious with her father. She called me her incredible hulk of a babysitter. But then over time . . . "

"Too much info, Dad," Max protested.

"No, hear me out. Once we realized that we had this chemistry, the real problem became that your mom was raised possibly the most class-conscious person I had ever run into. She actually thought loving me was wrong—that it couldn't possibly work out because of the differences in our backgrounds. I told her we should just go with the flow, but she thought her parents—especially her father—would lock her away in a convent if he thought there was anything going on with us. So we played this game—acted like we could barely tolerate each other whenever he was around."

"And when he wasn't?"

"Magic, pure magic." His dad sipped his coffee. "So you and Sarah? Is that magic? 'Cause I gotta tell you, son, if a girl like that comes along, you do not want to let her go."

She's going anyway. "Day after tomorrow she's off to Syria for six months on a relief mission. The timing doesn't work."

"Make it work. You of all people know how fragile and unpredictable life can be. The fact is that your mother was saying just last night how for once you seem almost content to be back home. She also believes that Sarah might have played an important role in that."

"I would hardly think that Sarah Peterson would be her choice for me." He immediately regretted the snide comment. "Sorry, but you know what I mean. Mom can be a little . . . "

"Max, you were little more than a kid when you enlisted—a teenager who was finding himself and thought his parents were boring and impossible. Practically from the day we left Brooklyn, you blamed your mother."

"Yeah. You've got a point."

His dad stood up but then lingered at the table for a moment. "Well, you're not that kid anymore. You've pretty much been absent from the family for over a decade now. It's time you stopped looking at your mother through the eyes of that angry boy and appreciated the fact that I was the one behind our move to this part of town. Mostly because I wanted to impress her parents. So how about considering that she didn't have great role models for parenting like I did and cut her some slack?"

He stood for a long moment staring out the kitchen window before continuing. "She loves you, Max—you and Grace. Grace knows that and accepts that your mom's always done the best she could as a parent. Try letting her into your life some and you just might be surprised." He carried his mug to the sink, dumped the last of the coffee, and rinsed out the mug, then he grasped Max's shoulder. "Got to get to work. Good to have you home, son."

Max watched his father climb the stairs. He couldn't help noticing that the man was a step slower than he remembered, and he felt the passage—and the wasting—of time.

* * * * *

The small church near Sarah's loft was packed for the concert. Sarah waved to Grace and Jack and Molly as they hurried down the center aisle to claim seats in the pews that had been reserved for family of the choir members. Then she saw Max escorting his grandmother down the aisle and was surprised to see his parents following. So they had come after all. She wondered if his mother's change of heart pleased him. Marilyn Wolzak had insisted on the need to stand with tradition at least in terms of Christmas Eve dinner with her husband's business partners. Yet here she was.

Sarah watched Max make his way upstream against more people crowding in to fill the pews. He glanced up at her and smiled. Next to her she heard Mary breathe a sigh of relief.

"He's late," she muttered, "but he's here."

"He is not late," Sarah insisted. "And stop worrying. Everything is going to be fine." But she understood Mary's case of nerves. In the end, Frank Stover had declined to sing the solo and others in the choir had suggested Max. He'd reluctantly agreed. The solo—an a capella rendering of the opening words to "O Holy Night"—would start the evening's performance. This had been Ned's last-minute suggestion, and everyone had agreed the idea was inspired. The sound of one voice singing without accompaniment would quiet the audience and set the tone for the entire concert. And at concert's end, everyone— choir and congregation—would raise their voices in song.

Max ran up the narrow stairway and squeezed into his place in the front row. "Show time," he said softly as he grinned at Mary and Ned.

Below them two children moved to the altar, each carrying a lit candle that they used to light a single larger candle situated on a tall stand below a beautiful stained glass window depicting the Nativity. A hush fell over the audience and Max stood, waiting for the signal from Mary.

There was a marked difference in the sound now that the church was filled with people. Max's lone voice seemed to resound through-out the space, and Sarah wondered if this was what Scripture meant when it spoke of the voices of the angels resounding throughout the hillsides that holy night so long ago. She felt a tear trickle down her cheek as Max sang, "It is the night of the dear Savior's birth."

Now the whole choir joined him in singing the remainder of the beloved carol, and when they had finished there was a moment of silence that rang throughout the church almost as powerfully as the music had. After that, the time seemed to fly by as they performed song after song until they reached the finale—"Silent Night." While the choir hummed the tune, the children came forward once again and lit tapers from that center candle. Everyone attending had been given a small candle upon entering the church. Now, one by one, neighbor turned to neighbor to pass the light until the whole church glowed with the light of their candles.

As the soft light spread throughout the darkened church, Mary made her way down from the loft and up to the front of the sanctuary, where she invited all to join in the singing of the much-loved carol. During the last verse, the entire choir filed down the choir loft stairs to the main floor, where they stood along the aisles as Ned moved from "Silent Night" to "Joy to the World." Then the choir members led those in the audience from the church, still carrying their lit candles as they gathered on the steps of the church and let their voices fill the cold night air reaching out to everyone in the neighborhood.

Above them Sarah saw windows raised as people leaned out and joined in. Patrons from those restaurants and other businesses that were still open crowded in doorways and pressed against shop windows to enjoy the moment. Sarah knew that if Mary and Ned had their way, a soft snow would begin falling, but above them the skies were clear and filled with stars—a much better setting to Sarah's way of thinking.

They sang the last verse of the carol and then extinguished their candles as in unison they all shouted, "Merry Christmas!"

Sarah blew out her candle and turned, surrounded by the excited chatter of others. Max was standing right behind her. Their eyes met and she realized that for the first time since they had begun seeing each other, his had lost that haunted look of a man who had been too long in a world of pain and misery. In his eyes she saw joy . . . and hope.

She reached up and cupped his cheek, and he caught her hand in his and pressed a kiss to her palm. In that moment she understood why she had been feeling so out of sorts and disoriented about leaving on the latest relief mission. She did not want to leave Max—ever.

Chapter Seven

. . . .

After the concert, Max's parents went back home to host their dinner party while everyone else in the family headed uptown to yet another church to set up for Molly's party. The minister, Stan Baker, had agreed they could come in following his congregation's Christmas Eve service and reception to get everything ready for the following day. To Sarah's delight, several members of Stan Baker's congregation stayed to help and told her they planned to return the following day with family and friends to assist with the party as well.

The men arranged tables and chairs as the women organized the kitchen for the meal they would serve their guests. They had decided on a kind of turkey stew since they had no way of knowing how many people might show up, and with stew they could stretch the donated food as far as possible.

"Loaves and fishes," Grace said.

"More like biscuits and turkey stew," Jack teased.

They had decided to bake the biscuits ahead of time and then warm them up for the meal. Meanwhile Molly and a few of her friends were filling small cellophane bags with cookies, a peppermint stick, and an orange. These would be the favors each guest would receive. In addition, there were large plastic bins of decorated cookies, which would be served with scoops of vanilla ice cream for dessert. The ice cream had been Max's idea, and Sarah smiled, knowing that if he had his way, the confection would have included a ladle filled with hot fudge. But his grandmother had squelched that idea.

"For the money you might spend on hot fudge—even if we made it ourselves—you can give them a small token. Something they can keep as a reminder of this night."

"Like what, Gramma?" Molly had asked.

"I don't know—something that they can look at and remember."

"I'll take care of it," Max assured her, and now as she worked alongside the other women, Sarah could not help but wonder what he had come up with. He certainly was being mysterious about it.

"The place is beginning to look like a party," Max said as he came into the kitchen carrying more bins of his grandmother's cookies. "Where do you want these?"

They were running out of counter space, so Sarah pointed to a table in the corner. "Stack them there. Tomorrow we can fill the platters from them and store the empty containers under the table."

He did as she directed, then instead of heading back out into the community hall, he lingered. "When we finish up here, are you up for a walk?"

"Sure, but aren't you wiped out after the concert and now this? And what about your family? It is Christmas Eve after all."

"My parents' dinner with the partners will go until well past midnight, and the truth is I'd like to spend some time with you." He glanced out toward the community hall, where Mary and Ned were putting up more decorations. "Unless you have plans . . . I mean, you're right—it is Christmas Eve and most people have their traditions and . . . "

Sarah smiled. "I'll call my parents tomorrow. Mary and Ned are catching the last train to Westport tonight to be with their family. Besides, I thought we were all about starting new traditions, thanks to Molly," she said with a wave of her hand to encompass all the preparations for the next day's party. "I would love to take a walk with you."

"I think we've done about all we can do before tomorrow," Grace announced. "Shall we call it a night? I know one little girl who needs to get to sleep if she expects Santa to come calling." She ruffled Molly's hair.

"Ah, Mom, it's early."

"Get your jacket," Grace said, and then she turned to Max. "Jack and I will take Gramma Karen home. I mean, I figure you and Sarah . . . " She actually winked at her brother.

"Thanks. See you tomorrow, okay?" He leaned in and kissed his sister's cheek. "Merry Christmas, Gracie."

"I think it just might be a special one," she replied. "For all of us." This time she winked at Sarah and then laughed as she hurried to the exit.

Once everyone had left and Sarah and Max were alone on the deserted street, she suddenly felt shy. "What a beautiful clear night," she said, gazing up at the stars just visible between the high-rise apartment buildings surrounding them.

"Ready to head downtown?"

"You mean walk all the way to Chelsea from here?"

"That's kind of the plan. I figure we can always catch a cab if one of us decides she's not up to the hike."

They were standing near a lamppost, and she read clearly the challenge in his grin. "You are on, buster." She was already several steps ahead of him when he caught up to her, took hold of her hand, and spun her so that she ended up in his arms.

"Truth is, Sarah, I don't care if we walk or not. I just wanted to have some time with you—without an entourage—either yours or mine."

"I'd like that." She placed both hands flat against his chest, and it seemed the most normal thing in the world to kiss him. He tightened his embrace, and she wrapped her arms around his neck. The kiss seemed to last forever and at the same time be over far too soon. She knew that once she was half a world away she would treasure this moment. "Now that's what I call a Christmas present," she said when the kiss ended.

He took her hand in his, and they started walking. The streets were pretty much empty. Both of them were silent for several blocks, and yet her head resounded with the one thing she wanted so desperately to ask him. She had just worked up her courage to form the words when he spoke.

"I read all the stuff you gave me about the relief mission and the job, but I can't come with you, Sarah. It's too soon, and I can't shake the idea that if ever I went back it would be to help those buddies still over there in the thick of things. I'm sorry."

Her heart felt as if it were breaking. She'd guessed that this might be his decision, and to that end she had placed a notice for the position with no results. She'd told herself that she understood. But now that the words were spoken she felt only sadness. "It's all right," she hurried to speak before he could say anything more. She wasn't sure why, but deep in her heart she felt that allowing him to try to keep explaining would only make things worse. Because it wasn't all right at all. She had allowed herself to imagine them working side by side, helping people make a better life for themselves and their children. She had allowed herself to believe that they could build a future not only for others but for themselves. She had allowed herself to fall in love with him.

* * * * *

Nothing was going the way Max had planned. He had so carefully rehearsed what he would say to Sarah. How six months wasn't that long, and while she was overseas he would get settled into a civilian life—a civilian job so that when she returned they could be together. He had allowed himself not only to rehearse what he would say but what she would answer. *"It's all right"* had not been in the script. *"It's all right"* sounded like she thought this was nothing more than him turning down a job she'd suggested. *"It's all right"* did not in any way indicate feelings—the kind of deep forever feelings he had begun to have for her.

It was an ironic twist on their past. After that first date when the towers had been hit and he'd gone without hesitation to enlist, Sarah had been the one he had called first. Before telling his parents or Grace or even Gramma Karen, he had called her. Why? Because he had been sure that she would understand—and she had. Now she was the one going off to save the world. He had allowed himself to imagine that she would plead with him to come with her, or better yet that she would tell him she would stay. He had allowed himself to imagine that she felt what he did—that she loved him so much that she could not imagine six months without him. And yet he had also known that she had a commitment— a duty to her work that it would be unfair of him to try and change. That's why he had decided to play the whole thing the way he had. He had it all worked out in his mind, but now his doubts nearly overwhelmed him.

He shoved his free hand in his pocket and felt the small jeweler's box he was carrying. Inside it was something he had ordered at the same time he ordered the tokens for the attendees at the party. It was a pendant on a silver chain that he'd decided to give to Sarah so she would always remember the day—and wear until they could be together again. He had taken the idea from what Gramma Karen had said about something for the homeless people—something they could touch and remember. But he had to face facts. He and Sarah were not at all on the same page. Her life was light years ahead of his in terms of friends and work she loved. His life was up for grabs. Was he so desperate to find someplace—someone—to change that? It wasn't fair to Sarah to expect that simply because he'd walked back into her life after all these years those feelings she might have had for him when they were in high school would still be intact.

He was an idiot. This was the way Sarah lived her life— seeing people in need and trying to help. She had obviously thought that by offering him the position on the relief team she was doing him a favor, giving him a purpose. *"Just friendship"* had been her only ground rule. But in his imagination he had taken things several steps beyond that. He didn't blame her. She was just being Sarah. After all, she had built an entire career—her entire life—around helping others find their way.

"Max? About the opening on the relief team . . . I mean, I just thought . . . Well, you'd be perfect, but I get it that it's too soon. I'm sorry if it felt like I was pressuring you. You don't need that right now."

"Thanks for understanding," he managed and then started scanning the street for a cab. "You know, I'm not sure this was my best idea—walking for miles. It's late and we've both got a full day tomorrow, plus it's getting colder." He spotted a cab, hailed it, and held the door open for her.

Her expression was one of confusion, but she got in and scooted to the far side, leaving room for him. Instead he handed the driver enough money for the fare to her place. Then he took hold of her hand and squeezed it. "Merry Christmas, Sarah. See you tomorrow." He closed the door, knowing the cabbie would take off at once, and then he stood in the middle of the street watching until the red taillights disappeared. "Wolzak, you're a total jerk," he muttered as he headed for home, his hand in his pocket clutching the small box.

* * * * *

What just happened?

For the second time Max had simply walked away. His actions were almost as confusing to her as her feelings for him were. She knew exactly why she had thought of him to fill the vacancy on her team. Two reasons: one, he knew the area and the intricacies of the various groups they'd be dealing with, and two, it was the only solution she could come up with to keep him in her life while she did her job. Reason number two had been primary, although she had not allowed herself to admit that until tonight.

Okay, so she had fallen for the guy—again. But this was no high school crush. What she felt for him now was the real deal. But as had been their history, their lives were on parallel tracks. Back then, he had been the one to follow the call of duty. Now she had to go and, for now at least, he needed to stay until he could figure out his next steps. Maybe when she returned in six months . . .

Sarah barely paid attention to the ride as the cabbie barreled down streets and avenues on his way to the address that Max had given him. She stared out the window, but the passing traffic and neighborhoods were little more than a blur. As they neared her building, she tapped the barrier separating her from the driver.

"Anywhere here is fine," she said. She pulled a five-dollar bill from her pocket in spite of the fact that Max had already paid the driver. "Merry Christmas," she said, handing him the tip as she got out.

"You okay, miss?"

The cabbie had rolled down his window and was looking at her with a worried frown. He was older with wispy white hair. He was wearing a faded red jacket. It was Christmas Eve, and her driver looked like Santa. Sarah smiled. "Just need to think," she said.

"Church back a couple of blocks looked like it was open for midnight services," he suggested. "Want me to take you back? No charge."

She smiled. "No. I'll be fine walking. Thanks, though. It's the perfect place."

She'd passed the old church many times, always admiring the way the light from inside illuminated the beautiful windows after dark. She'd already spent most of her Christmas Eve in churches, so why not this one? Only this time, instead of performing with a choir or setting up for a Christmas Day party, she could just be still and wait for her jumbled thoughts to settle. She could find her way again.

Inside, the sanctuary was crowded, and Sarah squeezed into a seat in the last row of pews. There was no choir or minister retelling the Christmas story. Someone was playing the organ very softly, as if to avoid disturbing those who had come. Around and across from her Sarah saw everyone had their heads bowed, so she bowed hers as well and waited for the prayers to come—prayers of thanksgiving for the many blessings in her life, prayers of request for the safety and good health and happiness of those near and dear to her, and prayers of wonder that she had been given this time with Max and Grace and little Molly.

Never had she dreamed that her very best present this Christmas would be a reunion with her childhood friend and the chance to reconnect with Karen Wolzak who had been like a second mother to her. Never had it occurred to her that this was the Christmas when she might fall in love.

I do love him, heavenly Father. I don't know what Your plan for us might be, but You have shown me how to love again—truly love without condition, and I am so very grateful for that.

It was true. The one reality that Sarah understood was that life came with no guarantees. The very fact that she had had this time with Max was indeed a blessing in itself. She would not ask for more.

The music had stopped, and for several minutes the church was completely quiet except for the occasional cough or rustling as someone shifted positions. Then a man near the front of the church turned to his neighbor and shook hands. "Merry Christmas," he said, speaking in a normal voice. That set off a chain reaction, as throughout the crowded sanctuary people greeted one another. Soon the church that had been so still just minutes before was alive with laughter and conversation. She shook hands and greeted those around her and then slipped quietly out to the street, the light from the church spilling over the sidewalk through the open doors.

Above her the stars were visible because in this part of the city most buildings were dark at night. Behind her the church bells chimed out twelve rings.

It was Christmas Day.

* * * * *

Christmas morning was chaotic at the Wolzak house. Grace, Jack, and Molly arrived early for the family's traditional gift-opening and breakfast. Mike took over the kitchen, where once they were all gathered around the table, he would turn out slices of his trademark eggnog French toast until the orders stopped coming.

"Help your mother cut up the fruit," Max's dad instructed. "She wants to talk to you about something. And play nice, okay? Don't get your guard up before you even know what's coming."

"Occupational hazard," Max muttered. He picked up a paring knife and moved to the other end of the large kitchen island. It occurred to him that the only time he'd ever seen his mother wearing an apron was on Christmas morning. "Need some help?"

She held out a mango. "I may live to be an old woman, but I will never understand how you cut one of these things without throwing two-thirds of it away. Here, you try. I'm much better with strawberries."

"Watch and learn," Max said as he set the fruit on the cutting board with its stem down. "Now, set your knife about a quarter inch from the center and cut straight down." He demonstrated then handed her the knife. "You do the other side."

"Here?" She positioned the knife.

"Perfect. Now slice."

The smile his mother gave him when her half of the fruit fell away was radiant. "Now what?"

"Okay, now turn your piece on its back—skin side down and cut into the flesh but not all the way through the skin."

She followed his lead. "You make it look so easy." She watched him turn his piece a half turn and cut horizontal rows until he had a checkerboard pattern. She did the same.

"And now you simply flip it, push the skin in so the fruit pops out, and either scoop out the fruit with a spoon or separate it from the skin with the tip of your knife."

"Oh, Maxie, where on earth did you ever learn to do this?" She picked up a second mango and began the process again. She had not called him by his childhood name in years.

"I had a buddy who grew up in Florida—he taught me. He was a terrific cook—very inventive." He realized that this was probably more information about his military friends than he had ever before shared with his parents.

His mother concentrated on the mango and then very softly she asked, "Is he, this friend, did he . . . ?"

"No, Mom. He died. Stepped on a landmine."

"I'm sorry . . . for your loss. He was obviously important to you."

Max did not know what to say so he concentrated on capping strawberries instead.

"Is Sarah important to you, Max?"

Okay, did not see that coming. "She's . . . It's good to have her back in our lives—mine and Grace's." *And speaking of landmines.*

"Grace seems to believe that it's more than just the return of an old friend. So does your father."

"Sarah's leaving tomorrow for her next assignment. She'll be gone for six months."

Having cut up the second mango, his mother turned her attention to rinsing and sorting through blueberries. But suddenly she grew very still as the water ran over her fingers and the colander filled with the berries. And then to Max's shock he saw that she was crying.

"Mom? Mother?" His hand hovered close to her shoulder. With anyone else—Grace or Gramma Karen or especially Sarah—he would have wrapped his arm around her and comforted her until she revealed the source of her tears. But this was his mother, who had resisted open displays of affection her entire life.

She batted impatiently at her tears with the back of one hand and only succeeded in splashing more water on her face. Max glanced back, hoping his father would notice what was happening, but he'd left the kitchen. They were alone, and Max saw no sign of reinforcement coming.

"Mom, tell me what's wrong. Dad said you wanted to talk to me." A horrible thought struck him. "Are you ill, Mom? Is there . . . "

She shook her head vehemently and then placed her wet palm against his cheek. "The only thing I ever wanted, Max, was for you and Grace to be happy. Grace has found her happiness with Jack. But you . . . you still seem so lost, and I don't know how to help you find your way."

Relief flooded through him, and it hit him how terrified he had been of the mere thought that his mother might have some deadly disease. "Hey, I'm all grown up, and it's not for you to—"

"Hear me out," she interrupted. "First, let's get one thing straight—I do not judge others based on their social or economic backgrounds. It's true that my parents tend toward that sort of thing, but I don't. Is that understood?"

Max actually felt himself blushing as he nodded.

"Good. Second, if Sarah is the one for you, then for heaven's sake, son, do not let her just walk away. I know she has a job to do and I respect her for her dedication, but there have to be some ground rules here—why are you smiling? This is no laughing matter, Max."

"I'm smiling at your use of the term 'ground rules.' It's an inside joke between Sarah and me."

"Well, that's a start at least."

"So what are the ground rules as you see them?"

"Sarah clearly cannot abandon her work. And Grace tells me that for whatever reason, you have turned down Sarah's offer for you to fill a vacancy on her team and go with her. But, son, you must stay in touch—and I mean in close touch. Surely in the six months she's over there she will have some breaks, so you meet her in Paris or Rome or Venice or . . . "

Max's grin spread even wider. In his mother's world, everything could be solved by a trip to Paris . . . and he realized that he loved her for that simple naïveté. "It is what it is, Mom," he said as he wrapped his arms around her. "It will be what it will be. God's will be done. Isn't that what you always taught us?"

His mother frowned but did not pull away from his affection. "Well, hopefully I never taught you to simply sit on the sidelines," she replied. "God expects us to do our part, so you'll speak to Sarah?"

"I will. I will text and e-mail and phone and—"

"I mean today."

"And say what, Mom?"

"What you feel for her. Be honest about that. Did you buy her a gift?"

"Not exactly." He thought about the jeweler's box.

"Oh my goodness. Here," she said as she dried her hands on her apron and then handed him the gold bangle bracelet she was wearing.

Max took hold of her wrist and replaced the bracelet. "Thanks, Mom—truly. And not just for the bracelet. I just realized that I have something else that might be perfect."

"Good. Now go tell your father that it's time to start making the French toast, or we'll never eat." She patted his cheek and dumped the drained blueberries in with the rest of the fruit then tossed the mixture lightly before taking the dish to the dining room.

Max watched her go. His dad had been so right. He'd held a grudge for far too long and had missed really getting to know this woman who had just admitted that her best Christmas gift would be his happiness.

Chapter Eight

Sarah was at the church basement early. She wanted to be sure that everything was ready, and someone had to get the coffee started and the stew simmering. Even so, she was not the first to arrive. The church organist was at his post playing a concert of carols that were broadcast to the outside and accompanied at intervals by the ringing of the church bells. Upstairs in the sanctuary, people had already begun to fill the pews to wait for the service that would start at four and precede the meal and party downstairs. It was amazing how Molly's simple idea had blossomed as the minister, his staff, and several members of the congregation pitched in to help and offer more ideas.

In a couple of hours, the hall would be filled with their guests sitting at tables, singing carols, joining in some simple word games that Molly had insisted were part of any party, and enjoying their Christmas dinner. By sundown it would all be over, and tomorrow she would be packing up the last of her things and preparing to head for the airport. It seemed like only yesterday that she and Max had started seeing each other. Yet in some ways it felt as if she and Max had always had a connection, even in all the years when she doubted either one of them had given much thought to the other.

The outside entrance to the basement opened, bringing with it a blast of cold fresh air as Molly announced, "We're here! And guess what, Sarah!"

"What?"

"My bestest Christmas present? I'm getting a baby sister—or maybe a brother." She didn't seem too sure about the idea of a brother.

Sarah looked up as Grace and Jack entered the room followed by Marilyn and Mike, Marilyn's parents, Karen Wolzak, and finally Max. "Is it true?" Sarah whispered as she relieved Grace of a box of supplies.

"It's true," Grace replied, cradling the bump below her waist.

Molly clapped her hands to gain everyone's attention and started handing out assignments. "Dad, you and Uncle Max are the greeters. Nana, Marilyn, and Papa Mike, you can serve along with Mom and Sarah. Gramma Karen will be in charge in the kitchen."

"And you?" Max asked.

"I'll float around and make sure everything is going exactly as we planned." She did a little twirl and then grinned. "Do you like my outfit, Sarah?" She turned to show off the green velvet dress over white tights and black patent shoes.

"Very festive," Sarah agreed.

"You look pretty too—doesn't she, Uncle Max?"

And there it was, the unmistakable moment when they had to make eye contact for the first time since their parting the night before. "She always looks beautiful, Molly." His eyes locked on her face, and yet she could not read his thoughts any more clearly than she had been able to the night before.

Molly heaved a sigh. "Well, I know that, Max, but today is special."

Max glanced at his niece and then back at Sarah. "That's a lovely dress, Sarah," he said and then checked with Molly for her approval.

"Better—not great," she said, rolling her eyes at Sarah as if between the two of them they understood that boys in general were clueless. Then she headed for the kitchen, calling out to her mother to come help her with the cookies and leaving Sarah and Max standing alone in the church hall.

Above them the organ music flourished into the prelude for the service.

"Looks like Molly's got everything under control down here," Max said. "I was thinking I'd like to attend the service. Would you like to come with me?"

Sarah accepted his invitation for the olive branch that it was. "Love to," she said.

Upstairs they took seats in the last pew closest to the exit. Sarah was both surprised and touched to see so many people filling the church. Not all of them were homeless, she realized as she watched whole families enter the sanctuary and take their seats. Furthermore the street people had clearly made every effort to look their best for the occasion. A woman next to Sarah wore a pillbox hat reminiscent of Jackie Kennedy's style and a pair of white cotton gloves. In front of them sat three men of various ages, all with that ruddy look and damp hair of the recently showered.

Reverend Baker had just called for the congregation to rise for the first hymn. Max opened the hymnal to the page and held the book so that he and Sarah could share. It was only natural to move a step closer to him. Their shoulders touched as Max balanced the hymnal on one large open palm and placed his other hand loosely around her waist.

Following the hymn, the minister called for a moment of friendship. The street people looked a little confused until they saw members of the congregation turning to one another to greet them. The three men in front of Max and Sarah turned and offered tentative smiles. Max stuck out his hand as Sarah turned to greet the woman on her right. And suddenly there were no strangers in the gathering. Everyone was exchanging a handshake or a wish for a merry Christmas until Reverend Baker tapped the pulpit to call everyone back to worship.

The friendship ritual was followed by a period of silent prayer that ended with the Lord's Prayer and then a second hymn. And as the service progressed, Sarah felt her heart swell with gladness and hope. Gladness that she was a part of this incredible moment. Hope for the futures of these desperate people. It seemed the most natural thing in the world for her to take hold of Max's hand. He linked his fingers with hers, and they stayed that way until the sermon ended and the last hymn was announced.

"We should go," Sarah whispered, nodding toward the stairway, and as they made their way back down to the church hall they were still holding hands.

* * * * *

Max was more confused than ever about his feelings for Sarah—and hers for him. It felt so right being with her. He started to pull her aside when they reached the downstairs hallway that led to the kitchen, but Molly spotted them and came running. "Uncle Max, did you bring the presents?"

"I did. They are all wrapped up and in that shoebox over there, but you are not to touch it, understood? There are some parts of this event where you are not in charge, okay?" He tweaked her nose the way he used to tweak her mother's and got the exact same reaction.

Molly giggled and pulled away. "Stop that."

In the meantime he had lost the moment with Sarah. She was in the kitchen laughing with Gramma Karen and the church ladies. She was wearing an apron over the blue dress that matched her eyes, and as always she looked completely at home in her surroundings.

Her surroundings that by this time a couple of days from now will be vastly different.

"Hey, man. Max, was it?" One of the men from the pew in front of them tapped him on the shoulder. "I'm Glen."

"I remember. How can I help you, Glen?"

"Just wanted to thank you and your missus for everything you're doing here today. We all get it that this is a one-time deal, but you have no idea what it means to us. So thanks, okay?"

Before Max could say anything or correct the notion that Sarah was his "missus" Glen moved away quickly, pulling out a crumpled bandana handkerchief to blow his nose as he made his way back to the table where his friends were waiting. Just then Reverend Baker moved to the front of the room and clapped his hands for attention. "Let us pray," he said and then uttered words of thanks for the food and the day and especially for Molly.

And a little child shall lead them, Max found himself thinking.

When the prayer ended, the minister raised his head, smiled broadly, and said, "Well, folks, shall we get this party started?"

For the next couple of hours, the hall was alive with conversation, laughter, and the smells of fresh evergreens and wonderful food. The street people took to Molly's games—which her mother and Max had thought might bomb—as if they were having the time of their lives. When the woman who had sat next to Sarah during the service began playing the piano, everyone gathered around for a songfest of popular songs of the season—"Rudolph" and "Frosty" and "Jingle Bells" . . . they sang them all. And Max and Sarah just naturally seemed to find their way to each other's side.

As the group started the verse for "Let It Snow," it was obvious that the weather outside had indeed turned frightful. There was no snow. Instead it was a downpour of cold rain that seemed to have set in for the evening.

"We can't send them out in this," Sarah said softly.

"Maybe by the time we serve dessert and coffee and give out the presents . . . " Gramma Karen suggested.

"The weather report is for this to keep up all night and well into tomorrow," Max said. "Let me see what I can do."

Gramma Karen looked at him as if he had suddenly lost his mind. "About the weather? Max, I really don't think—"

"About them," Max corrected as he nodded toward their guests.

He signaled for Reverend Baker and one or two of the church elders to join him in the kitchen. When Sarah followed them, Max had to smile. The woman was not to be denied when it came to taking care of those less fortunate . . . it was one of the reasons he loved her.

* * * * *

Sarah heard the end of Max's question to the church leaders and could not believe her ears.

" . . . shelter them for the night right here?"

The responses from the elders were immediate—and negative. The words *precedent* and *liability* were the centerpieces of their arguments. She did notice that Reverend Baker maintained his silence as he listened to each speaker.

"But to send them out in that downpour," Max argued. "It's almost like telling them this whole event has been nothing more than a show."

"Hey, plenty of people here gave up their own Christmas Day for this," one man argued. "If those people expect—"

Sarah stepped into the fray. "*Those people* were invited here, sir. They came with no expectations and they leave with none."

"And you are?"

"This is Sarah Peterson," Max said. "She works for the United Nations leading relief missions around the world. If anyone knows about situations like this one it's Sarah, so I suggest we listen to what she has to say."

With the spotlight fully on her, Sarah took a moment to send up a silent prayer for the right words to persuade them. "I fully appreciate your concerns," she began. "What if we agreed to stay overnight and monitor the street people? What if we took full responsibility?"

"Who is 'we'?" the other elder asked.

"The organizers of this event. Myself, Max here, and his family." She risked a glance at Max and was relieved to see him nod. "We can work in shifts so that someone you trust is awake through the night. Then first thing tomorrow the people will leave."

"Rain or no rain?" The man who had been the biggest critic of the idea actually seemed to be considering Sarah's idea.

"Those will be the ground rules," she agreed and saw Max smother a smile.

"There are no cots or sleeping bags," Reverend Baker pointed out.

"But there are chairs—straight-backed of course, but three of them lined up would make a cot as comfortable as any park bench," Max said. "And I expect this wouldn't be the first night these folks have slept on a hard floor."

The minister looked at the two elders. "I know it's unusual, but it is what we are about, isn't it? Helping those less fortunate?"

Just then Molly poked her head in through the half-closed door. "Uncle Max," she said in a stage whisper, "it's time for the presents."

"Coming," Max said before turning back to the church leaders. "So, what's the decision?"

One by one, the three men nodded. "You folks get yourselves organized for staying the night," Reverend Baker instructed. "Then I'll make the announcement and lay down the rules."

"Sounds like a plan." Max waited for the three men to leave the room before laying out a schedule. "I'll ask my folks to take the first shift say until eight while Jack and Grace get Gramma Karen and Molly home. Then, how about you and I cover eight to midnight and then—"

"You should be with your family, Max," Sarah protested. "I can do this, and Mary and Ned will be back later tonight. I'll call them to come straight here."

"I would like to do this, Sarah. More to the point, I would like to do this with you, okay?" He tucked a strand of her hair behind her ear.

"Okay."

"Uncle Max, are you coming or not?" Molly was standing in the doorway, hands on her hips.

"Coming."

* * * * *

There were thirty attendees at the party. To be on the safe side, Max had ordered three dozen of the tokens. The shop had gift-wrapped each one in a small, square, white box tied with a red bow. "Ladies and gentlemen!" Max shouted above the lively conversation filling the hall. "We're coming to the end of our festivities here for this evening. But it wouldn't be Christmas without gifts, so your hosts wanted to be sure you had something to carry with you that would remind you of this day—remind you that someone cared, that a seven-year-old girl was far more interested in making sure that you had a good day than she was in anything Santa might have left under her tree."

All around the room he saw people nodding and smiling and craning their necks to see Molly. Someone started a chant. "Moll-lee! Moll-lee!" And when Max motioned her to come stand with him, everyone stood and applauded, and he was pretty sure that he saw tears in the eyes of those closest to him. He lifted Molly onto the table next to him and handed her the first gift—a box just slightly larger than the rest.

"Molly, I have never been prouder of anyone than I am of you. You have given all of us a lesson in the true meaning of Christmas, and we are very grateful."

"Can I open the present now?" Molly asked, her fingers poised over the bow.

"Yes."

The room grew still as Molly untied the bow and opened the box. "It's a necklace," she said, holding it up to show them.

"It's a medal of honor," Max corrected her. He held out his hand, and when she gave him the necklace he fastened it around her neck.

"Like the ones you got when you were a soldier?"

"Just like that," Max assured her, and he stepped back and gave her a sharp salute.

Once again the room erupted into applause and cheers.

"And now if Molly will help me pass out these boxes, we have remembrances for each of you. We hope you will carry this token with you as you continue the challenging journey you face every day."

Quickly the gifts were distributed and the room grew still once again as everyone opened their little box and removed the coin-like token with the inscription that read *Christmas* with the date on one side and featured a shooting star on the other.

"And now I'd like to turn things over to Pastor Baker for one last announcement and the benediction."

Outside, the rain pelted the windows and the wind howled, and Max saw several of the street people glance toward the exit, their faces registering their acceptance that all too soon they would have to figure out where they might spend the night. He stepped aside to give the minister the floor, and immediately Sarah came to stand with him.

"They all want to help," she whispered.

"Good. So my folks will take—"

"No, Max, I mean *everyone* wants to help—the choir members, the church volunteers, your family, everyone. Mary and Ned are on their way back from Connecticut and plan to come straight here."

It was at that very moment that Reverend Baker made his announcement. A stunned silence fell over the room. He gave out the terms of the invitation as the news slowly began to sink in. No smoking or drinking. No loud or unruly behavior. Leave at first light. Respect for the premises. "You are in a house of God,"

Baker reminded them. "I'm afraid this is a one-time offer, ladies and gentlemen. We are not set up to be a shelter, but this is a very special night and we will not turn you away."

A woman broke down in tears of relief. Several people stepped forward to shake the minister's hand and thank him. And once the benediction had been given, without hesitation every one of the street people worked in tandem with Sarah and the other volunteers clearing away the remains of the party—gathering trash, folding and storing the tables, sweeping the floor—whatever needed to be done.

Max stood off to one side watching Sarah. She was facing a long flight the next day, and yet here she was looking as fresh and vibrant as she had hours before when he'd first arrived.

"Hey," he said as she passed him on her way to the kitchen. "With all this support, how about you go on home and get a good night's sleep?"

"I can sleep on the plane tomorrow," she said. "I wouldn't miss this for anything. Do you understand how grateful the folks are for what you've done?"

"What we've done—we make a good team."

She studied him closely for a long moment. "I tried to tell you that a few days ago," she finally said. "I didn't mean that the way it sounded, Max. Sorry. Maybe I am a little tired, but this is where I want to be."

"No apologies necessary. If you're sure about staying, then I'm just grateful for the extra time we'll have before you have to leave."

She smiled up at him. "Give me a hand setting up these chairs?"

"Lead on, my captain."

Together they staged the room, setting up chairs for the women at one end and for the men at the other. They were low on food, but there were still several dozen cookies left and there was plenty of tea and decaf coffee, so they made an arrangement of tables between the two sleeping areas and set out the leftovers. Some of the volunteers left, promising to return for their shift as the night wore on. One group of church members had decided to hold an all-night prayer vigil in the church's small chapel. By the time they had everything arranged, it was dark outside but the rain kept coming.

Max saw Sarah talking to his mother. They were laughing together, and he thought that he had never seen his mother looking more relaxed. She was wearing an apron and holding a broom, and she had pulled her hair back into a ponytail. She looked like a teen-ager, and he suddenly understood why his father had been smitten with this uptown beauty all those years ago.

"They seem to be hitting it off," his father said, coming out of the coatroom and nodding toward the two women. "I'm going to take your mother and grandmother home, and then I'll be back to stand watch with you, okay?"

"We've got plenty of help, Dad. Go on home and enjoy what's left of the evening. I expect there's still a small package hidden in the tree that Mom has pretended not to find yet?"

His dad chuckled. Max's parents had a long-standing tradition that one gift for his mom would be something small that could be hidden somewhere in the tree and not found until they were removing the decorations and storing them for the next year. It was always the very last present to be opened.

"Well, she's going to be surprised—that's for certain," his dad said. "Not sure if it will be a good surprise or not."

"Jewelry or gift card?" Max knew that some years the gift was a piece of jewelry or a gift card to one of his mother's favorite boutiques.

"It's a gift card, but not one she usually expects. It's a handwritten one to Bernie's Diner."

"In Brooklyn?"

"Yeah. That's where I proposed to her and I thought ... " He frowned.

"She'll love it, Dad." Max wasn't at all sure how he knew that, but looking at the woman leaning on a broom talking and laughing with Sarah, he was suddenly very sure that his dad had chosen exactly the right thing.

He patted his pocket, hoping that the gift he'd chosen for Sarah would be equally well received.

* * * * *

As the night wore on and the first hint of dawn lightened the sky, Sarah was relieved to see that the storm had passed. True to their word, the street people woke and stretched, lined up for one final cup of coffee and the last of the cookies, and then one by one made their way out the door and disappeared into the city. She stood at the basement window next to the stairway that led to the street and watched the last of them go, and she was sure that the tears in her eyes were as much the result of wishing she could have done more as they were of exhaustion.

She gave herself a moment to collect her emotions before turning back to the empty church hall. Mary and Ned had arrived in time to take the final shift and were now clearing the coffee urns and cookie trays while Max stacked the chairs and bagged the last of the trash.

"Well, this was certainly a Christmas that I will remember for the rest of my life," she said as she went to do her part to make sure they left everything as clean as possible.

"You and everyone who had a part in it," Ned agreed. "I just wish Mary and I had gotten here earlier."

"You were here when it counted," Sarah assured him. "Thank you."

"You look exhausted," Mary said. "Will you please go home and get some rest? I promise to make sure you're at the airport in plenty of time to make your flight."

"I am pretty beat," Sarah admitted.

"Another Christmas miracle," Ned teased. "The woman confesses to being human like the rest of us mere mortals. Now come on. I'll get our coats."

"You two go on. I just want to check the restrooms before we go to be sure they're clean."

"Ned and I will check the restrooms. You get your coat. Better yet, you sit down here and Max can get all our coats, okay?" He glanced across the hall to where Max was just returning from taking out the last of the garbage. "Hey, Max, Ned and I will pull latrine duty while you collect coats and make sure that Sarah stays awake long enough for us to get her into a cab, okay?"

"My pleasure."

By the time Max collected their coats and sat down next to her to wait for Ned and Mary, Sarah was having trouble keeping her eyes open. But when Max handed her a small box with a purple ribbon tied around it, she instantly perked up. "What's this? I thought we agreed . . . "

"We did no such thing, and besides, this is not a Christmas present. It's something I want you to open when you are on that plane tonight."

"Why not now?"

"Because . . . just trust me. It'll be better tonight." He tucked the box into the pocket of her jacket and zipped the pocket shut. "Okay?"

"Okay."

Mary and Ned were scrambling around finding cleaners to wipe out the sinks and polish the mirrors and gathering the last of the trash from the restrooms. All of a sudden she and Max seemed to have nothing to say to each other, so she said what was in her heart. "I wish you were coming with me."

"Maybe once you're there you'll find somebody for the team."

His comment irritated her. "That's not what I said." She stood up and shoved her arms into the sleeves of her jacket and walked toward the restrooms. "Mary? I'll catch a cab. Got to finish packing, so I'll see you later, okay?"

She didn't wait for an answer but walked straight to the door and out. A cab was just cruising by and stopped the second she raised her hand. She was already inside when she saw Max emerge from the stairwell and start running after the taxi.

Chapter Nine

. . . .

It was still early when Max let himself into the brownstone, changed clothes, and then took to the streets for his morning run. His feet pounded the pavement, marking out the cadence of his misery. She was leaving today . . . today . . . today.

She had said that she understood why he could not bring himself to return to that part of the world. He had gone back twice and to what end? Nothing had really changed except maybe the names of the countries killing each other's children. Sarah still believed she could make a difference, but he knew better. Maybe she could change the life of one child—maybe even a dozen— but there would be more in need. There always were.

But it wasn't just about the children or the work she did or the place where she did it. It was about them—Sarah and him— and the future he'd allowed himself to imagine for them. That morning he had stopped short of declaring his love for her— what would be the point? She was going. She *should* be going. It was her job, her calling. Why complicate her life?

He ran through the park and out onto Fifth Avenue. Soon the street would be filled with people out to shop the sales or to return gifts they didn't want or to get back to work. The city had been on pause for a night and a day, but now it was time to return to reality. Just like it was for Max. Deciding not to reenlist had been the easy part—a no-brainer once he really thought about it. Why tempt fate? He had made it through years of combat with life and limb intact. Going back would mean that he actually thought he could make a difference when the evidence was overwhelming that he couldn't—hadn't.

The trouble was that he had allowed the time with Sarah to rekindle a sense of hope—of possibility that things could be different. But somewhere, blocks farther downtown, Sarah was closing up her loft and packing the last of her gear for the six months she would spend overseas. Her plane was scheduled to leave from JFK airport early that evening.

Their parting had not been anything like he'd hoped it would be. The truth was that Sarah couldn't seem to get away from him fast enough. By the time he realized that she was walking out without him and went after her, she was already in the cab. She had not looked back.

Max slowed his pace—a full-out run—to catch his breath before continuing. As he sucked in the cold winter air, he realized that he was standing outside St. Patrick's—possibly the most famous cathedral in America and certainly a stop for tourists of all faiths. But at this hour of the morning, there were only a few people coming and going—a woman in a black coat with a shawl that covered her head and half her face was leaving as a man and a boy walked slowly up the stone steps and through the open doors.

Over the years Max had developed a habit of stopping at the grand old church whenever he was in town to light candles for his fallen friends. He was not Catholic, but he was pretty sure God didn't keep score—at least on something like that. He'd been so busy since coming home this time—and had gotten so caught up in spending every moment he could with Sarah—that the tradition had slipped his mind. Well, no time like the present to rectify that. He wasn't exactly dressed for church—desert fatigues—but again he doubted God would care.

He entered the church and stood at the back for a moment, allowing his eyes to adjust to the sudden shift from daylight to shadow. A memory washed over him—a time back in Afghanistan when he had led his company through a burned-out village. They had checked the ruins of every building looking for survivors. They had found only the charred bodies of the villagers who had not escaped. Max remembered it was that moment when he'd first thought that if he made it back to America alive, he would never come back. There were no answers, he had decided. Not for this part of the world anyway.

He'd been the last to leave the village, following his comrades through a narrow street, when he'd heard something in a small shed behind a house. One of his buddies heard it as well. Max had motioned for the others to keep walking, wanting whoever was hiding in the shed to believe that they had left. In the meantime he and the other soldier circled back, signaling each other with gestures as they got into position. Together they rushed the half-open door, throwing it all the way open so that the strong noonday sunlight lit the area.

There, crouched in a corner of the room, was a girl not more than fourteen, her eyes wide with fear but also determination as she clutched a bundle to her chest. Max had handed his rifle to his buddy and motioned for the girl to give him the bundle. He'd been certain that it was a bomb—how often over the years had he seen children used as carriers? The girl had scooted more firmly into the corner. She had shaken her head in a firm and universally understood refusal.

Now, in the church, as the sweat from his run dried and he felt a sudden chill race through his body, he remembered that it had been winter then as well, and that the girl had not worn more than a thin dress. Max had taken off his outer jacket and laid it carefully on the ground in front of her, then gestured that he would trade—the jacket and warmth for the bundle.

She had considered it but then once again firmly refused. All the while, Max's partner had kept his rifle trained on the girl, nervously looking around, spooked by the silence and the shadows.

And then the bundle had moved, and Max heard the weak but undeniable cry of a baby. His partner heard it as well and instinctively lowered his rifle. Max remembered how he had knelt on the dirt floor and inched his way close enough so that he could place his jacket around both the girl and the baby. All the while he had murmured the few words of Arabic that he knew and hoped they were the dialect that she understood. "Hospital," he had said softly. "Food. Medicine."

He had held out his arms and instead of the girl surrendering the baby as he had expected, she crawled to him and settled herself and the baby against his chest, her silent tears running unchecked down her dirt-streaked face. That was when he realized that she couldn't walk—that her legs had been badly burned.

Now as he stood at the back of the main sanctuary to the famous cathedral, he wondered what had become of that girl. They had gotten her to a MASH unit, where she and the baby had been stabilized before being airlifted to a hospital. He had tried to follow up a few weeks later when he got leave, but the staff at the hospital couldn't tell him anything except that she and the baby had been doing well, and then one day they had simply disappeared.

Max wondered if she was alive, and not for the first time he wondered if the newborn she had so fiercely protected had been her own child. He sat down in a pew, and because the kneeling pad was there, he slipped to his knees. He folded his hands and looked into the glow of lights in the distance—the glow surrounding the altar. And he prayed.

He prayed for the girl and her child. He prayed for all the children caught up in wars they had no part in. He prayed for his buddies—those who hadn't made it, those who had sustained such injuries that their lives had been forever changed, and those still there somewhere in that endless mountain and desert wasteland where borders were bitterly contested, where power mongers set family against family, friend against friend, all too often in the name of God.

He bowed his head, resting his forehead on his clenched hands as the images of all that he had seen in all the years he had spent over there flashed through his mind. He had never really permitted himself to remember those things—certainly he could not avoid the way they replayed in his dreams—but awake he refused to give them a single moment more of his life. And yet on this day the memories came freely—the faces, the names, the losses—so very many losses.

He stayed there for a long time after the memories had finally settled back into the recesses of his brain. He turned his prayers to the present—to Grace and Jack and Molly and the miracle of new life that Grace carried. He prayed for Gramma Karen to continue to enjoy good health and thanked God for the blessing of her in his life. He prayed for his parents, asking forgiveness for the years he had wasted in not appreciating his mother's fears and self-doubts when it came to parenting. And finally he turned his thoughts and prayers to Sarah. "Keep her safe," he begged. "I love her so much." This last he prayed aloud in a whisper that was barely more than the movement of his lips. "I love her," he repeated as if he needed to make the point—as if God didn't already know that.

After a moment more he raised his head and pushed himself back onto the pew. Then he stood and went to a bank of candles. He dug out the crumpled bills he had stuffed in his pocket—in case he got injured and needed a cab or decided to stop for breakfast—and left them in the donation box. Then he lit a wooden taper and slowly lit candles—one for his buddies who had died, one for those who were alive but so severely injured in body or mind that they might well wish they were dead, one for his family—his wonderful, intact, loving family—and then one last one for Sarah and her team that they would do their work and come home again.

When he turned to go, he saw the man and boy he'd seen enter the church before him. They were watching him as if waiting for him to finish his prayers and tributes before approaching him. He nodded and started for the exit. As he stepped outside the man and boy caught up to him.

"Forgive me, sir," the man said. "You are a soldier?"

Was he? Not anymore. "I'm a civilian now."

"Were you in Iraq?"

"No. Afghanistan mostly." He studied the man—older than he had first thought. "My name is Max Wolzak," he said and offered a handshake.

"Jahmir Rahman, and this is my grandson Sanjay." He had accepted Max's handshake with a slight bow. "We wish to thank you."

"I think you must have me confused with someone else," Max replied.

"No. I have told my grandson here that it was a man like you who saved him. My son and his family were caught in a firefight during the war. They were all killed, but an American soldier found Sanjay here lying under his mother's body. He was only seven. That soldier got him to a hospital, and how he managed this I will never know—for we never knew the soldier's identity—but somehow he learned that I was here in New York and made the necessary arrangements through a group working with the United Nations to bring the boy here. We have no words, Max Wolzak."

Now he was grasping Max's hand with both of his, and the boy was smiling at him. "I am American now," he said proudly, "and one day I will serve as well."

"But in peace," his grandfather hastened to add. "Always in peace. There has been too much war."

"When I finish school, I will work for the United Nations," Sanjay told Max. "I will work for peace as my grandfather wishes, but I will also do this work because it is the only way."

In the boy's eyes, Max imagined Sarah's smile. If only she could hear Sanjay speaking with such conviction. Here was someone who would believe in what she believed in, would follow her to the ends of the earth in his certainty that the work she and others like her did was the only cure for the world's woes.

"I know of many stories like our family's story, Max Wolzak," Jahmir continued. "And I know that had it not been for that soldier, my grandson would not be alive today."

Max straightened to his full height and turned to the boy. "Do you have something to write with?"

Sanjay nodded and pulled the stub of a pencil and a small notebook from his jacket pocket. He handed them to Max and waited while Max wrote down his name and cell number.

"When you are ready to go to work, call me. I may have a contact who can make sure you at least get an interview."

"Thank you, sir."

"And blessings be upon you," his grandfather added as Max waved and set out running again—this time back the way he had come. For suddenly he knew what he needed to do—for himself and for the possibility of a future with Sarah.

* * * * *

Sarah could not recall a time when she had been more reluctant to head off for a new relief mission. Usually she was filled with anticipation for the work she and the others on the team would do—for the surprises they were bound to encounter and the blessings that would come back to them tenfold. But as she packed the last of her things on this day after Christmas, she could not seem to focus on the mission. Instead, all her thoughts were on Max Wolzak—and for what?

She reminded herself that they had known each other for only a little over a month. Yes, they had known each other as teenagers, but that was way different from an adult relationship. The problem was that she had allowed herself to act as if they were those teenagers—starry-eyed with their whole futures ahead of them, blind to the dangers of the greater world and certain that no harm could ever come their way.

And then the planes had flown into the supposedly indestructible towers and into the Pentagon and into a deserted farm field in rural Pennsylvania—and the world had shifted on its axis for everyone. Within a week Max was off to basic training, and the single date he'd had with Sarah faded into a distant memory as she tried to decide what future she might choose that would truly make a difference.

And here they were—all grown up and no longer naïve about the capacity for evil. And yet she found hope in her work—a spark of possibility that drove her to return to troubled areas around the globe on the off chance that she could make a difference. Max had followed a different path, although he too had set out determined to put a stop to terrorism and violence against innocents. Once, he had been as certain as she was that good could conquer evil, but after spending so much time with him these last few weeks, she understood that he no longer believed that was possible.

The intercom buzzed, and she absentmindedly released the outer door without pausing to check who was there. She was expecting Mary. They had a long-standing tradition that whenever possible her friend would go with her to the airport and see her off. Mary was also a marvel at making sure she had everything she needed—passport, medicines, tickets—before she left the loft.

She glanced at the clock. Mary was early. Maybe she'd heard something about traffic and knew they would need extra time. She opened the door to her loft so Mary could just walk in and then hurried back to the part of the open space she had partitioned off with bookshelves as her bedroom. "Coffee's still hot, or at least warm," she called when she heard a light tap at the door. "Just finishing—" She turned and saw Max standing in the doorway. He looked as if he'd just run a marathon.

He dropped the military issue duffel he was carrying and held out his arms. She did not hesitate for even a second but ran to him, burrowing her face against his chest, where his heartbeat pounded out its rhythm against her ear. She could not remember a time when she had felt more secure in her life.

"I was wondering," he said softly, "if that job is still open."

She leaned back so she could see his face. "You're serious?"

"I'm here, aren't I?" He smiled. "I've tried saving the world my way. It didn't work out. So I got to thinking that maybe you had another way . . . a better way."

"You'll come with us? For the whole six months?"

"I'll come with *you* for as long as you'll have me."

She glanced down at his duffel bag. "You're ready to leave today?"

"If there's still a seat on the plane."

She nodded. The mission traveled on a UN cargo plane that carried supplies as well as the members of her team, and there was plenty of room. But his sudden change of heart triggered Sarah's innate caution. "Max, I . . . "

He put his finger to her lips to silence her. "I know it's too soon for happily ever after, Sarah, but how are we ever going to know for sure if we don't give it a shot?"

She so wanted this to work. The truth was that she had wanted someone like Max to share her life with—and her life's work— for far longer than she had allowed herself to admit. "Tell me what changed."

She expected an exasperated sigh. She expected him to release her and look away as he tried to put together the words it would take to convince her. Instead he tightened his hold on her and gazed down at her.

"I met a man and his grandson this morning. They were Iraqis. The boy lost his entire family, and the grandfather lost his son and other grandchildren. And yet when they saw my fatigues, they wanted to tell me their story—they wanted to thank me as a representative of the American military. At some point in that boy's life, a soldier made a difference, and I had to wonder

how many such stories there are. We were just doing our jobs—
our duty and yet . . . "

"You changed lives."

"In the process of our real mission . . . yeah." He told her about
his encounter with the girl and her baby. "I never knew if the child
was her brother or her son," he said. "I never knew what happened
to her."

"We could try to locate her," Sarah said. "My connections at the
UN could help."

Max shook his head. "No. It's pure selfishness for me to want
to know. Better to use time and resources to help others, don't
you think?"

Never in the weeks she had been with him had she been closer
to declaring her love for him, and yet such feelings had not yet
been tested. She bit her lower lip. He read the gesture as doubt and
released her.

"Sarah, if you'd rather I didn't . . . "

"I want you to come. I need you to be there."

"Because you're a man short?" This time his smile was bittersweet.

"Because I was trying to imagine going without you and I
wasn't succeeding." She stood on tiptoe and kissed him.

"I love you, Sarah Peterson," he whispered before kissing
her back.

Behind them, the freight elevator groaned into action, but Sarah
barely noticed. Max loved her and no, that love had not been tested,
but perhaps they had to start by admitting their feelings openly.

They were still standing in the open doorway when the elevator ground to a stop. The metal door opened and Mary stepped out.
Seeing them, she turned and got back on the elevator, obviously prepared to head back downstairs until she thought it proper to return.

"No, wait," Sarah called out before Mary could make her escape. "Max is going with me."

Tentatively Mary exited the elevator. "To the airport?"

"On the mission."

"Well, that is good news." But Mary was looking at Sarah as if she wanted to take her aside for a private discussion of the matter.

"I love him, Mary, and he loves me. We're going to try and make this work." She certainly had not meant to direct those words at someone else the first time she admitted her feelings aloud. She glanced up at Max, who was grinning now as if he'd just won the lottery.

"And we will," he added. "You can trust me, Mary. I would never hurt Sarah."

There was an uncomfortable moment during which Mary seemed to wrestle with her concerns. Finally she spoke. "Is this the place where I give the two of you my blessing?"

They both nodded.

Mary spread her arms wide. "Group hug," she announced.

* * * * *

While Mary stepped outside into the hallway to call Ned and tell him the news and Sarah went to finish packing, Max wandered into the galley kitchen. He turned off the coffeemaker after pouring himself a cup and stood at the window that opened onto the fire escape, staring out at the place where the towers had once stood.

"Max? You can't mean to give me this." Sarah was holding the box he'd given her that morning in one hand and his Purple Heart in the other.

He set down his empty coffee cup and took the medal from her. It was indeed a small purple heart framed by a gold border and engraved with a profile depiction of George Washington when he was a general. At the top of the medal was Washington's coat of arms—a white shield featuring two red bars and three red stars set between sprays of green leaves. The medal hung from a deep purple ribbon. "You were supposed to wait."

"But you're here now so I thought— Max, this is too much."

"I want you to have it. At first I planned on giving it to you because I believed you were going into battle. I believed you had already done battle with the forces of evil."

"And what's changed?"

"Do you remember what the history books taught us about George Washington? 'First in war, first in peace, and first in the hearts of his countrymen'?"

"Yes, but—"

"You are first in my heart, Sarah, and this is my very non-traditional attempt to give my love for you a tangible symbol." But then he realized that she probably would far rather have something more romantic—a heart-shaped pendant, perhaps. He closed his fist around the medal. "I wasn't thinking . . . Grace has always said that when it comes to romance, I am a total clod. If we leave now, maybe we can stop by a jeweler's and get you something you like."

"Okay, two things: Number one, I don't need symbols, Max. And number two, I think you may be putting the cart before the horse."

"I don't understand."

"Are you asking me to make a commitment here, and if so, what are the ground rules?"

"I'm asking you to build a life with me. If you agree there can be no ground rules other than that if there is ever a time when you change your mind . . . "

"What if *you* change your mind?"

"I won't."

"You're that sure?"

He smiled. "I think I was that sure Thanksgiving night when you showed up at my parents' house after walking several blocks in the cold because you were too kind to let the cabbie know that he had made a mistake."

She set the box down and slowly unfurled his fist until the medal lay flat on his palm. "Then this is all I will ever need in the way of symbols, and I will wear it with pride."

She turned away from him and fumbled with the clasp on the medal and her blouse. When she turned back, the medal was nowhere in sight. In answer to the question obvious in his raised eyebrows, she pointed to a place just above her heart. "It's here," she assured him. "It always will be."

They were kissing again when Mary came back inside the loft from the hallway. She cleared her throat loudly. "Time to go," she muttered as she headed for the kitchen, where she dumped the last of her coffee. "And we have to leave, as in right now, or you are never going to make your flight." She grasped the handle of Sarah's rolling bag. "Come along, children," she called as she pressed the elevator button.

* * * * *

Sarah had fallen asleep almost the minute the plane took off. Her head was resting against Max's shoulder, and he marveled at the way the two of them fit together so perfectly. He stared out the window at the black night and then he saw it in the distance. A star in the eastern sky . . . one they would follow to their new life. Their new life together.

About the Author

 ANNA SCHMIDT is the award-winning author of over twenty-five works of historical and contemporary fiction with over one million books sold. Her most recent works include the Women of Pinecraft series: *A Stranger's Gift* (4-½ stars from RT Book Reviews); *A Sister's Forgiveness* (an RT Book Reviews Top Pick); and *A Mother's Promise* (4 stars from RT Book Reviews).

Anna's novel, *A Convenient Wife*, earned her a third nomination for the coveted RITA Award for Inspirational Fiction from Romance Writers of America as well as the Holt Medallion Award for Short Inspirational Fiction. She has also been a finalist in the Romantic Times Reviewer's Choice awards four times and won twice. She splits her time between Wisconsin and Florida and gets to New York whenever she can.

Love Finds You

Want a peek into local American life—past and present?
The *Love Finds You*™ series published by Summerside Press
features real towns and combines travel, romance,
and faith in one irresistible package!

The novels in the series—uniquely titled after American towns with romantic or intriguing names—inspire romance and fun. Each fictional story draws on the compelling history or the unique character of a real place. Stories center on romances kindled in small towns, old loves lost and found again on the high plains, and new loves discovered at exciting vacation getaways. Summerside Press plans to publish at least one novel set in each of the fifty states. Be sure to catch them all!

NOW AVAILABLE

Love Finds You in
Miracle, Kentucky
by Andrea Boeshaar
ISBN: 978-1-934770-37-5

Love Finds You in
Snowball, Arkansas
by Sandra D. Bricker
ISBN: 978-1-934770-45-0

Love Finds You in Romeo, Colorado
by Gwen Ford Faulkenberry
ISBN: 978-1-934770-46-7

Love Finds You in
Valentine, Nebraska
by Irene Brand
ISBN: 978-1-934770-38-2

Love Finds You in Humble, Texas
by Anita Higman
ISBN: 978-1-934770-61-0

Love Finds You in
Last Chance, California
by Miralee Ferrell
ISBN: 978-1-934770-39-9

Love Finds You in
Maiden, North Carolina
by Tamela Hancock Murray
ISBN: 978-1-934770-65-8

Love Finds You in
Paradise, Pennsylvania
by Loree Lough
ISBN: 978-1-934770-66-5

Love Finds You in
Treasure Island, Florida
by Debby Mayne
ISBN: 978-1-934770-80-1

Love Finds You in Liberty, Indiana
by Melanie Dobson
ISBN: 978-1-934770-74-0

Love Finds You in Revenge, Ohio
by Lisa Harris
ISBN: 978-1-934770-81-8

Love Finds You in Poetry, Texas
by Janice Hanna
ISBN: 978-1-935416-16-6

Love Finds You in Sisters, Oregon
by Melody Carlson
ISBN: 978-1-935416-18-0

Love Finds You in Charm, Ohio
by Annalisa Daughety
ISBN: 978-1-935416-17-3

*Love Finds You in
Bethlehem, New Hampshire*
by Lauralee Bliss
ISBN: 978-1-935416-20-3

*Love Finds You in North
Pole, Alaska*
by Loree Lough
ISBN: 978-1-935416-19-7

Love Finds You in Holiday, Florida
by Sandra D. Bricker
ISBN: 978-1-935416-25-8

*Love Finds You in
Lonesome Prairie, Montana*
by Tricia Goyer and Ocieanna Fleiss
ISBN: 978-1-935416-29-6

*Love Finds You in Bridal
Veil, Oregon*
by Miralee Ferrell
ISBN: 978-1-935416-63-0

*Love Finds You in
Hershey, Pennsylvania*
by Cerella D. Sechrist
ISBN: 978-1-935416-64-7

Love Finds You in Homestead, Iowa
by Melanie Dobson
ISBN: 978-1-935416-66-1

*Love Finds You in
Pendleton, Oregon*
by Melody Carlson
ISBN: 978-1-935416-84-5

*Love Finds You in
Golden, New Mexico*
by Lena Nelson Dooley
ISBN: 978-1-935416-74-6

Love Finds You in Lahaina, Hawaii
by Bodie Thoene
ISBN: 978-1-935416-78-4

*Love Finds You in
Victory Heights, Washington*
by Tricia Goyer and Ocieanna Fleiss
ISBN: 978-1-60936-000-9

Love Finds You in Calico, California
by Elizabeth Ludwig
ISBN: 978-1-60936-001-6

Love Finds You in Sugarcreek, Ohio
by Serena B. Miller
ISBN: 978-1-60936-002-3

*Love Finds You in
Deadwood, South Dakota*
by Tracey Cross
ISBN: 978-1-60936-003-0

Love Finds You in Silver City, Idaho
by Janelle Mowery
ISBN: 978-1-60936-005-4

*Love Finds You in
Carmel-by-the-Sea, California*
by Sandra D. Bricker
ISBN: 978-1-60936-027-6

Love Finds You Under the Mistletoe
by Irene Brand and Anita Higman
ISBN: 978-1-60936-004-7

Love Finds You in Hope, Kansas
by Pamela Griffin
ISBN: 978-1-60936-007-8

Love Finds You in Sun Valley, Idaho
by Angela Ruth
ISBN: 978-1-60936-008-5

*Love Finds You in
Camelot, Tennessee*
by Janice Hanna
ISBN: 978-1-935416-65-4

*Love Finds You in
Tombstone, Arizona*
by Miralee Ferrell
ISBN: 978-1-60936-104-4

*Love Finds You in
Martha's Vineyard, Massachusetts*
by Melody Carlson
ISBN: 978-1-60936-110-5

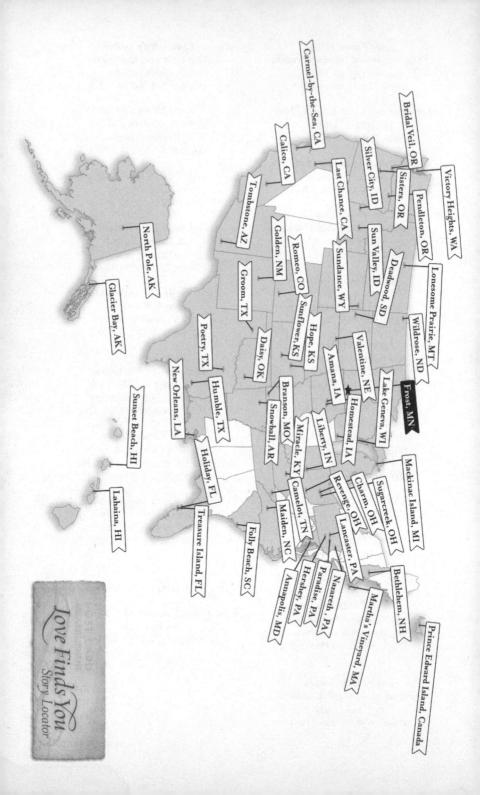